THE GOOD
SAMARITAN

ALSO BY TONI HALLEEN

The Surrogate

THE GOOD SAMARITAN

A Novel

TONI HALLEEN

HARPER

NEW YORK • LONDON • TORONTO • SYDNEY

HARPER

THE GOOD SAMARITAN. Copyright © 2025 by Toni Halleen. All rights reserved. Printed in the United States of America. No part of this book may be used or reproduced in any manner whatsoever without written permission except in the case of brief quotations embodied in critical articles and reviews. For information, address HarperCollins Publishers, 195 Broadway, New York, NY 10007.

HarperCollins books may be purchased for educational, business, or sales promotional use. For information, please email the Special Markets Department at SPsales@harpercollins.com.

FIRST EDITION

Designed by Jamie Lynn Kerner

Library of Congress Cataloging-in-Publication Data

Names: Halleen, Toni, author.
Title: The good samaritan : a novel / Toni Halleen.
Description: First edition. | New York, NY : Harper Paperbacks, 2025.
Identifiers: LCCN 2024016077 | ISBN 9780063070134
    (trade paperback) | ISBN 9780063070127 (hardcover) | ISBN
    9780063070141 (ebook)
Subjects: LCGFT: Thrillers (Fiction) | Novels.
Classification: LCC PS3608.A548294 G66 2025 | DDC 813/.6—
    dc23/eng/20240415
LC record available at https://lccn.loc.gov/2024016077

ISBN 978-0-06-307013-4 (pbk.)
ISBN 978-0-06-307012-7 (simultaneous hardcover edition)

24 25 26 27 28 LBC 5 4 3 2 1

For Mom and Dad, with gratitude and awe, with love always

tenure |ˈtenyər|
1. a guarantee
2. to be made permanent
From the Old French "to hold"

THE GOOD
SAMARITAN

One

MATTHEW

SUNDAY, SEPTEMBER 27, 1992

FIRST OF ALL, I DIDN'T KNOW THERE WAS A BODY ON THE PORCH. I barely knew what a *feedstore* was and it didn't matter because this was Sunday night and everything was closed. Anyway, I wasn't looking for fertilizer when I stopped at the quaint little hardware store for farmers; I was desperate for shelter. For the past half hour on I-35 South, I'd been white-knuckling it through heavy rain and low visibility while other cars had clustered under bridges. But when the hail started—pummeling my Subaru with ice pellets—my need for protection was urgent. Fortunately, I had reached my exit, the one I took on my weekly commute to campus.

As I veered off the highway, Hafemeyer's Feed & Seed was the first place I saw with an overhang. The moment I pulled under the carport, the racket stopped. Relief. I switched off the wipers and caught my breath. Then, in the glare of my headlights, I saw it: a lump on the porch.

It was covered with a tarp and it could have been anything: a bag of seed, a coil of rope, a mound of dirt. But as I stared at the shape, I understood it was a body. Humans recognize other humans, a simple truth I explained to my first-years every fall in Sociology 101. I didn't know whether this tarp-covered human was dead or alive, and frankly, which would be worse. All I knew was I couldn't take my eyes off that lump. Perhaps it was my training as a sociologist to be curious. Perhaps it was my instinct as a dad to be filled with dread. But I should have listened to Claire: I should have stayed in Minneapolis.

My daughter had tried to warn me. She was only sixteen, but she fancied herself an amateur meteorologist. Which only meant she watched the Weather Channel. Claire said they were forecasting rain, with possible hail. She said I'd be driving directly into the storm, but I was sure I'd outrun it. She'd accused me of minimizing her concerns, not taking her seriously. I assumed she was just being clingy. Lately she'd been having trouble going back to her mother's after our weekends. Still, Sunday was my travel day, and Claire should have understood by now that I needed time to prepare for my Monday morning lecture.

For a person like me, an assistant professor on the verge of promotion, every decision felt loaded, like there was a right and a wrong. I had to be careful. I was finally about to get tenure and I wasn't going to let anything screw that up. Not this time. I'd failed at my previous appointment—somewhat of a misunderstanding—over an omitted authorship credit. It was complicated, but the fiasco had cast a mark against me. But now I had a second bite at the apple, albeit in my forties, and I knew this was my last chance.

Tenure—the coveted goal of every serious academic, whether they admitted it or not—meant a promotion, a title, and a raise. These were obvious advantages; but for me, the most valuable part of tenure would be the guaranteed employment. I could not be fired. I could serve out my days without worry. I'd be protected. I would belong. I'd be home.

But tonight, I was staring at a tarp-covered body-shaped lump in the middle of Minnesota farm country, wondering what to do. What would the college expect me to do in this situation? What would a tenured professor do? My behavior, as a reflection of my judgment, was always subject to scrutiny. This was hard for non-academic people, like my daughter and ex-wife, to understand. They saw me, at times, as exaggerating my importance. But in the context of St. Gustaf College, I was held to a certain standard. From the top. From the student body. From the local community. I was expected to set an example.

Reluctantly, I opened the door. The rain made a racket around us, and hailstones peppered the parking lot. I was fighting with the seat belt, as if my Subaru was smarter than I was, suggesting I stay inside and not get involved. Once unbuckled, I extracted my long legs from under the steering wheel to stand up. I shivered outside the car and glanced around, scanning the situation. The lump and I were alone.

"Hey!" I called to the porch, but my voice was swallowed by the storm. Nothing from under the tarp. "Goddamn it," I muttered, zipping up my coat. I left my headlights on, driver door open, and engine running. I wasn't sure what kind of mess I might find. I climbed the three or four steps to reach the porch.

Everything was wet despite the overhang. In Minnesota, rain fell sideways if it needed to. I glanced back at my car; the amber interior light was on, beckoning me. Cautiously I stepped closer to the lump to examine it. Two wet shoes were sticking out. Sneakers. In one motion, I reached down and tugged at the tarp. It slid off easily, revealing a small person huddled underneath: a boy. He was curled up on a stack of seed bags. Alive, I thought. He had to be alive.

"Oh god," I said, pulling off my glasses and rubbing my eyes. Of course I thought of Finn. His ghost follows me everywhere. Pushing my glasses back on, I peered around the parking lot, as if this child's parents might be lurking out there in the darkness. I grabbed the railing, trying to contain my rising emotion, the choke in my neck. At the other end of the porch, I spotted a pay phone. I should call someone.

"Okay," I said to myself, summoning clarity. I knew I should call 911, but there were a couple of reasons why I couldn't. Not tonight. First, I'd only called 911 twice before, and those had been the two worst days of my life. Once was when my dad was having a heart attack and the other was when they pulled Finn unresponsive out of our neighbor's swimming pool.

I looked again at the boy on the porch. He was slim, his frame was small compared to his disproportionately large feet, probably a result of the onset of puberty. I guessed he was eleven, maybe twelve. I jiggled his shoulder gently. He was limp. I put two fingers on the side of his neck, picking up a pulse. Good. I didn't want to give CPR to anyone ever again. This kid didn't seem to need it, but what did I know? Maybe he had frostbite or hypothermia? Unlike my brother, I had no medical training, so I was only guessing.

I took a deep breath and exhaled slowly, one of the anxiety-reducing exercises Tammy and I had learned at a marriage encounter workshop that had failed to save us. For a second, I was tempted to bail. As if I'd never been here. Like I hadn't seen this kid. Just drive to my faculty apartment as I was meant to do and return to my purpose, my research, and the lecture tomorrow morning. All the ordinary things I should have been doing to clinch a yes vote at the Promotion and Tenure Committee meeting later this week.

I felt the urge to call Tammy, but what would I have said? That I'd found a lost child, a boy, like ours? That he seemed about twelve, the age Finn would've been if he'd lived? No. I shook my head and snapped out of it. My ex-wife would only have been annoyed with me. According to Tammy, everything bad was my fault, especially Finn's death, so no thanks. Besides, she was two hours away, and it's not like she would zip down here to save the day. Anyway, she'd probably be helping Claire with homework, or they'd be watching a movie, and I shouldn't bother my daughter. Not on a school night.

"For Christ's sake," I said, staring at the boy. He wasn't dressed for cold weather, or rain. Only a sweatshirt, no coat. No hat. I knew I couldn't leave him. This was someone's son. And I was a stranger. A stranger with a bad track record. Not that many people knew about that.

I strode to the pay phone and picked up the receiver, but then slammed it down, remembering. The second reason I couldn't call 911 was the police. If the police came, they'd ask if I'd been drinking, and why would tonight be different from any other? Yes, I'd had a few glasses of Chardonnay, perhaps a bottle. But I didn't feel drunk. I had a headache, but who wouldn't under these circumstances? The drive had been stressful. Still, I wasn't slurring. I probably looked okay. Could I walk a straight line? No, I didn't need to gamble with this tenure vote, the committee. Which meant 911 was out of the question.

So who else could I call? I had friends on the faculty, but I couldn't trust them. Academics were, in my experience, competitive and cutthroat. Surely, they'd gossip about this. Someone would find a way to use it against me. No. Better to spare the faculty.

I couldn't call a student, could I? I had some marvelous ones over the years. College kids who really wanted to make a difference in the world. Most of them didn't have cars, however, not in a rural town like Northwood where everything was walkable. So what could a student do for me? Anyway, it wouldn't be appropriate of me to ask. No, I shouldn't.

Who else? None of the women I was seeing were the type to expect a call from me on a Sunday night. Especially not a call for help. It just wasn't like that. I'd been avoiding actual relationships, at least until after the tenure vote, if ever.

I sure as heck wasn't going to call my brother. Not that he ever answered the phone. My sister was only a Realtor but she'd give advice to anyone about anything. Nah, she'd only tell me to call the cops. And I didn't want her lecturing.

So where did that leave me? I couldn't abandon the child. It wouldn't reflect well on the college if it came out that a faculty member had simply driven away. Left the scene without helping? Not a good look for a rising professor, especially one who studies the elements of society, of community, of family. Surely my students would expect more of me. Not to mention the P&T Committee or—for that matter—my own dear mother, who was battling health problems of her own.

I looked over at the boy.

"Screw it," I said. I'd drive him myself. The local hospital was only twelve miles away. I leaned down and picked up the kid, sliding one arm under his knees and one under his armpits, letting his limbs dangle the way I'd carried Finn. It still came natural to me even though it'd been eight years. My gut clenched with the memory of Finn's slight frame, how limp and heavy he'd felt, and I shuddered at the memory of moving my son's drenched body onto the carpeted floor of the neighbor's family room and administering CPR.

Tonight, the boy in my arms stirred and whimpered. I was glad he was alive, but I didn't want to drop him. I shifted him into a more secure hold, then concentrated as I navigated down the porch steps to my car.

Before I opened the door, it occurred to me that someone might be watching and assume I was kidnapping him. But I wasn't a creep, I wanted to tell them, whoever they were, if they were watching. I turned in a circle, still holding the passed-out kid, scanning the area in case someone was out there.

"I'm taking him to the hospital, that's all," I shouted to the emptiness, to the dark parking lot, shiny and scattered with melting hailstones. Behind the store, three grain elevators loomed tall like glaciers, shadowy guardians keeping watch, silently judging me, as if even they knew this was a bad idea.

Two

CLAIRE

FRIDAY, SEPTEMBER 25, 1992

I WAS TAUGHT TO STAY AWAY FROM STRANGERS, BUT I THOUGHT THAT meant avoiding people who were strange, like weirdos on the street. Or anonymous people, random criminals and monsters. No one warned me to watch out for the people I already knew or who knew me, nice people, or the boy I liked. No one said those might be the ones to hurt me.

The boy I liked was Evan Lewis. He had long eyelashes and a thick neck. We were lab partners in biology because of the alphabet—otherwise he never would have chosen me. Not that there was anything wrong with me; I wasn't ugly, just tall. And I got good grades. My hair wasn't long or styled smooth; it was bushy and tangled. Not like the girls Evan normally hung out with, the Cheryl Gundersons and the Julie Chesleys. Girls whose voices were loud and husky from smoking. Sexy girls with blue eyeliner and multiple earrings, tight jeans and clingy tops that showed their bras, and no jackets in the winter, even when it snowed.

I was more practical, and I hated being cold. I knew cigarettes killed cilia in the lungs and I did better on tests when I wore comfortable clothing. If we had chosen our own seats, I would have been in the front row so I could see the chalkboard better, but Mrs. Biggerstaff had a seating chart, so Evan and I shared a two-person desk in the last row, and we did all our experiments together. Testing water and making smoke. Microscopes and beakers. I loved everything about biology, except for cutting into dead things.

That was Evan's favorite part.

So far, we'd only done a worm. Next week would be a frog. I wasn't looking forward to it, but sitting close to Evan while picking at the insides of a worm had been surprisingly intimate. Evan's head so close to mine. I studied his thick hair, dark brown and hefty, unruly like Medusa's, and I wondered what it would be like to touch it. Evan fidgeted with his hair a lot, pushing it down and smoothing it, but it always bounced back like a spring.

As we worked on the worm, our faces were inches apart, and I could see hairs sprouting between his overgrown eyebrows. And acne scars. I could see the beginning of a cold sore on his bottom lip. I loved his long eyelashes. I wondered what Cheryl Gunderson and Julie Chesley thought about me and Evan sitting like that in such proximity, leaning together over the sandy worm guts.

His torso was so much larger than mine. How had that happened? His neck was very broad, and he had a pronounced Adam's apple that made it seem like he was in a constant state of midswallow, or that he might be choking, but he wasn't either of those things, and I wondered if that Adam's apple was part of what made Evan's voice so deep and throaty.

He didn't talk much, which gave his few words more impact. He told me he had practice after school every day and he lifted every morning in the weight room before class. It seemed Evan didn't mind staying at school and being away from his house, but he didn't exactly say that. He said his parents weren't together. I said we had that in common. He looked at me and nodded. His eyes were so brown, an intense hue, not like a yellowy tan or greenish brown, but real brown, like coffee. Truly dark.

I told him about my job at Bageletta. About how I was glad to be done with babysitting. And since I turned sixteen last summer, I could finally get a real job. It's not the most meaningful work in the world—it's just making sandwiches—but I learned about customer service and safety protocols and supply and demand.

Evan asked if I could get him free food. I said we throw out the day-old bagels on the third day. He asked when I was working next. I said Friday. He asked if my manager would be there. I said no, I would be alone.

"Cool," he'd said with a half smile. "Maybe I'll stop by."

When he smiled at me like that, a chill tingled in my nipples. I felt myself blush and I looked at the desk, my textbook, my lap. I knew it wasn't a date. But it was sort of like a date. It was a secret.

I'd thought about it all week. Was it wrong to promise him free bagels? No, they were the old ones. Was it wrong to invite a friend to visit me at the store? No, it was open to the public. But somewhere in my chest I felt something heavy, like I was moving toward danger, and I couldn't stay away. Something about his face, his whole way of being, was different and exciting to me.

When Friday came, I was nervous. I had no idea what I'd gotten myself into and I half hoped he wouldn't show up. But he did.

It had been slow that night at Bageletta. A woman came in for coffee around eight. I sold her a cookie to go with it. Then a couple came in. They were on their way to see a movie. They said they were sneaking their sandwiches into the theater. People told me things like that, things I didn't really need to know. I was watching the clock. I only had an hour until close. It seemed Evan wouldn't be coming.

I put plastic wrap on the stainless-steel pans. The coffee smelled like leather. I switched it off and opened my book from English class, *Lord of the Flies*, which I read while leaning up against the counter. Next time I checked the clock, it said only fifteen minutes to close. I thought, *Oh, I shouldn't have worried about Evan. He probably forgot.*

Then there was a thump against the window. I looked up but didn't see anything. Then commotion outside. Voices laughing. *Here we go*, I thought. Some drunks. More laughing and shuffling around. Then the door burst open, and Evan tumbled in. Then his best friend, Dom. Then Cheryl and Julie. They were hanging on Evan.

Whoa. He'd come!

But he didn't look like Evan from biology. He was acting weird. He didn't say anything to me. It seemed like he didn't even recognize me. They were being jerks and I didn't know what to do. I was mad he was so late. I was mad he wasn't alone.

"Can I help you?" I said to the whole group. I was noticing everything about them. I was planning to call Becca and tell her about it when I got home. Becca would know what this meant.

"Give us bagels!" ordered Cheryl like I was her maid. She was propping herself against the glass case, peering at the rack of bagels. "Oh shit, there's no cinnamon. Can you make me a cinnamon?"

"Sorry," I said, shaking my head. The bakers were the only ones who could make bagels. They usually came late at night or early in the morning. I'd learned about the process in the training videos. There was an order to it, hot ovens, the oil. It was complicated and I was strictly prohibited. Also, I didn't know how to do it. I knew it wasn't simply a matter of sprinkling cinnamon on a plain.

"Can't you like, sprinkle cinnamon on a plain?" whined Julie.

"We don't have, like, cinnamon to sprinkle," I said, but it was a lie. We had cinnamon for oatmeal during the morning shift. So technically, I could go in the back and get it. But something about the wildness in these kids made me think I shouldn't leave them alone in the store. I was responsible for what was happening. Dom was pulling napkins out of the holder like he wanted to see how long he could go, like he was daring me to stop him. Cheryl and Julie were touching all the containers of cream cheese in the refrigerated compartment. Evan was just leaning against the cash register and staring at the area behind the counter. Staring at me.

I touched my Bageletta cap and wondered how I looked with my hair tucked up. He knew it was me, right?

Finally, he said, "Got any bagel bites?"

I rolled my eyes. Of course we had bagel bites. "Yeah," I said, because it was obvious. But that wasn't the plan. "I mean, you'd have to pay for them."

He smirked and reached for his wallet.

"Okay," I said, getting to work on bagging the bites.

The other kids seemed to have lost interest in being there. Cheryl hit Dom and he stopped with the napkin excavation. They were laughing about something, and I wondered if it was about me. There was no way to find out, so I rang up the bagel bites and handed Evan the bag.

"Later," said Dom and he strutted out the door with the girls. I felt a whoosh of cold air and saw that the door had gotten stuck open when they left. I could hear them out there, still laughing.

I gave Evan his change and he put it in his pocket.

"Evan! You coming?" said one of the girls from the darkness.

"Yeah, wait up," he said, not taking his eyes off me. He picked a bagel bite out of the bag and ate it. I watched him chew. He picked out another one and tossed it at me. I ducked. He laughed and threw another one. It hit my arm and stung.

"Hey," I said, rubbing the spot.

"It didn't hurt," he said, as if I'd been imagining things. And then, like to prove it, he chucked another one.

I moved away, looking at the pieces of bagel on the floor. I'd have to clean those up later. Over and over, Evan hurled bagel bites at me, and I tried to dodge them, which he thought was funny. Like it was a game.

"Stop it," I said. Was I supposed to catch them? I wasn't sure what he was doing or why. He aimed harder, some of them hitting me, some hitting the wall. It was so stupid. It was like he didn't have any interest in eating the bagels. I wondered if the other kids were watching. It was dark outside and they'd disappeared. I backed away from Evan and tried to act like I wasn't scared.

Then he got really serious. He squeezed the dough so it was smaller and harder, and he threw like he really wanted to hurt me. Aiming for my body, laughing. He had a spooky look in his eye as he compressed the balls and pelted them. Like he was daring me to flare up and roar back at him. But I didn't. I shrank down. I waited for it to be over.

It wasn't over until he'd emptied the bag. And then finally, all thirteen bites were gone. "Later, Larkin," he mumbled, chucking the paper bag on the floor, glancing behind me, and ambling out.

I stood there, in shock, like, what just happened?

When I heard a noise behind me, I jumped.

Three

MATTHEW

SUNDAY, SEPTEMBER 27

IT WASN'T EASY GETTING THE KID INTO MY SUBARU. I HAD TO PROP him up against the passenger side of the car while I opened the door. Then I saw my briefcase was on the seat, but I still had the kid in my arms so I had to attempt a grab-and-switch, replacing the bag with the boy, Indiana Jones–style, and let him plop into the seat. His head jostled a bit as he landed and settled at a crooked angle that looked uncomfortable. As I pulled the seat belt across him, I flashed on a memory of Claire as a baby and Tammy nagging me to support her head, our first time as parents. A vivid memory, even these many years later. I latched the belt across the boy's crumpled body and closed the door. The sooner I got out of there, the better.

My heart was pounding as I climbed into the driver's seat and buckled up. I cranked the heat and switched on the overhead light as if we were the ambulance. I could keep an eye on the kid, and anyone outside could see us if they really wanted to. I wanted the world to know I had nothing to hide; I was doing good. Gently, I pulled out of the lot and onto CR-15 East, the small county highway that led to St. Gustaf. This was the route I usually took alone, but tonight I had a passenger. The road ahead was empty and everything was black outside.

"Hang in there, Bud," I said to the boy, surprising myself with the name. "Bud" had been my dad's nickname for me. He'd called my older brother "Partner," but I was Bud. I'd always been jealous of Gregory, including his nickname. People always said Gregory was just like Dad, while I took after our mom. I accepted it as gospel without fully understanding how I resembled Mom or why people didn't see my similarity to Dad. Anyway, the name Bud just popped out of my mouth, but the kid slumped next to me hadn't heard it. He appeared to be passed out, even in that awkward position, the seat belt cutting against his neck and his mouth slightly agape.

My passenger and I snaked around the curves of the county highway, passing a few farmhouses, then onto the next stretch that was a straight shot for about four miles through dark fields. I'd taken this road dozens of times since I'd gotten the job at St. Gustaf four and a half years ago, when I was lucky to land a tenure track opportunity with partial credit given for my prior accomplishments. This late in the season, the crops had been harvested and the plants were mostly cut down. One of the things I'd noticed in all my years of commuting was the way that farming felt out of sync with the college rhythm. For example, this was late September, the beginning of our academic year, but it was the end of growing season for the acres of farmers who surrounded us.

In the dark, there wasn't much to see except the occasional security light outside a barn, casting a beam onto a dirt driveway, a broken-down truck, or a small tractor. I kept my speed fairly low because it helped me concentrate on staying between the lines. I didn't want to give anyone—that is, any police lurking in the darkness—a reason for pulling me over. The wipers were set to intermittent, and I tried to relax. Riding like this late at night reminded me of rides with Gregory and Dad on the way home from some adventure. Usually at the lake or one of the fishing creeks, somewhere in Wisconsin. We'd be gone all day, fishing in a canoe or off the dock. We'd have caught a bucket of bass or sunnies. Sometimes we cleaned our fish in the light of Dad's headlamps. Gregory and I would sit on the ground, with knives and newspaper set out in front of us. It was a messy, smelly job, and I hated it, the dead fish with their sharp scales and bulging eyes, but Gregory took it as a challenge to clean them. He didn't mind getting dirty. I pretended to be bad at it so Gregory would have to do more. Then we'd load everything up and drive home, tired, wet, and fishy. But it was okay, because we were together and we had nothing else to worry about.

I glanced at the boy. His face was pointing upward, a smudge of dirt on his cheek, his eyes closed. He could have been any child. He could have been Finn. Suddenly he shifted to the other direction, slouching against the window. In that moment I wished I'd gotten the wool blanket out of the wayback and put it on him.

I checked the rearview mirror but no one was following us. I looked at my watch. Everything would be fine. I could drive this boy to the hospital not far from campus, drop him at the Emergency Room, then get to my apartment by nine fifteen or nine thirty. Good deed accomplished. Plenty of time to review my notes and prep for my lecture.

I must have been lost in my thoughts, because I didn't see the stop sign until it was too late. I slammed on the brakes, and the kid and I both lurched forward. He slapped his hand onto the dashboard, ninjalike, as if to catch himself from hitting it, shook his head, and looked at me. His eyes were wide and worried. He was awake!

"Sorry about that," I said. We had landed halfway into the intersection. The cross street didn't have a name; we were completely alone in the boonies. I probably didn't even need to stop. Just a habit, I guess, to comply with the rules.

"What the fuck?" said the boy.

"Hey, now," I said, as if offended by both his language and his critique of my reckless driving. I explained, "I didn't see the sign."

He squinted at me. "Are you drunk?"

"No," I said, looking around, like maybe he was talking to someone else. Technically, I could have been drunk. I still felt a bit foggy-headed.

"Who are you? Why am I in your car?" the kid asked. He'd started fussing with the seat belt.

"Matthew Larkin," I said. "I'm a teacher at the college. I found you at the feedstore."

The boy's head and body were twisting as he struggled to unbuckle as quickly as possible. He spotted the farmhouse up ahead and he said, "Are you taking me there? To the Ogletrees?"

"What trees? Huh? No. I thought you needed help," I said as he struggled with the lock. "Wait a second." I grabbed his shoulder and he flailed a hand at me and hit my face. "Ow. Hey, I'm taking you to the hospital, you jerk—"

"—No!" The kid was grasping at the door, opening it. "No hospital."

"Wait. No, you can't go," I said, putting my arm out to restrain him.

"The hell I can't," he said, fighting me off. He heaved the door wide open and damp air rushed in.

"What are you doing? Stop it," I said, shoving the gear shift into park and switching off the ignition. "Get back in the car, please."

He turned and walked along the shoulder, unsteady on his feet.

"Hold on now," I said, unbuckling myself and opening my door. I muttered as I climbed out of the car, "Where are you going?"

He sidestepped down into the ditch at the edge of the road. He slipped on the wet grass and scrambled to his feet, climbing up the other side of the ditch.

"No, stop," I said, but the boy was wedging his way under the fence that surrounded a giant soybean field, dark and dangerous. "Please come back," I begged. "You have hypothermia. You should see a doctor."

He stood on the other side of the fence and stared at me, like he was wondering if it was true. After a moment, he shook his head and shouted. "Leave me alone!"

He was only twenty yards away, but I knew I couldn't chase him. I looked down at my Hush Puppy shoes. Without traction, I'd never get out of that ditch. "Hey, wait!" I hollered. "You can't stay out here!"

The kid heard me, I knew it, but he didn't look back. Just kept moving farther away, and as he scampered on, he got smaller and smaller in the dark field.

"Where are you going?" I hollered. There was a white farm-house across the street, kitty-corner from us. I pointed at it. "Are you going to that farm over there?"

He stopped and looked back at me but said nothing.

"Are you going to that house?" I yelled, cupping my hands around my mouth.

"No!" he shouted, moving toward me again, like a threat. "Don't go there! Just leave!"

"Why?" I shouted back.

He turned and ran, but not fast. He was moving with a limp.

"Shit!" I said, because I'd blown it. My only plan had been to take him to the hospital, but now what? This kid was messing everything up. None of this was my problem, but he was making it my problem.

I stood there for a minute, angry. At myself, at the kid. Helplessly, I watched him, unsure what else to do. The rascal seemed to know his way around the fields. Good. Maybe that meant he'd be all right. If he got hurt out there, would that be my fault? I could just hear Tammy scolding me. She always found out about my failures. And she was terrific at hindsight.

"Hey!" I called out one last time. Why was this stubborn boy afraid of the hospital? And why didn't he want me going to that farmhouse? Maybe he'd stolen something. I wondered as I watched him recede into the distance, his petite frame hobbling away in the nubby remnants of the harvested soybean stalks. "Little shit," I muttered.

I looked around. Were there any witnesses? Any allies or foes? Was there anyone else tromping around in the dead crops? God forbid a crazy farmer was out here with some dangerous nighttime machinery. Or a wild horse or a sleepwalking cow. Anyway it wasn't safe. It was a disaster. I looked at the farmhouse again. A light was on in the barn. I hadn't noticed that before.

Back in the Subaru, I switched on the ignition and turned onto the side street that led to the farmhouse. Pulling into the long driveway, I spotted a truck outside the garage. The barn stood beside the main house, set back slightly. I parked in the circle drive at the front of the house, triggering a motion-sensor floodlight and the sound of barking dogs. The front porch light went on as I got out and walked toward the front door.

"Can I help you?" asked the big man who appeared on the top step. He had gray hair and gray stubble, and he wore a white T-shirt and flannel pajama pants. His girth was healthy, and his arms seemed strong enough. He was frowning as if impatient because I'd interrupted Sunday night football.

"Hello," I said, raising one arm to indicate I'd come in peace, wishing I could start this whole night over.

The man nodded slightly, looked me over, and waited. For a moment, I wondered if he had a shotgun within reach. Finally, he said, "You lost?"

A woman appeared behind him, peering at me like this was a matter of great interest. They both seemed about ten or fifteen years my senior, putting them in their early sixties, I'd guess, but farming might have made them seem older.

"No, I'm not lost," I said. "I'm a professor . . . at the college."

"Oh?" said the man, as if that told him everything he needed to know, like he encountered pesky professors all the time and we were all the same: nerdy, ignorant pains in the neck. "Outta gas?"

"No, uh, it's not the car," I said, smiling briefly. Certainly, scholars like me had a reputation for being absent-minded and not mechanical, but I was actually pretty comfortable under the hood. I explained, "It sounds strange, but I saw a boy run into your field."

"What field?" said the man with a twinge of defensiveness.

"Just there," I pointed across the gravel road to the field where the boy had disappeared.

"That one ain't mine," said the man, glowering at the field like it had insulted him.

"Oh," I said, taken aback that this farmer seemed more concerned with property rights than the fact that a lost boy was running around all by himself in a cold, wet field at night. "Well, I mean, whoever owns the land is not really the point."

The man tilted his head as he studied me. "You had a few too many, pal?"

I scoffed, offended.

"What's going on?" said the woman stepping out and wrapping her fuzzy cardigan closed. She'd obviously been listening to our conversation. She surveyed the driveway and said, "Is this about Seaver?" Then into the night she called, "Seaver! You out there?"

"Get inside," scolded the man.

"Seaver!" she yelled again. Her voice rang in the stillness, and she glared at me like she was making me a promise. Whoever Seaver was, this woman wasn't giving up.

The man ushered her back inside and shooed her away from the storm door. She disappeared before I had a chance to tell her I didn't know the boy's name.

"Oh, is he your, uh, grandson?" I guessed. "Or son?"

The man ignored my question and simply said, "She's got it in her head that Seaver's in trouble. I told her he's probably at his friend's. He's run away before."

"Okay, well, how old is Seaver? Or, I mean, what does he look like?" I asked, wondering if we were talking about the same kid, but I wasn't sure how much this guy would share. Also not sure how much I should share with him. He didn't answer my questions.

"Is that all?" asked the man, halfway into his house, clearly indicating the conversation was over.

In the window next to the door, the curtains parted, and the woman appeared again, peeking. I glanced between the man at the door and the woman in the window.

She gestured something, pointing in the direction of the man or something on that side of the house, but what? The truck? The barn? I didn't understand. I shook my head at her.

"Whataya looking at?" asked the man, stepping outside, looking where I was looking.

"Uh . . . nothing," I said, instinctively covering for the woman, although I still had no idea what she was trying to communicate. I reached in my coat pocket and handed the farmer my card. "Let me give you this. Got my phone number there, my address. Would you give me a call if you see anything? I sorta feel responsible, ya know."

"Oh yeah?" said the guy, taking the card. "Why's that?"

"Well. I mean . . . I was giving him a ride," I said.

The man looked at my card. "A ride, huh?"

I sighed. "Nothing nefarious. I found him passed out on the porch at Hafemeyer's, and I was gonna take him to the hospital. I was worried about hypothermia."

The man nodded but said nothing else.

"I just hope he's okay," I said, retreating down the steps. "It can get pretty cold at night."

"Okay then," said the man, closing the door.

"Good night," I said, returning to my car. I took another quick look around, wondering what that woman could have been pointing to. I couldn't very well stroll into the backyard and take a peek inside the barn. The man was definitely watching as I opened the car and strapped in. Maybe the woman was too. As I drove out, I studied the truck, then squinted up at the barn. Could the boy be in there somewhere? The dogs were outside now, still barking and escorting me off the property. I hoped the boy had found his way somewhere warm. And that he'd be all right.

At the end of the driveway, before I turned onto the side road, I noticed the mailbox. The name at the top, spelled out in block letters, was OGLETREE.

Four

KIRA

THE FIRST RULE I BROKE WAS GIVING OUT MY HOME PHONE NUMBER to every kid on my caseload. I wasn't supposed to do that. As a social worker, I was supposed to have boundaries. Understandable, but these kids needed someone they could call. A trusted adult. Did my phone ring a lot? Yes, but it was okay because I used caller ID.

The calls I avoided were from my landlord and the bank. Creditors went to the machine. They'd leave a message letting me know an amount was "owing." Every month I did a juggling act with the bills. After rent, my biggest expense was that student loan from grad school. My VW Rabbit was paid off, but gas was expensive, especially with how much I drove between the agency and the high school. My main employer was a private foster care agency, but the agency contracted me out to a public high school where I spent half my time. So I basically had two jobs and I did a lot of driving. And I let my kids call me at home, big deal. I could handle other people's problems. I was good with troubled kids. I was good with frustrated parents, and I liked to help. Besides, I wasn't home much anyway, and when I was, it was just me and Orange Perry, and Perry didn't care about anything but his food bowl and a clean litter box.

So I let the kids call me. These were children who'd been

taken from their homes and placed in foster care. They'd been traumatized. And I had to look them in the eye and promise they'd be okay. After doing that a hundred times, you'd break a few rules too.

When June called me on Sunday night, I'd just gotten home from the movies. It had actually been a relaxing weekend. I worked late on Friday, but I'd gotten in a run on Saturday, then did paperwork Saturday night. I'd missed the hailstorm on Sunday by being at the local discount movie theater for two and a half hours, and it was just what the doctor ordered. A romantic comedy. Nothing serious. With a job like mine, I don't need drama on the screen. I go for the full escapist experience in cinema. This was a Julia Roberts flick with a happily ever after. I'd been told I look like her, but it's probably just the hair. Long and wavy, auburn. Usually unbrushed. Maybe it's the smile? I've been blessed with straight teeth, but I certainly don't consider myself a great beauty. Anyway, I shed a couple of tears at the end when Richard Gere returned to her, and they "rescued" each other. The orchestration worked like a charm on me. I guess you could say I'm an old softie.

But I must have been distracted on the drive home because I got pulled over. Apparently, I was going fifty-five in a forty-five-mile-an-hour zone. Whoops. The cop asked me where I'd been, and I told him. I mean, I didn't offer that I'd been to the movies by myself. Or that I actually enjoy going alone. The nice officer simply wrote me a ticket and I thanked him. He asked if I'd been drinking, and I laughed. Only this, I'd said, showing him the supergiant-size diet fountain drink I still had with me, almost too big for my VW's compact drink holder. He waved me away, which was good because I had to pee and being pulled over wasn't helping the bladder situation.

When I got to my apartment building, all I wanted was to beeline to the bathroom. However, I heard my phone ringing all the way from the stairwell, so I had to hurry up the steps and down the hall.

"Coming," I called to the door, but by the time I unlocked it and dumped my stuff, the phone had stopped ringing. As I ran to the bathroom, I listened for the answering machine to pick up. No message. When I was done, I checked the caller ID. Unknown number. Oh well. If it was important, they'd call back.

Meanwhile, food! Lunch was seven hours ago and movie theater popcorn was not dinner. I opened the fridge: a can of Mountain Dew, a few slices of cheese, and an unopened jar of homemade strawberry jam, a gift from one of the foster parents on my caseload. I checked the freezer: two lonely Lean Cuisines and a nearly empty container of chocolate chunk ice cream.

"Kira Patterson, you need to go to the grocery store," I said to myself, as I grabbed a frozen dinner and tossed it in the microwave. Four minutes on high. I surveyed the cupboard, which held a half-eaten box of Lucky Charms, a container of instant rice, and a bag of potatoes that were growing feet. I held my nose as I tossed the potatoes in the trash. Just then, the cat rounded the corner, arching his back as if he'd just awoken. I greeted him and he rubbed against my shin.

"Perry Boy," I cooed, leaning down to stroke him.

He moved away and stood by his empty bowl.

I grabbed the Lucky Charms and poured him some. "There ya go, kitty."

Perry gave me a look, but ate.

The phone rang at the same moment the microwave started beeping. Without checking the number, I picked up the phone and said, "Hi, can you hang on?"

I set down the phone and retrieved my mac 'n' cheese, lifting the film and stirring, then I returned it to the microwave and pressed two more minutes. Grabbing the phone, I exhaled and said, "What's up?"

"Kira, it's me. We have a problem," said a worried voice. Instantly I knew it was June Ogletree, the most-experienced, most amazing foster parent on my roster and definitely my favorite. Of course, I was biased when it came to June—she was like a pseudo-mom to me—but I trusted her completely. If June said we had a problem, we had a problem.

"Okay," I said, bracing myself. I'd gotten through the whole weekend without any kid-related hiccups; I could handle this. I pulled my hot dinner out of the microwave. "What is it?"

"Seaver," said June. "He's gone."

"Oh shit," I said, burning my finger on the steaming mac 'n' cheese. I let it drop to the counter.

"I'm so sorry!" June cried.

"It's not your fault, okay?" I said, giving her the benefit of the doubt because it wasn't uncommon for kids to run away. I grabbed a pen from the junk drawer and an unopened envelope from the pile of mail, ready to take notes. "Let's figure this out. When did he go?"

"This evening," said June. "Around suppertime."

I looked at my watch and made a note. "Okay, so he's been gone for what, five hours?"

"About that, yes," said June.

I found a fork from the sink and returned to my tiny kitchen table. I took a bite of mac 'n' cheese. While chewing, I said, "So he still might come back tonight, right?"

There was a pause on the other end of the line. Finally, June said, "I hope so, Kira, but what if he doesn't? We had a terrible storm down here. He wasn't dressed for it."

"Okay. So you had bad weather down there too?" June lived two hours south of Minneapolis.

"With terrible hail," she said.

"Shit. Okay, have you called around, checked with the parents of his friends, anywhere he might have gone for shelter?" I asked.

"I've called everyone I could think of," said June. "No one has seen him since he left Michael's sleepover. He was at a sleepover this whole weekend."

"Okay," I said, stuffing another forkful into my mouth. Eating helped me think.

"Tell her about the man," said another voice gruffly. Knowing her husband, I never assumed my calls with June were private. He often listened in, and he'd clearly picked up the other extension. I could hear him breathing into it.

"Hi, Grady," I said, reminding him how I liked to communicate: Directly. Honestly. Respectfully.

"Hmph," he grunted in response.

"What man is Grady talking about, June?" I asked, appropriately concerned. It couldn't be Seaver's father. He was in jail in Texas.

"The one that came to the door," clarified Grady.

June explained about the evening's events, including the professor who'd seen a boy running. As I listened, I ate the rest of my dinner and looked out the kitchen window. My view was of the apartment complex parking lot. The wooden sign at the entrance was illuminated by a weak spotlight.

"As soon as the professor left, I checked the barn again. Not a soul in sight," said June, her voice catching.

I'd jotted some notes, then ran my pen across the envelope, as if crossing out the big nothing that was there.

Finally, Grady said, "We need to know who this professor is and why he's nosing around."

"He gave us his card, Grady," said June. She read from the card. "It's Matthew Larkin and he teaches at St. Gustaf."

My alma mater. I'd received my MSW from St. Gus.

"I don't give a crap what his title is. I wanna know what he was doing snooping around my farm," said Grady, clearly unhappy. "Mind you, I'm not responsible for what happens on the Dozier acreage."

Grady was referring to the field across the gravel road from his property line. The Ogletrees didn't do any farming anymore; they leased out their land to others. Grady kept a few horses and several acres for grazing and hay. But old farmers like Grady were touchy about who owned what.

"All right," I said. "I'll look into the professor."

"You'd better, or I will." Grady's annoyance was clear. Finally he huffed and said, "I'm going to bed."

I checked the clock. It was almost ten. We heard Grady's line click off, then it was just me and June.

Quietly, she said, "I put a few blankets out for him."

"In the barn?"

"Yes," said June. "We've still got that hay bale out there. For late arrivals. And I left the light on."

"Okay." I made a mental note to check out the barn for any hideaways, and I threw away my empty mac 'n' cheese carton. I leaned against the counter and filled a glass with water. As I took a sip, something caught my eye. There was a stain on the ceiling where the roof must have leaked. The light fixture was yellowed and out of date and one of the bulbs had burned out.

"Changing the subject," said June. "Your birthday's coming up."

"I'm aware." I smiled at how June loved me.

"It's a big one," added June. "Thirty-five. We should have a family dinner."

The number stung. I wasn't old, but there was something urgent about being halfway through my thirties. I said, "Yes, I know my age."

June said, "Well, if you want, we'll have cake and candles."

"Sure," I said because I couldn't say no to June.

After a pause, she said, "I'm sorry about Seaver, Kira."

"I know." I inhaled deeply, as if trying to pull all the worry out of the air. I was frustrated, but I didn't want to make her feel any worse. Gently, I asked, "Was there anything that changed recently? Something that might have made him want to go?"

After I'd said it, I felt the burn of the question. Finally, she answered, "No, Kira. You know he's run before. I can't lock him in the house."

"You're right," I said. And we both knew Seaver would likely come back on his own. Or someone would spot him and notify the police. "Have you called Rice County?"

"No, I wanted to talk to you first," said June.

"Okay, so you'll call tonight?" I asked.

"You realize the sheriff's department won't do anything until tomorrow," said June.

"I know." Of course I hated siccing the hounds on Seaver. Ideally, I could find him before the cops did. I knew a few spots to look. But still, I reiterated, "We need to report it."

"Kira, I will call Rice County as soon as we hang up," said June.

But I knew that she was lying. And I had to figure out why.

Five

CLAIRE

ON SUNDAY NIGHT I WAS STILL THINKING ABOUT EVAN AND THE BAGEL incident. I was sitting on my bed at Mom's (and Brian's) town house and I was supposed to be doing my biology homework about dominant and recessive genes, but all I could think about was Evan pitching bagel bites at me and laughing bizarrely. I'd already talked to my best friend, Becca, about it, and her theory was that Evan liked me and didn't know how to express it. Becca's mom was a psychiatrist, so Becca knew a lot about people's emotions. It was a good theory but I wasn't sure.

My bedroom at Mom and Brian's has one window and it faces south. I'd been watching the sky as the storm passed over, black-and-green cumulonimbus clouds, and I was doodling on my spiral notebook. When the phone rang, I wondered if it was Dad calling to say he'd made it safely to Northwood. Maybe he was calling to say I'd been right and he'd gotten caught in the hail like I said. He'd been so stubborn and ignored my warnings as usual. Maybe it was the police calling to say my dad had been in an accident and if that was true, he would have deserved it. He would have deserved to hit a slippery patch of road and run into a tractor trailer and smash the front end and break both his legs and go into a coma. But then I felt bad for thinking that and of course I hoped my dad was safe. I'm not a horrible person, I was just mad. In a flash I was off the bed and down the hall to Mom's room. She'd already answered the phone and was sitting on their new king-size bed, her head in her hands, listening.

"Mom?" I half whispered, my face in the door ajar, like Jack Nicholson in the movie poster Becca had on her wall. "Is it Dad?"

Mom shook her head and frowned. She mouthed *It's work* and waved for me to go away. I went back to my room.

But I could have gone to the guest room and listened through the vent in the wall. That was where I'd eavesdropped on lots of Mom's private calls. Sometimes I heard her crying in there. Or arguing with Brian. Sometimes they were talking in hushed tones. But I could usually hear enough to piece together the big picture on stuff I wasn't supposed to know. Last year I knew I was getting Reeboks and a new Walkman for Christmas. And overall shorts and silver turtle earrings for my sixteenth birthday. I liked knowing what gifts I was getting because then I knew how to react. But there were other things I wished I hadn't heard because I knew I was supposed to keep it a secret. Like, how I found out about Mom and Brian being engaged before Mom officially told Dad about it. And I heard them arguing about how expensive their wedding had been. But mostly it's just boring things like my mom having to fire someone because she's a big shot or Brian's ongoing stomach problems or their debates about who should gas up the car tomorrow.

They both work at the same place; it's where they met. They carpool but use separate entrances, for "optics." It's so dumb. He goes to the legal department and she goes to the executive wing. They work at the corporate headquarters. I've gone there for family functions a couple of times, like when they'd set up mini golf in the atrium, or when they had a carnival in the parking lot. It was all right.

Mom and Brian talked about work a lot. Mergers and acquisitions, corporate restructuring, executive compensation, succession

planning. I knew so much corporate lingo, it was like a second language. And I knew I'd never get an MBA or go into the business
world where everything was focused on what can we build and
how much will it cost. I was more like my dad: I cared about the
underneath parts, the why is this happening and could it be different somehow.

Sometimes Mom and Brian talked about Dad, his situation, the
college. And the custody schedule. About child support payments.
And spousal maintenance. I know all the legal terms and all the
numbers because I've read the divorce paperwork that Mom tried
to hide in a cardboard box in the basement. It was easy to find
because she'd labeled it "Divorce" and kept it in an unlocked storage closet along with miscellaneous tax records, old photo albums,
and clothes that were too small but that Mom hoped to someday fit
into again. Brian had his own closet, but it was locked. His private
belongings, I assumed, but I didn't know what. I haven't yet found
the key.

All the Finn stuff was stored at the house on Zenith Avenue.
The Zenith house was where we all lived when Finn was alive and
my parents were still married. Now it was half empty and occu-
pied only on weekends and for part of the summer for my visitations with Dad, as per the custody schedule. After I graduate from
high school or on my eighteenth birthday, whichever comes first,
my parents will be allowed to sell Zenith and split the profits, even
though the title is in my mom's name.

I was glad they kept the Zenith house for Dad and me to have
our visitations, but I would have liked it better if he lived here year-
round. I've told him this many times, but he insisted on taking an
apartment down in Northwood, like, two hours away, because he
believed it would "greatly improve" his chances at tenure. And
tenure is all that my father really cares about.

Ever since he moved to Northwood, Dad stopped doing dad

things with me, like coming to school events or picking me up from theater class or watching the Weather Channel. We stopped drinking chocolate milk for breakfast and singing good night to the stars. He couldn't read my essays or quiz me on my vocab words. He hasn't seen me working at Bageletta. He didn't teach me to drive. It was Mom who took me to my driving test when I got my license this past summer.

But Dad tried to make up for it on weekends. He usually made soup. He loved making wild rice soup (with chicken). There was usually an outing to the movie theater if anything good was playing. Always a trip to the Y, where we went our separate ways, Dad to the treadmill and me to the pool. The rest of the time we spent at home; he was reading or grading papers, and I was doing homework. Sometimes I'd ask what he was reading, and he'd give a mini-lecture about motivation theory or the sociology of belonging. It was supposed to be quality time with Dad, not quantity. And then the weekend would be over and I'd watch him drive away.

Dad was just so excited about his supposedly amazing superbig-deal "faculty apartment" because, wow, it was on campus. And he claimed that all our sacrifices would be worth it when—very soon, he promised—he'd get tenure. The way my dad talked about tenure made it sound like winning the Academy Award or something, like, oh my god, no one has ever achieved anything like this before, like the ultimate honor of the universe. And that was why he had to leave us every Sunday.

Not that anyone needed him for anything now, after five years of him commuting like this, after we'd gotten used to it, because I'd had no choice and basically had to raise myself. And if Finn were still alive I'd have raised him too, except if Finn hadn't died, I'm pretty sure my parents would still be married and my dad would still be living at Zenith because he wouldn't want to leave us, especially Finn. But no one will admit that. No one will even talk about the fact that Finn died and that it ruined our lives. It was the Big Topic that we didn't address. In the hopes that it would what, go away? Pointless.

So on Sunday nights I just stood there and watched my dad drive away like always. I used to wonder what it would take to make him stay. I'd tried different things. Being sick, crying. Eventually I gave up.

Now I was in high school. I had a lot of other things to focus on. Like storm systems. And my stupid biology homework. And bagel bites. And Evan.

Six

MATTHEW

WHEN I GOT TO CAMPUS, I WANTED A DRINK. ALL THE GOOD PARKING spots were taken in front of my building, so I drove around to the back. The streets were wet and the sidewalks were empty. Everything was dark and quiet. Students were tucked in their rooms, studying or not studying, or whatever college kids did on Sunday nights. All I wanted was to get inside, have a drink, and forget about the ungrateful kid and the surly farmer.

I grabbed my briefcase and trudged to the front door. Breezing past the mailboxes, I took the elevator to the second floor, and headed down the corridor to my apartment. As usual, my neighbor across the hall, Doug Mozelle, was blaring Led Zeppelin. Doug was an art teacher who often painted in his apartment late at night. A bit of a rebel, Doug was one of the most popular professors. He used to be a drummer, which made him cool. And he was tenured, so he had it easy.

I unlocked my door and dumped my things on the futon, headed straight for the fridge, and pulled out a can of beer. The sound of the top cracking open was like an old friend saying *It's okay, I've got your back.* I took a long swig and closed the fridge. Moved to the futon and sat. When I was finished, I got up and paced around. Looked out the window to the dark patch of lawn covered in wet leaves, the big oak, sagging with drippy leaves that refused to fall. I couldn't stop the thoughts about that stupid kid running around in the cold field. I opened the fridge and took out another beer. Halfway through, I picked up the phone.

I chose Nancy, a nice woman I'd slept with a few times. She'd been divorced, like me, so we had that in common. She answered on the second ring.

"Hi, it's Matthew," I said, adding, "Larkin."

"Oh hi, Matthew," she said, sounding pleasantly surprised. She lowered her voice when she said my name, as if trying to find privacy from someone in her vicinity, probably her kids. I'd found that divorced moms generally didn't let their kids know about their dating life—or whatever I was to them—until much further along. Hence, I'd never met Nancy's kids, nor those of any of the other women I'd seen, for that matter.

"How're you doing?" I said to Nancy, because I didn't want to just jump in with the whole boy-running-in-a-field thing.

"Fine," she said, but she seemed to sense that I was calling about something else, which was one of the magical abilities about women that I'd both admired and somewhat feared. She said, "Is everything all right, Matthew?"

"Everything's great," I said, perhaps overselling it. "I was just thinking about you and I thought I'd call and say hi." This wasn't true. I only wanted to talk about the boy.

"Okay," she said, definitely not believing me.

"Yeah, I'm down in Northwood. Big storm. Commute was tough," I said, faking the small talk badly. "And what are you up to tonight?"

"Sorry, hang on," she said, and I heard another voice in the room. Her two daughters were still young. A small voice said, "Mama, will you read to us?" To the child, Nancy said, "Mama's on the phone." I heard a door close. To me, she said, "Sorry about that."

"I thought they'd be asleep by now." This wasn't true either. I had no idea what their bedtimes were.

I heard the door again, then children murmuring. To the children, Nancy said, "Pick out some books and I'll be right in." To me, she said, "Matthew, can you hang on?"

"Sure." As I waited, I remembered how I used to read to Finn. Illustrated books about trucks and trains. He'd point to the pictures and I'd make up stories about the construction projects or the loads the trains were carrying. He'd ask, "Whaz in dere?" I'd answer, "Big logs for building," and if he liked that story, he'd smile and point to the next one and ask, "Whaz in dere?" But if he didn't like my answer, he'd say, "No's not," and I'd have to come up with something else.

"Okay, I'm back," said Nancy, breathless.

"Look, I should let you go," I said, suddenly not wanting to talk about it.

"Really?" She sounded both disappointed and relieved.

"Yeah, it's fine. You've got your hands full."

We said good night. I promised to call again and maybe I would, but this was a busy time of the semester. After I hung up, I tossed my empty beer can and opened another. I sat on the futon and unzipped my briefcase. I pulled out my notes and placed them on the coffee table.

Flipping through the pages, I scanned my lecture outline but couldn't concentrate. I sat back and pinched the spot between my eyes, trying to squeeze away my thoughts. I switched on the TV, but channel-surfing didn't help. Pacing my six-hundred-square-foot abode didn't help. Neither did staring again at the dark lawn or listening to the muffled sound of Led Zeppelin. I picked up the phone and dialed.

"What is it, brother?" said Audrey, who had answered after six rings, moments before I was about to give up.

But it wasn't Audrey I was calling for; it was her husband, who happened to be a lawyer. "Is Hal there?"

"This isn't your *One Phone Call*, is it?" said Audrey, never letting me forget that Hal had helped me out of a DUI.

"It doesn't have to be law-related, Aud. Hal and I talk about other things," I said, which was true. But it was mostly legal things: my divorce, child support, being fired, to name a few.

"Relax. I was joking," said Audrey. "Hal's right here."

I waited and my brother-in-law came on the line. "Hey, Matt, what's up?"

"Um, I've got a situation I wanna run by you," I said. It was nice having an attorney in the family.

"Okay. Hang on," said Hal. "Let me switch phones." I waited until Hal came back. "You there?" he said after a few seconds.

"Yeah, thanks. It's not that I don't want Audrey to know, exactly, it's just . . ." I said.

"No problem. Attorney-client privilege and all that," said Hal.

"Thanks," I said. But I knew that people didn't always keep things confidential even when they've promised. It's too hard for humans—even lawyers—not to share. Plus, Hal and Audrey had been married a long time. Hal would probably tell his wife and make her swear not to tell.

"What's on your mind?" asked Hal.

As I described the night's events, Hal listened, only interrupting to ask a question here or there. He wanted all the facts and I gave them. Finally, I asked, "What do you think?"

"You've had an eventful evening," said Hal. "That's what I think."

"Yeah."

"Let me ask you this," said Hal. "Why didn't you call the police? Couldn't find a phone?"

"No, there was a pay phone," I said. "It was just, um, with the storm, I figured it'd take a while for the ambulance to get to us."

"Uh-huh," said Hal, as if he knew that wasn't the only reason.

I added, "And I'd had a few drinks."

Hal sighed. "Gotcha. Okay."

"Yeah."

"Well, all right, that's fair," said Hal, clearing his throat. "So what's your question?"

"I guess I just wonder—"

"—about the legalities of putting a kid in your car and driving him off into the night?"

"Well, right," I said. "But I was trying to help the poor kid."

"So listen," said Hal. "This isn't my area. I do real estate law."

"I know."

"But," he continued, never letting his lack of knowledge keep him from taking a stab, "as a general starting point, there's no legal obligation to help, okay?"

"Uh-huh."

"But once you affirmatively step in, so to speak, as a volunteer, to rescue someone for example, then the law imposes a duty of care."

"Which means . . . ?"

"Basically, negligence. If you're negligent in how you rescue, you can be liable. Even though you weren't obligated to help in the first place. Make sense?"

"Sure," I said, thinking about all the negligent things I'd just done. I lifted and carried a passed-out kid without checking first for injury. I drove said kid while tipsy. I didn't lock the car, which made it easier for him to jump out. Slammed on the brakes, jarring him. Had he hit his head? Grabbed his shoulder, then let him run away into a dark field. Hmm.

Hal added, "You should be fine as long as you acted, quote-unquote, reasonably."

"You're talking about the Good Samaritan law." This was something we covered in my Society and the Moral Code workshop over January term.

"Right," said Hal.

"And what's reasonable is up for debate, I guess." I took a swig of beer. "That's how you lawyers get paid."

"Fair." Hal chuckled. "But in all practicality, who's gonna sue you over this—the runaway? I mean, where were the kid's parents tonight?"

I thought about the Ogletree farmers. Were they his parents? They didn't exactly act like it. "Yeah, I guess."

"Was the kid worse off after you helped him?" asked Hal.

I thought about it. "He was limping, I guess, but—"

"—not because of anything you did, right?"

"Sure," I said, unsure.

After a beat, Hal said, "A buddy of mine had a Good Samaritan case you wouldn't believe."

"Oh yeah?" I didn't think I wanted to hear it.

"A car accident, real bad, car's on fire," said Hal, unable to resist. "A bystander runs to the burning car and pulls the guy out. Drags him away before the car explodes. Saves his life, right?"

"Okay," I said, listening intently.

"But in the process of dragging the guy out, the bystander somehow broke the guy's arm. So the guy sues for damages. And wins."

"Wow." I paused and thought about it. "I don't think the kid broke any bones, but still . . ."

"Yeah, you're probably fine," said Hal, but it wasn't the most comforting thing he could have said. After a beat, Hal asked, "Any reason you can't call the cops now? Let them know what you saw. Maybe they can send a car out there."

THE GOOD SAMARITAN 41

"I guess," I said, but the kid didn't seem to want anyone to know he was there. "I'm not sure."

"I suggest you call the cops," said Hal. "Cover your ass."

"Yeah, I probably should," I said, but I didn't want to deal with their questions either. I wanted this all to be over. To have never happened in the first place. I took a swig.

I heard Audrey chirping in the background. Hal said, "Your sister wants to talk to you."

Audrey came on the line. "Matty?"

"Yes," I said dutifully.

"Don't forget to visit Mom this week."

"Oh, Audrey," I moaned. Our mother, aged eighty-one, was sick with cancer. On top of that, she'd fallen and then developed pneumonia. Her condition had worsened and they'd moved her to the hospital attached to her nursing home in Burnsville. "I'll try but it's tenure week and I have a full teaching load."

"We all work, Matty," said Audrey.

"Yeah, but . . ." I said.

Apparently, Audrey felt she needed to increase the guilt level because she said, "Matthew. I see her every day. I don't think I should be the only one."

"You're not the only one," I said, hating the defensiveness in my voice. "Claire and I went to see her two weeks ago and she was asleep the whole time. Anyway, what about Gregory?"

"Greg's at the Mayo. I think his schedule is a bit more difficult than yours and mine," said Audrey and the truth of it stung a little.

"Fine," I said. "I'll try."

After hanging up, I stared at the phone for a while, meditating on the hunk of plastic and metal. I picked it up. The dial tone blared its endless monotone. I could at least call in an anonymous tip. I started to dial, then set it down. The kid was afraid of the hospital, and that's exactly where the police would have taken him.

Morality dictated I honor his request, right? Also, the kid seemed to know his way around. He was probably close to home. He was probably fine. And I was slightly drunk.

I could call tomorrow.

I leaned against the kitchen counter and noticed the calm of my apartment. There was a drip from the faucet I kept forgetting to report to faculty residential services. I tightened the handle and jiggled the spout, and it was quiet again for a moment.

Seven

CLAIRE

MONDAY, SEPTEMBER 28, 1992

BECCA SUGGESTED I SNOOP THROUGH EVAN'S FILE IN THE COUNSELING Office, but I had already thought of that. We were sitting at lunch at the far end of one of the cafeteria tables. We'd finished eating and we were discussing the whole bagel-throwing thing. Becca leaned in conspiratorially as we talked. I must have been nervous, because I was tearing off tiny pieces of my napkin and letting them fall onto my tray, bit by bit until a small scattering appeared there, like dandruff.

As she listened, Becca was sucking on her straw, casually slurping up the last of her Diet Mountain Dew. I showed her a bruise I had on my arm.

"From the bagel bites?" she said. "Weird."

"I know," I said. We glanced around the cafeteria in case any of Evan's friends were spying on us, but the place had emptied out. We were safe.

Becca lifted her straw and stabbed at the ice in the bottom of the red plastic glass. "You should definitely look at his file."

"Yeah, I know," I said in a low voice. I had access to the student files because I worked in the Counseling Office during sixth hour. My "job" was to sit at the front desk, answer the phones, do filing, and greet students who came in to meet with the counselors. It was a position of honor only given to responsible students who had good grades and integrity. I'd snooped through Evan's student file two weeks ago after he and I had dissected the worm and I'd wanted to know more about him. But now, I didn't know what I was looking for and I wanted Becca to tell me.

"Maybe he has terrible parents or something," she guessed.

"Maybe," I said, although that wasn't the type of thing I would find in a student file and I knew that because I'd seen tons of student files, including my own. Including Becca's, and her parents weren't great. I said, "I'll try."

A sophomore walked past us to get to the vending machines that were lined up in the corner. We watched and waited. Becca slurped some more. I tied my shoe. Our trays were covered in crumpled napkins and there were remnants of hamburger buns stained with ketchup and abandoned on the beige plastic plates. I swiveled around on the cafeteria stool and kept an eye on the vending machine user. Their coins had jammed, and they were banging on the glass. Heavy sighs. We exchanged glances and I raised my eyebrows in recognition of my fellow student's helplessness in the situation.

"Report it to the front office," Becca suggested to the sophomore. Becca knew everything about school.

The disgruntled student slouched away, and we were alone again.

"Evan definitely likes you," said Becca, as if she'd been holding her breath.

"You think?" I felt my face heat up.

Becca nodded with a knowing expression. "You just need to find out everything you can. Be prepared."

"Yeah. I'll look today," I said. I'd only seen Evan's basic student file. Those were the easy files for me to get access to. I could read everything in the basic student files but there hadn't been much there about Evan. It made me wonder if he had other files somewhere. If he had a counseling file or a disciplinary report or something like that, those were confidential. Confidential files were kept in the counselor's offices and would be harder to get.

Our high school had two kinds of counseling. The first type was education related, which was handled by Mr. Peoples. Mr. Peoples was generally considered to be mean. He was not automatically confident that you would get into the college of your dreams. He did not make exceptions if you missed deadlines. He was the school disciplinarian and most kids hated him. But Mr. Peoples was nice to me, probably because my dad was a college professor, so in his eyes I had special status and it worked out all right for me.

The other type of counseling was basically therapy for kids with emotional problems, and it was done by the school social worker, Ms. Patterson. Ms. Patterson was so nice and cool, and everyone loved her. She was easy to talk to; she believed in us and she actually tried to help. She even got along with Mr. Peoples, but that was probably because he had a crush on her, and I know that because everyone had a crush on Ms. Patterson. Also, Mr. Peoples was always making up reasons to talk with her and ask her personal questions and a couple of times he brought her an extra piece of cake when there was a birthday party in the teachers' lounge or whatever.

On Monday afternoon when I got to the Counseling Office, it was quiet. Mr. Peoples was away, probably blabbing at an assembly in the auditorium. Ms. Patterson was on the phone in her office. So I went to the main file cabinet and found Evan's name. Evan's student file was just as I remembered from the last time I looked. Bad grades. Excessive tardies. Basketball stuff, nothing of note. But then it occurred to me what was missing. There wasn't any mention of his parents coming to the parent-teacher conferences.

There wasn't any form filled out by his parents about their Hopes and Dreams (the form we all had to take home for our parents to fill out at the beginning of high school). And there wasn't anything yet about his college wish list.

Maybe Mr. Peoples had told Evan he'd never get into college. I mean, his highest grade was a B-minus, which was my lowest grade of all time. I always assumed that getting a D would be insurmountable, but Evan had several of them and I wondered how he felt about that. He certainly didn't act devastated. Maybe he was but didn't show it. He just acted like everything was fine and he didn't have a care in the world.

It occurred to me that Evan might not be able to graduate on time, so I counted his credits. He'd already repeated math and English. I checked his birth date. He was almost two years older than me. He'd either been held back or had to repeat a grade. His birthday was December tenth and I liked knowing that. It was so different from mine; I was a summer baby.

Then I saw the file marked "IEP." I knew what IEPs were: Individualized Education Plans. Ms. Patterson had a lot of them for me to file and make copies of and staple. I opened Evan's IEP folder but there was only a blue piece of paper that said "Peoples" in large print. This meant the actual file was in Mr. Peoples's office. I sat back and sighed, frustrated that I'd reached a dead end.

Just then the door opened, and a person walked in who was someone I never expected to see in my high school. My mouth must have been hanging open. I was confused. In shock.

"Hi, Claire," he said, and my two worlds collided.

What was Adrian, my co-worker from Bageletta, doing here, at the Counseling Office? I'd only ever seen him at Bageletta and he was always wearing the Bageletta uniform. I almost didn't recognize him in civilian clothes. But it was him. Adrian must have been as surprised as I was, because he said, "I didn't realize you went to South."

"Uh, yeah, I do. I go here. Hi," I said, standing up.

Adrian smiled. He was so nice. He was the one who'd walked in on Friday night and seen Evan throwing bagel bites. Adrian had startled me, though, because he was a baker and bakers usually worked in the wee hours. I hadn't expected a baker to be at Bageletta so early in the night. Anyway, I'd jumped when I saw him and that was embarrassing. But then I was relieved he was there so I wasn't alone, and he helped me clean up. I'd never thought about Adrian coming to the high school for any reason. In fact, I thought he was in college. *Oh crap*, I thought. *Did this have to do with Evan?*

I tried to act cool. I smiled and asked Adrian, "So, what're you doing here?"

Eight

MATTHEW

I DON'T PROVIDE SEATING CHARTS FOR MY CLASSES. IT'S A SOCIOLOG-ical experiment every time: where to sit, whom to avoid. After the best seats were taken, students had to work harder to find an accept-able spot. In this context, the freedom over seat selection increased their stress, and many would have preferred being told where to sit. I found it fascinating. Reliably, most students congregated in the last few rows. They tried to leave an empty seat or two between them and the next person. And because humans resist change, the majority of students gravitated to the same spot each day if they could, which was why I encouraged them to pick a seat opposite their default choice.

"Come on down," I called out to the lecture hall as the Mon-day morning class filed in. I was standing at the base of the audi-torium, rocking back and forth, watching as the seats filled up. My favorite part was this anticipation, when all was possibility. But to-day was different: the observers would be there, listening and tak-ing notes on my lecture, so naturally I was distracted with thoughts about how it would go.

Already I was off my game. I'd awakened later than usual and had to rush across campus to make it to Lindberg Hall in time. I had a throbbing headache and I hadn't slept well last night, prob-ably because I was worried about the kid and about what Hal had said. I should have called the police. I would call them today, right after class.

"Plenty of seats up front," I announced, gesturing to the empty rows. For the most part, the students ignored my suggestion. A few glanced in my direction when they heard my voice. One or two trickled halfway down and I smiled at them absentmindedly. There were four more minutes until the start of class, but still no observers. I picked up the chalk and turned to the board.

I wrote, "Analyze circumstance => improve life?" This was an introductory course, and we were in week four. On the first day, I'd written, "What is society?" That question usually triggered a good entry to the preliminaries. Over the years I'd noticed that many of the students enrolled in Sociology 101 were only there because Psychology 101 was full. Others had (wrongly) assumed sociology would be easy. Many were interested in criminology, which often meant they were intrigued with crime and criminals. Others were passionate about deconstructing sexism or racism, or they had strong views on family systems, cultures, and communities. We covered it all, but it was a long road and we followed a syllabus. First things first.

Today's reading was by Auguste Comte, so I wrote his name on the board. Then I wrote, "What is positivism?" and a few other key concepts to dwell upon during the class. As I wrote on the board, I wondered who the observer would be. I guessed either Wesley Granger or Carolina Crossthwaite. Both were well-respected teachers who were influential with the P&T Committee.

I wiped the chalk dust from my hands and turned around. When I looked up, I startled. Wes Granger, my observer for the day, was sitting in the front row, notebook open, pen in hand. He winked at me, and I caught my breath. Even though I figured it might be Granger, I hadn't expected him to sit so close, but okay. Fine. I smiled at Granger and gathered my thoughts. *Time to shine.*

"Take your seats, please," I called to the students still milling about, and I switched on the overhead machine. The warmth from the projector and the familiar hum it emitted gave me focus, pulling me to my purpose. As if on autopilot, I started the lecture.

"Thanks to the French philosopher Auguste Comte," I said, projecting my voice to the back of the room, "we can study social systems using methods of the *natural sciences*."

I paused for effect. Wes Granger's face was neutral. Granger considered himself a master of the art of lecture. He was certainly talented, and he'd led several faculty training sessions. As I taught, I was ticking through some of Granger's tips in my head. One of them was about projecting confidence with nonverbal cues. For example, how one presents oneself. Not just in terms of clothing—today I'd chosen a pale blue button-down, pleated khakis, and comfortable shoes—but also, in mannerisms, body language, and facial expressions. I stuck out my right arm, a wide gesture of invitation. With my chin raised, I asked the two hundred students, "Who can tell me: What is Comte best known for?"

As I waited for a volunteer, I tried to relax my shoulders and soften my eyes, keeping my palms open. I was conveying *confident openness*.

No one answered and most were ignoring my question, but that was all right. It usually took a while for the class to warm up. I pointed at the chalkboard, underlining words as I spoke the answers. "Comte is known for the theory of positivism, the human ability to analyze our circumstances and improve our lives. Right?"

There were a few nodding heads. A flicker of life, come on! It was like coaxing a cold engine to start in winter. I couldn't lose them; I'd just begun. Granger was already jotting down notes. I wished he wasn't sitting in the front row; I didn't need to hear him scribbling like that. My neck flushed warm, and I remembered that I'd nicked myself while shaving this morning. I touched my neck. The bit of Kleenex was still on the spot. I wiped it away and glanced at my hands. No blood. Good.

The thought of bleeding brought to mind the boy from last night. Had I seen any cuts on him? I hadn't thought so. As I placed the next transparency on the overhead projector, I thought about the Good Samaritan statute, the obligation to act reasonably. Had I been negligent? Made things worse for that kid? I wished I hadn't given my card to those farmers. I was thinking about moral relativity and personal motivation theory. Why do we help one another? Is altruism real? Or are we always acting out of enlightened self-interest? Would the farmers tell the college about me?

"Professor Larkin?" said a voice.

"Huh?" I glanced up. The light of the overhead projector had blinded me, and I stepped back and rubbed my eyes. "What is it?"

A student in the fourth row said, "Are you okay?"

"Of course," I said, glancing at Granger. He was looking down. I asked the student, "Why?"

"You stopped talking," said another student. "Like, you were frozen."

"We thought you were gonna pass out," said the first student.

"Oh," I said, as if snapping awake. "No, I, uh . . . I didn't get a lot of sleep."

The students snickered and glanced at one another as if I'd made a titillating revelation. Students were always curious about us single professors and our dating lives.

"No, not what you're thinking," I said, which might have made it worse. Now they were really interested. To stunt their speculation, I blurted out the truth, saying, "There was a lost child in the storm last night. I think he might have had hypothermia."

The class went silent, as if they weren't sure they'd heard me right. Maybe they thought I was joking. They seemed to be waiting for further instruction on how to react.

Suddenly the bell rang, and class was over. I was at the end of my overheads, but I didn't remember what I'd said. I didn't remember moving through them, but I must have. The transparencies were sitting in a pile upside-down, which was how I stacked them after I was finished.

"Okay, that's it for today," I said, but I wasn't sure anyone was even listening.

There was a moment of hesitation, like when a crowd holds its breath to see if the trapeze artist will grab that next bar, and then a release. When we'd all snapped back into reality, I heard the familiar sounds that signified the end of class: slamming books and shuffling feet, zipping up backpacks, laughing and yawning. General chatter and the jubilation of being set free.

I pinched the bridge of my nose and switched off the projector. I might have been mumbling something to myself. That whole episode was strange.

When I lifted my eyes, Wes Granger was standing in front of me, waiting dumbly.

"Hi, Wes," I said, extending my hand.

"Hello," he said, shaking my hand a bit too long. The handshake was an odd formality in this setting, but it broke the ice. "Thanks for letting me sit in."

"You bet," I said, looking down at his chubby face, scrutinizing it for clues. I flashed a smile, then began packing my briefcase. "Just an intro class."

He watched me load my materials into my briefcase. Finally, almost conspiratorially, he leaned close and asked, "Is everything all right?"

There it was. A jab about my blanking out. "Oh, sure," I said, deflecting. "Just needed a power nap, I guess."

Wes chuckled. "May I walk with you?"

Did I have a choice? I hoisted my briefcase on my shoulder, nodded and gestured to the exit.

Together we climbed the steps and pushed out of Lindberg Hall and out onto the green. Leaves scattered the campus with yellow and red. A few broken branches littered the ground, as if certifying that yes, there was a storm last night, and I admired the curvy boughs rising from the surface like the Loch Ness Monster.

"What was that all about in class?" said Granger as we set off down the path together.

"What do you mean?" I said, but I knew what he was asking. And it wasn't about Auguste Comte.

"The kid with hypothermia? Was that real or—or—or some sort of a thought experiment?" said Granger. His short legs moved quickly to keep up with me.

"Oh, that," I said, but I didn't remember mentioning that the kid had hypothermia. "Huh . . . a thought experiment? Interesting . . ."

Granger made a face as if trying to follow. I wasn't sure how much to share with him, but I was intrigued by his suggestion. This quandary could be used as a teaching device, perhaps. Still, I didn't want to discuss it with Wes Granger. Not now.

Just then I caught sight of someone approaching us. It was my neighbor Doug, the rock 'n' roll art professor. He was striding toward us as if he had something important to say. He had a mysterious grin on his face.

"Doug," I said, stopping at the T in the paths. Wes hadn't anticipated the halt and nearly crashed into me.

"Hey, Matt," said Doug, planting himself in front of us. Seeing Granger, he added, "Wes."

"What's up?" I said, hoping to speed things along.

"Oh, not much," said Doug, hands on hips. "Only that there's a homeless kid living in your car."

Wes's eyes went wide. Doug stood there with a pleased expression, as if he couldn't wait to see my reaction. I wasn't sure I understood. I hoped I'd misheard him. I said, "What did you say?"

"Yeah, I just saw a homeless kid in your car," repeated Doug. He smiled and slapped me on the shoulder as if congratulating a new father.

I rubbed my shoulder because he'd hit me a bit too hard.

"A homeless kid?" asked Wes. "Could this be the boy you picked up last night?"

"You picked up a boy last night?" Doug furrowed his eyebrows. "What the hell, Matt?"

Nine

KIRA

WHEN KIDS WANT TO LEAVE, THEY FIND A WAY TO GO, AND SEAVER WAS no exception. It wasn't June's fault and I didn't want her getting into trouble over this. Worst of all, I didn't want my supervisor to refer the Ogletrees for possible disqualification as foster parents. That would be a sad day for us all, especially me. I'd placed many kids with them over the years. And June had literally been my own foster mother twenty years ago. The county had overlooked our personal relationship because of the long time gap, and also in light of the high demand for foster families in their area. I didn't want anything to mess that up. So I woke up Monday morning hoping I could fix the situation. Which meant I had a busy day ahead.

First, I called the St. Gus professor and left him a message. I gave him the heads-up that I'd be stopping by later in the day.

Next, I drove to the rehab facility in Otsego to pay a surprise visit to Seaver's mom. Maybe she'd heard from him. Maybe he was hiding near there, at a park or something? He was determined to be reunited with his mom, but I had my doubts about Nicole. She was nearing the end of yet another ninety-day treatment program, but the reports had been lukewarm. It sounded like she'd been phoning it in, only meeting the minimum requirements.

"Hi, Nicole," I said after they buzzed me through and led me to the activity room. My appearance wasn't on the schedule and the receptionist had given me a short lecture about the importance of calling ahead.

I spotted Seaver's mom sitting at a round table with a half-completed puzzle on it. Funny how rehab facilities resembled old folks' homes and day care centers. Nicole didn't look up until I got close. I said, "Hey, how's it going?"

"Oh, it's splendid," she deadpanned.

I plopped my briefcase onto a chair and took off my jacket. I sat down next to her and studied the puzzle. I said, "Working the edges first, huh?"

"This ain't mine," she said, pointing to the puzzle she had clearly been working on. "I just happened to sit here."

"Okay," I said, surveying the scattered puzzle. I found an edge piece and snapped it into position. I sat back and exhaled, resting my elbows on the arms of the chair. After a beat, I leaned forward and touched Nicole's forearm. I asked, "So, really, how's it going? Good?"

She shifted in her seat as if to signify she'd be giving me her full attention. "It's going just the way you think it's going," she said, as if speaking to a real dummy. "It sucks. I'm trapped here. I can't work. They took my son away. I can't drink. Ever again in my life, apparently. I can't take any of my medicine that I need. So I'd say everything's great."

"Yeah," I said, not intending to argue with her. I looked around the room and admired the woodwork, the bookshelves. A large television was on, but the sound was off. Another resident was relaxing on a worn sofa. There was a coffeepot and Styrofoam cups on a counter in the corner. "Want some coffee?"

Nicole scoffed and shook her head. "Just tell me why you're here."

"I will," I said, holding up my index finger as I rose and scooted over to the coffee station. I poured myself a cup and sprinkled in some powdered creamer, watching the color lighten. I took a sip and made a face. When I returned to the table, Nicole had added an edge piece to the one I'd put down. "Oh, look at that. Are there any more?"

I scanned the pieces. It was a scene of ducks on a small lake surrounded by cattails and evergreen trees and eagles overhead. An idyllic scenario, with a landscape that could actually be found not too far from this building. And yet, everything about it seemed out of place.

"I don't care about the stupid puzzle, Kira," she said. "When am I getting my kid back?"

I let go of a piece I'd been hanging on to and leaned toward Nicole. I sighed and said, "That's for the court to decide. After you finish your program. And get a job."

"Such bullshit," she said, pushing the puzzle away. The whole thing moved like a wobbly frame, but we could still make out the edges, the misshapen outline of an empty square.

"How are the parenting classes going?" I asked.

"Oh, they're a joy," said Nicole dryly, sitting back in her chair. She was slouching with her legs spread, the posture of someone who really didn't care. "Taught by an idiot."

"Yeah, it's hit or miss, isn't it?" I said, studying her, seeing her frustration. I knew she wanted to be a good parent. I grimaced. "You gotta go to those, Nicole."

"I know," she said, suddenly picking up a piece and trying to force it where it clearly didn't belong.

I watched her struggle with the pieces. Finally, I said, "Speaking of Seaver . . ."

"Yeah?" She looked at me, a misfit piece still pinched in her fingers. "What?"

"Have you heard from him? Does he ever try to call you?"

"No," said Nicole, a tinge of annoyance in her voice. And in her face. "You said he wasn't supposed to call me. Unless it's scheduled."

"Yeah, I know," I said, hiding my disappointment.

"So why are you asking me?" she asked suspiciously.

"No reason," I lied. Trying to act casual, I fussed with some puzzle pieces, hoping to distract her from my face. I said, "I'll bring him up here for another supervised visit next month."

"Great. Can't wait for that," she said sarcastically. "So you can watch how I am with my own child. Judge me. Make sure I don't do anything craaazy." She held out the vowel sound and made a gesture like she was out of her mind. "The scary addict mommy, that's me."

"Come on, you know I want you to succeed," I said. But just in case, of course I'd been working on backup plans, including an aunt who lived in Minneapolis but who had previously said she couldn't do it. Convincing the aunt was a work in progress, but I didn't need to bring that up today.

Nicole ignored me and stared at the puzzle. Her walls were up.

"Will you let me know if Seaver tries to contact you? That's the kind of thing I'd like to have a heads-up about. In case the judge catches wind of it."

"How would the judge know?" she asked. She wasn't stupid.

"Oh, I dunno. Maybe the rehab director puts it in your report or something." I pulled that one out of thin air.

"Ridiculous," said Nicole, shaking her head. "So that's it? You came all the way up here to ask if my kid has been calling me. Against the rules?"

"Well, that and just to . . ." I said, trying to cover myself. I reached in my briefcase and pulled out a file. It was her file, but there wasn't anything I needed to show her. "Just wanted to update my notes."

"Well, it's not exactly Thrillsville up here, so I don't know what to tell ya."

"That's what we like to hear."

"Well, I'm glad you're happy," she said, clearly annoyed. "Now if you don't mind, I'd like to take a shit before Group."

"Perfect," I said, checking my watch. "I gotta get back anyway." It was a forty-five-minute drive from Otsego back to the Cities. I had an older student coming in to enroll at the high school. He needed another credit to graduate, but I had a different reason to see him: Adrian Wallace had lived with Seaver at the Ogletree farm but had recently aged out. He was my next stop on the search for Seaver. As I stood, I gave Nicole a half hug. She tolerated it, and I caught a whiff of cigarette smoke in her hair. I said, "Good to see you."

"Okay," she said, rising.

"Talk to you soon," I said, hoisting my briefcase strap across my body and heading for the door.

When I got to the front desk, I thanked the receptionist again for letting me see Nicole without an appointment. She flashed me a fake smile and it seemed that no one was happy to be in that place.

As I left the facility, I scanned the parking lot, hoping to find Seaver hiding under a bench or something. He'd been very clear he wanted to live with his mother whether the court thought it was a good idea or not. Just to be sure, I walked around the building, checking the secluded areas for makeshift campsites. But I was alone in Otsego. Nicole didn't have any other visitors. My first guess hadn't paid off.

But I had one more hunch to scope out: a young man named Adrian.

Ten

CLAIRE

ADRIAN SMILED AT ME. A BIG, WARMHEARTED GRIN. HE TILTED HIS head and flashed his eyes as if he were delighted by my question, and he shook his head gently and I already knew this was a person who wouldn't tease me, betray me, or lie to me. He was a good person, and I believed that if Adrian liked a girl, he would never in a million years throw bagel bites at her.

He said, "I'm going here now."

"Here?" My eyes widened. "To South?"

"Sort of." He nodded, still smiling and mirroring my big eyes.

"For high school?" I said. "But aren't you, like . . ."

"Old?" he said. "Yeah. I get that a lot."

"No, I mean, yeah, but," I said, "like, I thought you were in college?"

"I'm nineteen," he said. "But I have one more high school class to take before I can get my diploma."

"One class?" My face scrunched up on its own accord. How could he have miscalculated his credits like that? He was so good at baking.

"I had to drop out. It's a long story," he said, smiling again, as if he'd be happy to tell me whenever I had the time.

I pulled my face back to normal, trying to be polite. Trying to be patient. But I really wanted to know the story.

"Adrian!" Ms. Patterson's voice floated high in the air behind me. She emerged from her office and practically ran to greet him. Adrian seemed shy and sort of bowed to Ms. Patterson, who had one hand on her chest as if honored to receive him. "I'm so glad I got to see you before your meeting with Mr. Peoples. He's the one who'll get you registered."

"Great, thanks," said Adrian.

The three of us were standing there in a triangle, as if no one knew whose turn it was to talk. Behind Ms. Patterson there were guest chairs, two against each wall, with a small table in the corner. A lamp and a couple of old college catalogs sat on the table. Beside my desk there was a giant display rack with information on ACT prep classes, financial aid, college fairs, and more. One of my jobs was to replenish the supply and keep it organized. Behind Adrian was the door and the big windows that looked out on the hallway that would be packed with kids as soon as the bell rang. But for now, it was just us three.

"I was just explaining to Claire that I'm enrolling for one class," said Adrian to Ms. Patterson.

"Oh, you met Claire?" said Ms. Patterson, and they both looked at me.

Adrian smiled. "We work together."

"Yeah, sort of," I said, trying not to blush.

"Oh, great," said Ms. Patterson. "Then you'll already have a friend."

Adrian and I smirked. This was getting embarrassing. He was so much older than me. And taller! Tall with perfect brown skin and big brown eyes. Without his Bageletta cap and bandanna, I could see his short hair, which made his shoulders seem wider, I don't know why. And without his safety glasses, his whole face was there and it was like he was a different person.

"I only sell sandwiches," I said, trying to explain the Bageletta hierarchy to Ms. Patterson. "Adrian is, like, a baker."

Adrian smiled like he was flattered.

Ms. Patterson nodded dumbly, like she didn't care what our ages or titles were. She said, "He's going to be a chef someday."

"Someday, maybe." Adrian grinned. Turning to me, he said, "But, um, yes. In fact, we both were working at the bagel shop last Friday."

Why was he bringing that up? To Ms. Patterson, I explained, "We sort of overlapped when he came in for the night shift."

"Good thing I got there when I did," he said.

"Why?" said Ms. Patterson, suddenly more interested. "What happened?"

"Some guy was hurling bagels at Claire," said Adrian.

"Bagel bites," I corrected him.

"Oh my goodness," said Ms. Patterson. "That sounds terrible."

"It was a joke," I said, but I still wasn't sure.

"Who was it? A customer?" asked Ms. Patterson.

"No one," I said, suddenly protective of Evan. "Just a kid."

"You said you knew him," said Adrian.

"I did?" God, this was so weird. Why was Adrian dwelling on this?

"Yeah." He shifted his weight. "You said he went here."

My neck was hot. I said, "Oh, I don't remember saying that. Anyway."

Adrian inhaled deeply, like he didn't want to argue. He said, "Well, I'm glad I was there. So you weren't alone."

Ms. Patterson asked Adrian, "So you got this guy to leave?"

"Uh-huh," said Adrian.

"I mean, he ran out of bagel bites," I explained.

"Still," said Adrian, not letting it go. "When I showed up, he was just throwing the empty bag on the floor. He saw me and took off out the door."

"Wow," said Ms. Patterson, but she was easily impressed.

"You scared me though," I said to Adrian. "I didn't even know a baker would be working that night. I mean, I jumped when you came in. Remember?"

"Yeah. You were kind of upset." Adrian reached over and touched my elbow.

I looked at Ms. Patterson. She was giving me those kind eyes.

"Anyway," said Adrian, "after the guy left, I locked the door."

"I'm glad," said Ms. Patterson.

"Me too," I said. "But I mean, it was fine."

Ms. Patterson gave me a long look, like she really understood how I felt. Then I was afraid I might cry. And then I was embarrassed. It was uncomfortable, the caring. I wanted it to stop.

As if sensing my request, her eyes moved to my desk. There was a spindle on the corner where I kept her messages. Pink while-you-were-out slips. She picked up the messages and then looked at the file that was sitting there. Evan's file.

"Oh, if you were wondering," I stammered, "that's Evan Lewis's file. I was just doing filing and I, um, noticed this blue IEP folder. It says Peoples. So I guess that means it's in Mr. Peoples's office?" I held up the blue paper.

"Claire, that's confidential." Ms. Patterson pushed the blue paper down.

The door opened and Mr. Peoples walked in. I didn't think he heard us talking about him but I didn't know for sure. Adrian stepped aside to let him pass. Mr. Peoples stopped when he saw Ms. Patterson. It was an awkward moment and we were all staring at Mr. Peoples.

"Did I fart?" he asked, and I laughed. That was his sense of humor. "What's going on?"

Ms. Patterson said, "Adrian Wallace is here to register."

"Oh?" said Mr. Peoples, as if he'd forgotten his meeting. Then, to cover his tracks, he nodded at Adrian and said, "Yes, of course."

"And I was just asking about this student's IEP file," I said. "I believe this blue paper means you have it?"

"Uh, yes, that's what it means. Do you need the file, Kira?" Mr. Peoples asked Ms. Patterson.

She was shaking her head. "We don't have to discuss this in front of our new student."

"Just let me check," said Mr. Peoples, heading into his office.

Adrian and I watched as Mr. Peoples pulled a set of keys out of one of the potted plants on top of the bookshelves in his office. Then he opened a smaller file cabinet close to his desk.

"Actually, let's get it later, Ted," said Ms. Patterson, as if Mr. Peoples was making everything worse. "Thanks."

"You sure?" The way he looked at her was exactly like a puppy dog.

"Yes, it's fine," she said, waving him off. "You have a meeting with this young man."

"Indeed, to register," said Mr. Peoples. Gesturing to Adrian, he said, "Come along."

As he left with Mr. Peoples, Adrian gave me a glance, teen-to-teen, as if we were the only ones who could possibly understand how embarrassing this was.

I watched Mr. Peoples return the secret keys to the secret spider plant and everybody went to their respective desks. I looked around for the watering can. Suddenly I had an urgent need to water the ferns.

Eleven

MATTHEW

"YOU'VE CLEARLY GOT YOUR HANDS FULL," SAID WES, REFERRING TO Doug's startling news about the kid in my car.

"Yeah," I said apologetically. If this was a test, I was failing. "I'm sure it's not as dramatic as it sounds."

Doug gave me a look as if he begged to differ.

"You'd better go take care of that," said Wes with a pained expression. He patted me on the back.

"Okay, sure," I said, trying to keep it together. "Thank you for being in class today."

"Yes, well, good luck to you," said Wes, and I wasn't sure if he was referring to the kid situation or the tenure vote. Maybe both.

We watched him walk away. As soon as Wes was out of earshot, I turned to Doug and said, "What the hell, Doug?"

"I'm sorry but you gotta trust me." He took off down the path, gesturing for me to come along.

I groaned and followed him.

He was walking fast and turning back occasionally to tell me the story. He explained, "I was moving my van to the studio."

"Uh-huh," I said.

"And when I came back, that's when I noticed it."

"Noticed what?" I said.

"The fogged-up back window of your car," said Doug.

My Subaru GL wagon had a wayback space that was similar to the classic station wagons from my childhood. That's one of the reasons I'd been drawn to the Subaru when Finn was born. Perfect for a family of four, and I imagined Tammy and I would take our kids on long car trips, like my parents had done with me and my siblings. Back then, Gregory and I slept in the wayback, and Audrey had the entire middle bench seat. I'd wanted to do the same with Claire and Finn, but Tammy and I had always been too busy to take any long trips. Then we lost Finn before we'd ever had the chance to re-create those memories, which suddenly felt quite sad to me.

Doug and I turned at the Y in the path. As we walked, Doug explained, "So I looked closer and saw a mess of, like, a blanket, and then, like, an arm and the top of a head and I sort of freaked out."

Doug was telling me the story, layer by layer, like this was a painting he was building. He was a talented artist, not that I would know good art from bad. His work featured wall-size canvases and multimedia. He'd shown at many galleries, and his pieces had been photographed and included in several major books about painting and sculpture. His research was about new ways to use paint, to create larger murals and recycled sculptures.

"It was weird, you know? To see a kid sleeping in your car like that. So out of place," said Doug, slowing down. The apartment building was just across the street and we paused, looking both ways. There was never any traffic on these campus roads, but we stopped anyway. He turned to me, his face completely earnest and said, "But don't worry. The kid seemed to be okay."

"How do you know that?" I asked.

"Because he rolled over and saw me looking at him."

I inhaled. As we stepped into the street, I took the lead, moving quickly ahead of Doug.

"And I talked to him," added Doug, almost like a brag.

"You talked to him?" We were just repeating each other.

"Well, I mean, I was saying words. I don't know if he heard them," explained Doug. "I mean, how do you define 'talking'? I guess that's a sociological question?"

How original, I thought, *a dig at sociology*. "Ha ha," I said dryly. Sociology was an easy target, but I'd become inured to the taunting long ago. Doug and I swerved like race cars along the side of the building, then around back to the parking lot. I was anxious to see if this was the same kid as last night.

As we approached the car, I patted my front pocket, confirming that my keys were safely within my possession. But hadn't I locked it? The Subaru looked untouched, nonsuspicious. Nothing out of order. I glanced at Doug. He walked to the back end of the car and I followed. We leaned close to the glass. There was nothing to see. No kid. No one.

"He must have taken off," said Doug. "He was here, I swear. Less than a half hour ago."

My heart rate was accelerating. Without pause, I swung open all the side doors, as if to air out the trouble. I leaned in and looked for clues. Nothing. I opened the rear hatch to examine the way-back. The wool blanket was in a pile. I usually kept it folded, for emergencies. I also had a window scraper, a candle, and an empty coffee can. They were intact.

I glanced around at the shrubs, the dumpster, then up at the apartment windows. Not sure what I was looking for. A cat was staring at us from the third floor. I thought of Snowball, a kitten my brother and I had rescued from a paper bag at the bus stop one morning. Getting a pet for the family was another thing I'd always planned on doing but never did.

Doug and I stood in the empty parking lot for a bit, as if the solution might arise from the cracked pavement. Doug pulled out his pipe and lit it. I stared at the dumpster, then up at the cat in the window. Perhaps the cat had seen where the boy was hiding? The tobacco smoke was sweet in the air between us.

"I wonder where that kid went," said Doug, looking again at the four corners of the lot. His pipe was clamped in his teeth like some kind of hip, edgy Popeye. "Can't have gone far."

"Why do you say that?" I asked.

"Because he's a kid and has no way to get around," said Doug.

"Unless he stole a bicycle or something. Better check the rack," I said, nodding to the side of the building where the bike rack sat. We scurried to the bike rack but nothing looked amiss.

"He probably just needed a place to sleep for the night," said Doug.

"Sure, but how'd he get into my car?" I said. A few students passed by and I nodded at them. Nosy, they whispered something to one another and continued on their way.

Doug meandered over to the dumpster and peeked in, as if the kid was hiding in there. Then he let the lid slam and I jumped. "Not in the dumpster," said Doug. "He's probably gone. Better lock your car just in case."

"Okay," I said, but I had a sense the kid was still nearby, hovering, listening to us, like from a tree. Like he was watching me for some reason. I felt it.

Puffing on his pipe, Doug strolled back into the apartment building and I followed. But I left my car unlocked.

In case the kid needed a place to sleep again.

Twelve

CLAIRE

WHEN MR. PEOPLES LEFT FOR THE MEN'S ROOM, I DASHED INTO HIS office and unlocked his file cabinet. Evan's file was thick. I pulled out a section of it, including the one marked IEP, and I took the papers to my desk. If I got caught, I could say that Ms. Patterson had asked me to return them to her.

I sat at my desk and flipped through the pages. Lots of academic struggles. I wondered whether Evan would be able to graduate this year. Then I remembered he was a star on the boys' basketball team and there'd been scouts from D1 colleges watching him play. I scanned the pages looking for anything from the athletic director, letters forgiving the poor grades and memorializing Evan's physical prowess as part of his permanent record. I didn't see anything like that, but I did find a report from a doctor.

It wasn't a regular doctor. It was an educational psychologist with a lot of letters by his name, meaning he had a lot of degrees. And I had Evan's full name: Evan Mark Lewis. *A good name*, I thought.

I read the first page of the doctor's report then flipped to the second. Evan had ADHD and dyslexia. The doctor recommended reading support and extra time. Evan was taking medications including Ritalin. That was interesting. Evan never talked about that. This seemed like a major secret. Then I found an even more personal item: the interest questionnaire. Evan had filled it out in his own handwriting, in pencil.

It felt very intimate to be reading his penciled answers to questions about what he wanted to be when he grew up, and what he thought were his best strengths. I wondered why he wrote in pencil. Didn't he have a pen? Maybe he wasn't sure about his answers. Some of them weren't complete. Others he'd skipped. But there was enough there, scrawled in Evan's uneven handwriting. It was kind of sweet and gave me a better sense of who he was. He wanted to be a professional basketball player, but if that didn't work out, he'd written, then he wanted to be a plumber.

So Evan wasn't interested in college. That was unusual, but I understood it better now that I knew about his learning difficulties. It was hard for him to read and take tests. No wonder he didn't want to spend four more years in school. It was different for me. School was easier, and my parents made it clear I was going to college. So when I'd taken my interest inventory, I assumed I'd be going. It was only a matter of where and what I'd study. According to my interests, I was going to be a meteorologist, teacher, or therapist. Hopefully not a teacher, because my dad would be weird about that. His mother was a retired teacher, so there would be three generations and that might make his head explode.

I glanced at the clock. Ten more minutes until the end of sixth hour. Mr. Peoples was still in the men's room, presumably. So I took the opportunity to page through the rest of the file, searching for anything interesting, and then I found it: a disciplinary report. And another one. And another. A fight in the cafeteria. Swearing at a teacher. Smoking. And then something else, a "physical incident" he'd been accused of. It had been flagged a "concern" and referred to Ms. Patterson. Why hadn't they just called it a fight like the others?

So strange. Evan didn't seem like someone who would get into all these fights. He seemed quiet. Yes, he was aggressive on the basketball court but that was expected in sports. And yes, he threw bagel bites at me, but that was just goofing around. I couldn't imagine him being an actual problem. I also couldn't imagine him being a plumber. But that's what the file said. I wondered how I could find out more.

Just then the door opened. Mr. Peoples waltzed in. He'd taken a long time in the men's room, if that's where'd he'd been, not that it was any of my business. I hurriedly pressed the papers together and closed the file. To cover the evidence, I slid a box of college flyers over the file and said, nonchalantly, "Hello."

"Hello," said Mr. Peoples, suspiciously. "Are you all right?"

I wanted to ask him the same question. He was the one who'd been in the bathroom for twenty minutes. "I'm fine," I said. "Just cleaning up. Almost time to go."

He frowned. "I stopped at the principal's office. If you were wondering where I went."

"I wasn't wondering," I said, standing up and awkwardly shifting the papers and the box of brochures.

Mr. Peoples watched me for a beat, then asked, "Any messages?"

I glanced at the spindle. It was empty. I shook my head and wondered if he was jealous because Ms. Patterson's spindle was full.

But as he turned to go back to his office, I realized I'd left his file cabinet unlocked. And I still had the key.

"Hang on," I said, scurrying to beat him into his own office. "I was watering your plants and, um . . ."

He spun around as I passed him, and I knocked into the plant that was his secret hiding spot. The plant wobbled but didn't fall over, so I gave it a shove.

"Hey!" he said. "Now look what you've done."

Dirt was spilled on the carpet and the plant was sprawled out like a victim.

"Sorry!" I said, scooping up the dirt, but it was still a mess.

Mr. Peoples huffed and turned around. Marching toward the closet, he said, "I'll get the sweeper."

When he was gone, I grabbed Evan's file, replaced it in Mr. Peoples's file cabinet, and locked it. Then I tossed the key back into the pile of dirt on the floor and got back onto my knees.

When Mr. Peoples returned, he was searching for an outlet. "You wanna tell me what you were doing in my files, Claire?"

My heart sank and I stopped breathing for a second. I looked up at him and swallowed. I pushed a clump of hair behind my ear. I started to stand up. "What do you mean?" I said.

"Claire"—he sighed—"I wasn't born yesterday. Okay?"

I picked up the plant and quickly repotted it. "I know."

"I saw the IEP on your desk."

"Oh. Ms. Patterson asked me—" I started in with my story.

"You left the file drawer open."

I glanced at the cabinet.

"And I saw you knock over this plant. On purpose," said Mr. Peoples. "So you wanna tell me what's going on?"

"U-u-um," I stammered. "I'm sorry about all the mess."

"Mm-hmm."

"I must have forgotten. When I was, uh, looking for the file. Um. That she wanted," I lied.

"Claire." He was standing there next to the vacuum cleaner, and I wished he would just turn it on so it would make a loud noise and we wouldn't be able to talk or be heard. But he just stood there with it off and everything quiet, and he waited for me to say something, but I didn't know what to say. As if reading my mind, he suggested, "Just tell the truth."

"I don't know what you mean . . . I mean, I don't know . . ." I said. I imagined Mr. Peoples telling the principal. And the school calling my parents. My dad would turn it into some kind of lesson. He'd give me a lecture about the nature of rules and our compulsion to break them and the need for order in society and the need for disruption to order and it would just be a bunch of theoretical gibberish.

But my mother! She wouldn't let me off the hook. No way. My mother was the Queen of Compliance. That was literally, like, her job. Her title was, like, Chief Compliance Officer, or something. She made sure an entire corporation followed the laws. She trained hundreds of managers herself. She wrote the policies. She wasn't about to make an exception for me. She was going to be Very Disappointed in me. I really didn't want her to hear about this. Finally, I asked, "Am I in trouble?"

"Claire, what would your dad say?" said Mr. Peoples. He was always focused on my dad because of his status as a college professor. Mr. Peoples was probably hoping he could deliver the news about my ethics infraction to my dad personally. I bet Mr. Peoples had wanted to be a college professor himself.

"My dad is too busy to even care," I said, suddenly certain of my words. Certain I was telling the truth.

"Too busy to care about what?" said a woman's voice.

We turned and saw Ms. Patterson standing in the doorway.

I said, "Oh, nothing."

Ms. Patterson made a face like she didn't believe me, then surveyed the dirt on the floor. "What happened here?

Before Mr. Peoples could answer, I blurted, "I got those files you asked me for, and then I knocked over the plant and I was just saying how sorry I was for everything and—"

"—Claire," Mr. Peoples scoffed and shook his head.

Just then the bell rang and I'd never been happier to leave for my next class, which was Intro to Accounting. I looked at the adults, like, *oh well*. Then I ran out the door and blended into the crowded hallway as quickly as I could, hoping Mr. Peoples would be too busy or too lazy to report me and that everyone would just forget about it.

Thirteen

MATTHEW

MIDMORNING ON MONDAY, AFTER CHECKING MY CAR WITH DOUG, I went to my office in the Old Library Building. As I got closer to my door, I saw a yellow Post-it note stuck to the glass. The note seemed to glow like an ominous beacon. It said, "Come see me plz. G." I snatched the sticky note from the glass and sighed. Gloria Jamieson, the chair of the sociology department, wanted to see me.

"Ugh. What's this about," I muttered as I unlocked my office. I switched on the lights and took off my jacket, then trudged down the hall to see Gloria.

Her office was four times the size of mine and featured three large windows and bright overhead lights. When she wasn't teaching, dutiful Gloria was in her office. She was the model professor. The students loved her. The faculty mostly loved her. She was an icon at St. Gus, having run the social work program for over twenty years before taking over as chair of the whole department almost ten years ago. She must have been seventy years old, yet she seemed never to age. Her bushy black hair had only a few white strands sticking out and her rectangle glasses were only needed for reading. And she was always reading.

As I approached her office, I could see that her door was open. Gloria was sitting behind her massive desk, a desk so large and ridiculously cluttered, it would make anyone look disproportionately small by comparison. By nature, Gloria Jamieson was petite in stature, so she appeared absolutely teensy behind the behemoth desk. What she lacked in body size, however, she made up for in political savvy and intellectual gravitas.

I knocked on the open door and she looked up. "Matthew, come in," she said, setting down a stack of papers and removing her reading glasses. "Sit."

I took a chair and crossed my legs. "What can I do for you, Gloria?"

"Tell me," she said. "What's going on? This isn't like you."

"What do you mean?"

"I've just been on the phone with Wes Granger."

"Oh god."

"He was in your class this morning."

"Yes. He sat in the first row," I said. I'd thought that was a bit aggressive.

"Yes, well, he says you blanked out."

"Blanked out?"

"Said it was like you went into la-la land for a few minutes."

"That's ridiculous. I might have lost my place for a moment, or maybe I went on autopilot. When you've been doing this as long as I have—and you, certainly, have been doing it longer, teaching, that is—it's bound to happen. Hazard of the job."

"Well, at any rate. Wes thought it was out of the ordinary, noticeable enough to mention it."

"He's nitpicking," I declared.

She pulled her face back. "Matthew, I didn't expect you to be this defensive."

"Sorry. You're right."

"There was another thing."

"From Wes?"

She nodded. "Do you know what I'm referring to?"

"Do you want me to guess?"

"No. This isn't a game. I'm simply assessing your awareness of the level of concern."

"So it's about the boy?"

"Why, yes, it is."

"That was a blip."

"It was a blip that you picked up a boy on the side of the road or that you felt compelled to unburden yourself about the whole thing to your students?"

I paused, taken aback by her sarcasm. Finally, I said, "I didn't tell them about the 'whole thing.'"

"So there's more?" She peered at me.

"Gloria, where are you going with this? Certainly not the P&T Committee?"

"That's for me to decide. Wes intends to include it in his report, which makes sense. Frankly, his rating was not flattering. And this incident, these incidents, are unusual, to say the least."

"Let's not make this into a big deal," I said. "I picked up a hitchhiker."

"Except he was unconscious. And a child. So not really the same as picking up a hitchhiker, was it?"

"First of all, he was passed out, but I don't think he was unconscious. But yes, he is a child. The point is, I was trying to help."

"But you should have called the police."

"Perhaps I should have. But I didn't."

"Why not?"

I paused, wondering what to say. "I made a mistake, I suppose."

"And then what?"

"He bolted out of the car. Not my fault. No one could have seen that coming."

"Really?"

"Yes."

"But Wes Granger said the boy was still in your car this morning."

God, this was annoying. Wes Granger was digging into areas he really needn't bother with. I said, "I have no idea how that happened. The boy must have followed me back to campus."

"On foot?"

"Either that or he snuck into my car when I was talking to the farmers. What does this have to do with anything?"

Gloria furrowed her brow, then let out a big exhale. Finally, she said. "So a minor child was in your car, on campus property. Overnight. That's accurate?"

"Yes, it seems."

"Which might expose the college to liability."

"For what?"

"I don't know—harboring a runaway?"

"Sure. I guess. But it's not like I invited him to sleep in my car. He simply appeared there."

"Okay, Matthew. Are we playing semantics here?"

"No. You're right. I get it."

"Look. I'm concerned. I've worked hard steering your application. I don't want to see it get sidetracked over a thing like this."

"A thing like this?"

"Yes. Something personal. That affects your teaching. And casts a shadow over your reputation."

I knew she meant a shadow over my reputation *again*. We were both thinking it. I said, "My reputation is intact."

"All right," she said, sighing. "Let's keep it that way."

I nodded and got up. That was the end of that.

After talking with Gloria, I went back to my apartment intending to eat lunch. Before I went inside, however, I jogged around back to check on my car. Part of me wondered if the kid would be there. To my surprise, he was.

The little shit was sitting in the driver's seat and there were wires dangling from the steering column.

"Hey, you!" I hollered and rushed to open the driver door. The kid had been fumbling with something under the steering wheel, like he was trying to hot-wire it. "What are you doing?"

He said nothing, just stared up at me, which was infuriating. I said, "You're trying to steal my car!"

He shrugged. Not a denial.

"Get out of there!" I shooed him out of my car and stepped aside as he climbed out. I leaned in and checked for damage. "What did you do?"

"Nothing!" he said.

"Doesn't look like nothing," I said, pointing to the steering column. I pointed at the wires and said, "Put those back."

He squeezed past me and returned to the driver's seat. I watched him fold up the wires and replace the panel cover. He knew what he was doing. The rascal. When he was done, he stared up at me again, a slight smirk on his face.

"I should call the police right now," I said.

"And I'll tell them how you kidnapped me," said the kid, threatening me.

"What?!" I said, horrified. The nerve! "Get out of my car!" He hopped out, and I slammed the front door. "I wasn't kidnapping you." I was practically hissing the words. "And you can't go around stealing cars," I added, but when I heard myself talking, my words sounded ridiculous.

The kid gazed off into the distance, as if suddenly fascinated by the college's bronze statue of Martin Luther on the other side of the street.

"Hey, listen to me," I said, snapping my fingers. I didn't like how paternalistic I was acting toward him and I didn't like the anger that was rising in me. But I also didn't like his threats and his snotty attitude. It was all rather unpleasant and uncomfortable. "What do you have to say for yourself?" God, I sounded like my father.

After a beat, he said, "I need a ride." The kid was nonchalant, as if he'd said the most obvious thing in the world.

"Well, okay," I said, lowering my voice. "So you thought you'd just steal a car?"

He gave me a blank look.

"And you know how to drive, I suppose?" I said, assuming he did not.

"Yeah," he said, meeting my gaze before he turned and started walking away, toward the Luther statue.

I followed him. "Hey, I wasn't done talking to you," I said, glancing around in case anyone was watching us. He kept walking. I called, "Seaver!"

He stopped and turned around slowly. "So it is you. Your name is Seaver," I said.

"So?" he said, glaring at me skeptically.

Calmly, I said, "I was only going to ask where you needed to go."

"Why?" he asked in a surly tone.

"Because maybe I can take you," I said lowly, checking our surroundings. I didn't want to be overheard and misunderstood.

"Why would you do that?" he said, then answered his own question. "So I won't call the cops on you?"

"Come on," I scoffed. "I didn't kidnap you. I was taking you to the hospital."

He squinted, then spat back, "But you screwed up. You feel guilty about something."

"I do not," I insisted, but my reaction felt overblown. I guess I did feel guilty. I said, "Just tell me."

Finally, the kid admitted, "I need to get to my mom's."

"Okay, and where does she live?" I said, encouraged by this progress, although I wasn't sure what we were progressing toward.

"Minneapolis," he said, shifting his weight.

"Minneapolis?" I said, surprised. "So you were gonna, what, drive my car from here to Minneapolis? Do you know how far that is?"

"Two hours," he said. "Will you take me or not?"

"Hold on," I said. "Your plan was to steal my car and drive two hours on the highway by yourself?"

"Yeah. It's easy," he said, scowling as if offended at my lack of faith in his abilities. Something about his confidence made me believe him. Drew me toward him. Made me want to know what made him tick. This kid was different. He intimidated me, demanded to be treated as an equal. In a way, he reminded me of someone. Maybe he reminded me of myself at his age? Or of the kid I wished I'd been.

In the bewildering next few moments, I decided, there in the parking lot behind my building, that I would help him. Something told I wouldn't be rid of this boy until I did. As if helping him would somehow solve the other quandaries I'd been bumping up against. And I wondered if it could be as simple as making that choice.

"Okay, kid," I said. "I'll do it." Suddenly it was only a matter of putting up a sign on my office door to alert any potential visitors that my afternoon office hours had been canceled. To be honest, hardly anyone ever showed up anyway.

We left Northwood around noon.

"When have you driven a car before?" I asked the kid. "And why?"

He shrugged.

We'd just pulled out onto the county road that led from the college to the highway. This was the stretch I'd taken last night after the brat had jumped out. Now, in the light of day, I was fairly certain he wouldn't do it again. To be sure, I said, "Please don't jump out of the car."

He looked at me and smirked, ever so slightly.

After a beat, I asked, "But seriously, whose car did you drive?"

"My mom's," he said, chewing on something that looked like a string.

I shook my head in disbelief. Tammy would never have allowed Claire to drive at such a young age. "Are you tall enough to see over the dashboard?"

He sat up straight, as if that were proof. But he clearly wasn't tall enough.

"Why were you driving? Did your mom know?"

"She was tired from her pills," he said. "So she couldn't drive."

"Oh," I said, gripping the steering wheel a bit tighter. This was sensitive. I'd have to handle it gently. I decided to leave it alone. "Okay."

Over the next stretch of road, I thought about my mom and how, after my dad died, she began to drink. Many nights, our aunt came over to take care of us, make us dinner, and put Mom to bed.

Now Mom was in a nursing home. A senior care center. Assisted living. I wasn't sure what they called it. I didn't like it there. It reminded me of visiting our grandfather as a kid. He was always slouched over in a wheelchair, sitting out in the hallway, and he never recognized me or my siblings. The center smelled awful, like Lysol and body sweat. But we grandchildren were forced to visit him every Sunday. Until he died. And then I'd felt guilty because instead of sadness I'd been overcome with relief that I wouldn't have to visit that place anymore. But I should visit Mom more. I would.

As we passed a sunflower field, I noticed the flowers had shrunken and the stems were leaning. Pointing to the field, I said to Seaver, "Look at that. They're just past their blooming."

He looked in the direction of the drooping plants. No reaction.

I pointed to a spot on the other side of road. "Once I got a flat tire right there."

Seaver glanced over, taking it in.

"Don't worry," I said, remembering. "Someone pulled over and drove me to the gas station. And I called my wife."

"Uh-huh," he said, not interested.

"Ex-wife now," I added.

Seaver nodded slightly. Why was I talking? I wanted him to like me, I suppose. I wondered about his parents, but decided not to ask. We passed the vegetable stand, the half-collapsed gray shed with the rusty green tractor out front. There was a wooden sign propped up against it with the words *For Sale* spray painted in red. It was always like that. It never changed.

I noticed a horse and buggy ahead of us. They hugged the shoulder as I slowed down to pass them. I pointed and said to Seaver, "Look, they're Amish, I believe."

But Seaver wasn't curious at all, which seemed odd. Most kids would love to see a horse and buggy. Finn would have. Finn loved animals.

"What's wrong?" I asked.

Seaver shook his head. He'd taken a Rubik's Cube out of his pocket, and he was fussing with it. "Nothing."

I squinted at the road. We were coming closer to the Ogletree farm, I realized. And the intersection where I'd lost him. He must have noticed it too, because he sunk down in his seat. I could sense his fear.

I pretended not to notice. I slowed down for the stop sign, but this time I didn't stop. I rolled through it, then sped up. I didn't say a word.

A few miles later we were at the entrance to the highway, the grain store on the left, the gas station on the right. At this intersection there was a stoplight. The light turned red, and I stopped.

"That's where I found you," I said, nodding at the feedstore.

"Uh-huh," he said.

"Can I ask . . ." I said, "what were you doing there?"

He looked at me as if judging my worthiness. If I measured up, it seemed, he might tell me something important. Then he said, "Hitchhiking."

"Oh," I said, oddly relieved. I wanted to know more but I sensed I should hold back. Tentatively, I asked, "Hitchhiking to your mom's?"

He nodded.

I left it at that and the light turned green. I asked, "Are you hungry?"

He made no response.

"I'll take that as a yes," I said, pulling into the gas station. I parked and said, "Stay here."

He shrunk down, and I locked the doors. Taking the keys with me, I scurried inside and got us a couple of ham and cheese sandwiches. Everyone likes ham and cheese. And two cans of Sprite.

When I returned, I handed him the food. He was still crouching in his seat. He gathered up the food and said, "Just go."

I did as instructed and merged onto the highway.

I opened one of the sandwiches and took a bite. After a few chews, I said, "Why are you hiding? Did you rob someone or something?"

His eyes flashed, and I dropped the topic. Watching him bite into his sandwich, I considered what awful things this kid might have done. Sold drugs? Set fires? Gotten into fights? Maybe he'd been to a juvenile detention center. Maybe he had a knife or god forbid, a gun. He could be a real criminal.

Or maybe he was a victim. Maybe he'd been abused or neglected. Maybe he'd witnessed domestic violence or drug abuse or murder. I really had no idea. Anyway, he didn't want to talk. Maybe he had a secret.

All I knew was this kid wasn't acting the way I thought he was going to act. He wasn't interested in my ideas of help. He only wanted what he wanted. Despite my being the adult, this boy was in charge, and to be honest, that made helping him much less enjoyable for me. I would still help, but I didn't want to be taken advantage of. I didn't want to be accused of kidnapping. And I didn't want to get mixed up in anything bad.

I decided to stop speculating and simply focus on driving. We were passing some of my favorite landmarks. There was the John Deere dealership with its rows of giant green machines, and the Pine Bend oil refinery that resembled a futuristic city, and finally, Buck Hill Ski Area, where I'd taught Claire to snowplow when she was six years old, and Finn was only two.

I passed the exit that led to the cemetery where Finn was buried. Usually, I took the exit and stopped at the grave. Not today, obviously. But I felt the pull at my chest as I drove by, a pain that swelled around my heart and choked in my throat. I took a deep breath.

Soon I would need to know exactly where we were going. I looked at the kid. His eyes were closed and his head was leaning against the window, the crumpled wrapper in one hand and the Rubik's Cube in the other. His hair needed washing. So did his face. His mouth was hanging open and I noticed his teeth. He was at that age when some of his big teeth had come in (and were crooked), but he still had some gaps where the baby teeth had fallen out.

"Hey, kid," I said, but he didn't stir.

I jostled him and he flinched awake, punching me in the process. He had a look of terror in his face and I wondered if he always woke up that way.

"What the fuck?" he demanded.

"Hey, relax," I said. "I need the address of your mother's house."

"It's not a house. It's an apartment."

"Okay," I said. "What's the address?"

He shifted in his seat, straightening himself. He looked out the window as if trying to recognize something. "Where are we?"

"Burnsville," I said. We were going over the river. "Do you at least know the cross streets? Anything?"

He glared at me like he hated my guts. Finally, he said, "I can find it."

And I believed him.

Fourteen

KIRA

TED PEOPLES WAS UPSET. OUT OF PROPORTION TO THE SITUATION, IN my opinion. Usually when someone is disproportionately upset, it says something more about them than the person they're upset about. A master's degree in social work taught me that. But I'd also lived it a thousand times. Now I was watching Ted spiral out.

I was standing in his office at the end of sixth hour listening to him rant and rail when all I wanted was to discuss ideas for helping Adrian Wallace finish high school and attend culinary school or study food science at a local college. But no, Mr. Peoples wanted me to hear all his complaints about Claire.

"Claire Larkin snoops and Claire Larkin steals," Ted was saying, and suddenly I realized why that name rang a bell.

"Hang on," I said. "Is Claire related to a professor at St. Gustaf, by any chance?"

"Yes, of course she's related," said Ted. "Haven't you heard me at the staff meetings? I've been saying we should use that connection at the college fair."

"Oh, yeah," I said, vaguely recalling. The college fair was his area, not mine.

"But that doesn't mean his daughter can get away with all this misbehavior. She can't violate other students' privacy just because her dad's a professor."

"No, of course not," I murmured, but I'd stopped listening. Claire's dad? I dug around in my purse for my notes from my call with June last night. Sure enough. "Is her dad's name Matthew?"

"Huh?" said Mr. Peoples, off in his own world of outrage at the audacity of today's youth. "What, who? Claire's dad? Yes, Kira. Keep up!"

"Hmm," I said. Very interesting.

Mr. Peoples continued ranting. "We can't allow a student, even a good student like Claire Larkin, to waltz around our file cabinets, steal our keys, and read the files of all the boys she has a crush on or whatever. It's a breach of confidentiality. We have our licenses to protect, and our reputations. We have a responsibility."

"Yes, all of that," I agreed, and I wondered what was really bothering Ted. Perhaps he was upset with himself for hiding the key in such an obvious location.

"We can't be influenced by who her father is," said Mr. Peoples. "We need to report it. No exceptions. There must be consequences."

"Okay, okay," I said, but I wasn't a fan of arbitrary punishment. I believed consequences happened naturally, and sometimes these things took time. "Relax."

Ted sat down and his shoulders dropped slightly. I sat next to him and patted his knee. The vacuum was still standing there by his desk. Remnants of soil remained on the carpet. We both had other things to do.

"All right," he said. "I'm calm."

"Good," I said.

"But I'm going to write this up."

"That's fine," I said. "I can't stop you."

After a beat, Ted said, "Did you happen to notice whose file she was looking at?"

I shook my head. "Whose?"

"Evan Lewis," said Ted, rolling his eyes.

This was a student who'd been keeping us all busy for years. He was exasperating. *What a tortured soul*, I thought. "You should have asked Claire to clean up," I said, which was how I would have handled it.

"I was going to ask her," Ted protested, "but the bell rang and she ran off!"

"So what? If she'd been late to her next class," I suggested, "that would be a natural consequence."

Ted smiled and stood up. "You're right. As usual."

"That's why we get the big bucks," I joked, and he laughed.

I went back to my office while Ted was running the vacuum. Very soon everything was back in its place, the carpet was clean, and Ted was sitting at his desk. "Hey." I knocked on the doorjamb. "I'm heading down to Northwood now."

"Oh?" he said. "Gonna see your favorite parents?"

"Something like that," I said. I didn't tell him I wanted to find Matthew Larkin. Or that I was hunting for a runaway foster kid and planned to check the local campground and the park and all the other typical hiding spots. I simply said, "Before you write Claire up, maybe sleep on it? Time is miraculous for perspective."

He let his head hang, then looked up and said. "I already wrote it up." He waved a paper at me. "But don't worry. I'll wait until tomorrow to turn it in."

"Okay," I said.

"Drive safe," he said.

"I always do," I said. But that wasn't true.

On the way to Northwood, I stopped at the McDonald's drive-through. I was balancing a Quarter Pounder with fries on my lap as I merged onto the freeway. Hoping to beat the rush-hour traffic, I kept the pedal to the metal and arrived in Northwood while the sun was still up, giving me enough light to look around. Unfortunately, I didn't find anything at any of the hiding spots. No evidence of Seaver having stayed at the park or the campground or in the garages or barns of any of his friends.

Finally, I pulled into the Ogletree driveway. June was standing on the front stoop. The moment I got out of the car, she asked, "Any news about Seaver?"

"I was gonna ask you the same question," I said, shaking my head as I shut the car door. I approached the house, and we hugged. After a beat, I asked, "How'd you know I was coming?"

"Carolyn called me," said June. Carolyn was Michael's mother. Michael was one of the school friends Seaver had met in the few months of sixth grade that were left before summer and after he was placed with the Ogletrees. I'd just been over to Michael's house poking around, and Carolyn had seen me. I'd had to talk to her. Naturally, she'd felt compelled to call June. It was hard to keep a secret in a small town. But at the same time, it was hard to get folks to talk about certain things because the locals were protective. So it was a double-edged sword. "I've got a pot roast in the slow cooker."

"Of course you do," I said. "But I already ate."

"What'd you have?" she asked, peering at me skeptically. It was like she had a psychic power to detect poor dietary choices.

I wasn't gonna win. And her pot roast was incredible. "All right. I'll eat."

June held open the front door for me.

I waved her off and said, "I want to take a look around. I'll just be a minute."

"Do what you need to do," said June, retreating and letting the door close.

First I padded over to the garage. Grady was tinkering away at his workbench, but his back was turned, and he didn't notice me.

I treaded along the side of the barn to the rear entrance. I wanted to see the place as it was, without Grady's commentary. I pushed open the door and crept in. Immediately confronted with a mess, I stepped over buckets and rocks and piles of scrap wood and rope and debris of all kinds. This was not the safest place for kids. I blamed Grady. He should keep it tidier if he wanted to continue to be a foster parent and keep getting the money that was so important to him. In my view, June did it for the love. Grady did it for the money.

When I reached the end of the barn, I noticed a walled-off area to the side, a room that hadn't been there before. The walls were made of Sheetrock, but they hadn't been taped or mudded yet. This was newish construction. There was no door yet, so I went inside. A long string hung from the bulb on the ceiling. I pulled on the string and switched on the light. It was a bedroom. A cot with blankets and a pillow. A small sink and a toilet. A space heater. Trash lying around. Potato chip bags and Coke cans. Dirty clothes. I switched off the light and went back to the main part of the barn, near the big door at the back.

I turned to leave and something caught my eye.

On the floor. A dark stain. Partially covered in hay. I kicked away the hay. What was it? Oil? *No*, I thought.

It looked like blood.

Fifteen

SEAVER

JULY 1992

SOMETHING HAPPENED THIS SUMMER WHEN I WAS RIDING MY BIKE with Michael and Connor. It wasn't my bike; it was the bike that Mrs. Ogletree let me use. She kept two in the garage for the kids that lived with her. I went riding with Michael and Connor. They were my two best friends from the school I went to in Northwood. But this was summer and school was out. Eli was also my friend, but he stayed home that day.

First we stopped at Eli's house to eat some Hostess Cupcakes. Then we went back out on the roads. They were gravel roads with no cars. There were lots of miles we could ride. We had the roads to ourselves. Michael, Connor, and I spread our bikes out across the gravel road and we were alone. I was riding no-hands, watching out for bumps and holes in the gravel. It was sunny so I was squinting. Then my eyes adjusted.

None of the gravel roads in Northwood have names. I never saw any street signs. We knew our way around by things like the sunken barn, the twisted tree, or that burned-out spot where a car on fire had left a big black mark.

On this day, just before we got to the burned-out spot, Michael said, "Watch out."

All three of us pulled over and stopped. Up ahead there was a cloud of dust and a white pickup truck. It was headed straight for us. We straddled our bikes, waiting for the truck to pass. But it didn't. It kept coming at us fast, and I wondered if the driver was drunk. Suddenly he slammed on the brakes and turned his wheel. The truck skidded sideways, blocking the whole road. It wasn't a wide road, so if another car had come, they wouldn't have been able to fit around him.

We stood there in the dust. We didn't know why he'd stopped like that. We didn't know what to do or if, like, he was in trouble. The guy opened the driver's-side door, hopped out, and stood next to his truck. He was wearing a baseball cap and holding a paper bag.

He took off the cap and rubbed his head. He had a scarred patch above his ear where no hair grew. It looked like he'd had a piece of his brain taken out. We stood there staring at the scar but also trying not to stare.

"You okay, mister?" asked Michael. Michael was the oldest of us. He thought he was in charge.

"I'm just dandy," said the guy, "now that I found you boys." He took a drink of whatever was wrapped in that paper bag. He said, "But I'm gonna need your help."

We looked at one another: me, Michael, and Connor, still on our bikes. I kept one foot on the ground and one foot on a pedal. I wanted to take off, but none of us was sure what to do. He'd asked us for help and something was definitely wrong with him.

"It's okay, come over here," he said.

We waddled our bikes forward until we were close enough to talk. We were facing the truck. It was a four-door extended cab. The guy opened the door to the back seat and rustled around with something. He started telling us a story. "I was just up at the store, you see . . . and, uh, I seen these kids on the sidewalk, there, and, well, it's hot today, ain't it?"

"Yeah," said Michael, but his voice sounded nervous.

"Nice and hot," said the guy. He kept on with his story. "Anyway, them kids at the store were eating some ice-cold Popsicles. Bomb Pops, I think they were. You boys know what a Bomb Pop is, right?"

We nodded.

"Red, white, and blue," he said, pulling something out of the back seat. He turned to us and showed us a box of Bomb Pops. "So I went in and bought me some."

Connor's eyes went wide because he loved Popsicles. I loved Popsicles too. And it was a hot day.

"Here." The guy opened the box and started handing us each a Popsicle. "Take 'em. You like Bomb Pops, don't ya?"

"Sure," said Connor. Michael and I nodded. We took them and just stood there not sure if we should open them or what.

"Go ahead, open 'em," said the guy. "I need you to eat them because I bought too many and they're gonna melt. So please, go ahead."

We looked at one another and shrugged. Connor had already unwrapped his. Michael was next, and then I decided I might as well.

"What should we do with the wrappers?" asked Michael.

"I'll take that," said the guy. When he came over to get the wrapper, I got a good look at his scarred head, the pink and white part that wasn't hidden by the baseball cap. He had a long thin ponytail in the back. When he noticed me staring, he jerked his head toward me, like he was trying to frighten me. I shrunk back and he laughed.

The three of us were still on our bikes and the sun was burning. The guy was standing in a small square of shade next to his truck. "Come over here in the shade," he said. "Your Bomb Pops are gonna melt over there in the sun."

He had a good point, so we did as he said. We let our bikes fall to the gravel and we moved closer to the truck.

Connor was done with his and handed the stick to the guy. The guy gave him another Popsicle, so Connor unwrapped it.

The guy kept talking the whole time. He said he had a kid about Connor's age but he never got to see him.

"You have a kid?" said Connor. We were all surprised.

"How old are you?" asked Michael. This guy didn't look like a dad age.

"Old enough." The guy laughed and we saw that his teeth were yellowed and darker, like when someone smoked cigarettes. He said, "I'm twenty-nine."

"How old's your kid?" asked Michael. We couldn't believe it.

"Well. Let's see now," said the guy. "How old are you boys?"

"I'm eleven and they're twelve," said Connor, pointing to himself and then to me and Michael.

"You're older than my son," said the guy. "What are you, in fifth grade? Sixth?"

"I'm going into sixth," said Connor. "Michael and Seaver are going into seventh."

"Seaver, huh?" said the guy to me. "Like the baseball pitcher? Tom Seaver?"

Other people had said that to me sometimes when they heard my name, so I knew about it. I nodded.

"Nice to meet you," said the guy. "Mind if I take a snapshot to remember this?"

We looked at one another. It was weird but the guy had set down his paper bag and was already holding a camera. He clicked the button and made a goofy face.

"Line up there," he said, pointing to the truck.

We sort of clustered together, holding our treats. The guy had the same kind of camera our teacher had used for Student of the Week photos. The kind that spat out an instant photo that you had to wave around until it dried and the picture appeared. The guy took a photo of us eating our Bomb Pops. Then he moved closer and took a close-up photo of each one of us, alone. Just our faces, but we had to have the Bomb Pop in our mouth for the picture. He said it was proof he'd done a good deed.

"Okay, now turn around and face the truck," he said. "Just lean up against it. So you're more in the shade. So your Bomb Pops don't melt."

"You want us to turn around?" said Michael, not sure he could believe it. "And lean against the truck?"

"Yeah," said the guy. "Is that too much to ask? Jeez, don't be like them ungrateful boys at the store. I just gave you jerks a bunch of Popsicles. Come on now. Turn around."

Slowly we turned, not knowing what else to do.

I heard the camera click and the faint motorlike sound of the photo sliding out. He took another. And another.

"Yeah, okay," he said, and he placed the photos on the back seat, along with the camera, picking up his paper bag again. "See. I knew it. I knew you were nice boys."

I motioned to Michael and he nodded.

"We gotta go," I said.

"Oh, yeah, Tom Seaver?" said the guy, leaning toward me. He took a drink from the paper bag. Turning to the group, he said, "Hey. I can throw your bikes in the back and give you a ride home if you want? The least I can do."

"Uh, no thanks," I said. I didn't want him to know where I lived but I didn't know why.

"Okay," he said, pretending to be sad. He got in his truck and started it up. He rolled down his window and said, "Hey, guys. Don't tell your parents about the Popsicles."

"Okay," said Connor.

"They might get angry that you've spoiled your appetites," said the guy.

"Sure," said Michael.

"You know how parents can be," said the guy. Then he peeled out of there, going back the way he came.

We were already on our bikes. We watched him go, then we turned and went the opposite direction, like we were going back to Eli's.

But it was the summer, and we didn't know where we were going.

Sixteen

MATTHEW

MONDAY, SEPTEMBER 28, 1992

I PULLED OFF THE HIGHWAY IN BLOOMINGTON, JUST SOUTH OF MIN-neapolis, and we made our way north into the city. The kid watched as I drove slowly through neighborhoods. He sat facing the window and said, "Not here, keep going."

I proceeded up Lyndale, then Portland, then Park Avenue, and eventually, back onto Portland. When we crossed Lake Street, Seaver started recognizing landmarks. We were on the lookout for a White Castle, then a Kmart, and finally a Shell station.

This was not a good neighborhood. The houses were worn and sagging, needing paint and repair, their yards overgrown with weeds. Windows were broken or boarded up. I knew Portland Avenue had once been a grand boulevard; the homes were large three-and-four-story gems, built in the nineteenth century by some of the city's founders and early leaders. But now they were dilapidated old relics, poorly maintained. Apart from its history, there was nothing grand about this place.

"Pull over here," said the kid.

"Where?" There weren't any open spots along the street, so I pulled into the Shell station.

As soon as I put the gear into park, the kid unbuckled himself and jumped out.

"Hey!" I said. "Where is it? Which one?"

He looked back at me with a frown and kept walking along the sidewalk. Then he crossed the street, jaywalking.

"Hey!" I hollered, struggling to unbuckle myself. "Hold up!" I ran after him, but at the crosswalk I stopped at the light. The boy ducked into an alley. When the coast was clear, I crossed and ran to the alley. What was I supposed to do in this situation? I hadn't expected to just drop him off and drive away. But I also didn't feel like I should chase him.

When I caught up to him, I was frustrated. I didn't like being in this position. He should have told me what his plan was. He shouldn't have jumped out of the car like that. I didn't like anything about this, including the neighborhood.

He glanced at me but didn't speak. Around the corner he went and so did I, speed walking to keep up. Clearly, he knew his way around these alleys, but I was going to stick with him. I was also trying to memorize the route so I could make it back to the Subaru after I'd successfully escorted him to his mom's.

"Seaver, I just want to make sure you get to your mom's, okay?" I said sharply.

He ignored me.

We passed a house with a chain-link fence around the yard. I heard a dog growling a warning but didn't see the animal. Suddenly, a white pit bull charged toward me, barking and growling. The dog was halted only by the chain-link fence. My heart was pounding as I scurried away, nearly stepping into the street to escape.

"Seaver!" I called. "Are we close?"

Finally, he stopped in front of a three-story apartment building. The exterior was stucco and wood-framed with a flat roof, with air conditioners sticking out of the windows unevenly, like ears, and weakly supported by aging brackets. The stucco was off-white, stained and chipped, with brown trim around the door and windows.

"This is it?" I asked, looking for house numbers, but there were none. Only the outline of where they used to be. They must have fallen off.

Seaver tried the handle, but the front door was locked. He leaned on the glass and peered into the entry.

Meanwhile, I examined the intercom and various buttons on the tarnished buzzer panel. There was a motley list of names, some scrawled in ink, some with a typed label, and others covered with masking tape or left blank. I asked, "Which one is yours?"

His face was expressionless.

"This is the place, though, right?" I asked, peering in.

It appeared Seaver wasn't sure. He squinted down the block farther west. I wondered how long it had been since he lived in this neighborhood.

"You think it's down there?" I asked.

Seaver shook his head. Was he losing his nerve? Embarrassed by something? Just then a figure emerged behind the glass and the front door swung open as a thin man breezed out. The man wasn't paying attention and brushed against my shoulder.

"Sorry," mumbled the stranger. Then he glanced at Seaver for a moment.

After the man turned to leave, Seaver darted into the building and, before the door closed, I squeezed in behind him, following him down the hall and up the stairs.

"Did you know that man?"

"No."

I took two steps at a time to keep up with the kid. "What's the apartment number?"

"It's up here." On the second floor, Seaver turned left and walked to the end. He stood outside the door marked "7."

So there it was. To give Seaver privacy with his mom, I stood back several feet. I wasn't confident I'd be welcomed there. I was definitely out of place. What was my role? I mean, I drove him here, kept him safe. I'd given him a ham and cheese sandwich. Surely, I'd discharged my responsibility in the situation under the law and any other measure of right and wrong. Right? I squeezed my hands into fists, then relaxed them, as if circulating my blood would help answer these questions. And I fervently hoped that whoever opened that door would be happy to see this boy.

Seaver knocked on the door, loudly. No answer. He knocked again, then leaned in to listen. Nothing.

We stood silent in that dim hallway and as my eyes adjusted, Seaver appeared more fragile to me. His shaggy head was hanging forward and his neck seemed narrower, his shoulders smaller and bony, like a tall bird. The bottoms of his pants were frayed, and all his clothes needed washing.

"Hey," I said, noticing a stain that looked like blood. "What's that on your pant leg?"

"Huh?" said Seaver, looking down. He saw the spot and brushed at it, but it was soaked in. "Nothing," he said.

I furrowed my brow, not believing him. But it could have been anything. My brother and I were always getting odd stains on our clothes, holes appearing without us knowing how. I didn't recall Claire ruining any of her clothes, but she was a more responsible kid. A bit indoorsy, my daughter hadn't been the type to trudge through the mud or climb a tree. Seaver was definitely a different kind of kid from Claire.

"Did you hurt your leg?" I asked.

He lurched at me like a threat and I got the message. I wasn't gonna force the issue.

No one was answering the door, so I said, "Seems like your mom's not home."

He glanced from me to the door, with a mixture of defeat and defiance. Suddenly, his face brightened, and he ran to the neighboring unit, marked "8."

Seaver knocked on number 8, loudly like he'd done on his mother's door.

This time, it opened.

Seventeen

MATTHEW

THE WOMAN IN APARTMENT 8 OPENED THE DOOR BUT KEPT THE CHAIN on, so we were forced to talk through a five-inch gap. Her eye makeup was heavy and a burning cigarette dangled from her mouth. She peered at me and said, "What is it?"

Seaver didn't say anything and the woman didn't seem to notice him. She was glaring up at me and bouncing a baby on her hip. Seaver peered through the gap as if searching for something—or someone—inside. Did he think his mother was in there?

The woman sighed impatiently and raised her eyebrows at me. I pointed to Seaver and she finally spotted him.

"Oh, for Christ's sake, Stinker," she said, annoyed. "It's you."

"I'm locked out," said Seaver, unfazed. "Can you give me your key?" He pushed on the woman's door but it caught with the chain lock.

"Hey, easy there," said the woman, glancing at me like I was somehow responsible for the boy's poor manners.

"Seaver," I said, pointlessly. They both ignored me. I was wondering how long I needed to stay. I wanted to get back on the road if I was to have any chance of salvaging this day. I had papers to grade and so much reading to do.

"Aren't you supposed to be with your foster family?" The

woman looked at me suspiciously. She pointed at me and asked Seaver, "Is this your foster dad?"

Seaver turned and looked at me like he'd forgotten I was there.

"No, I'm Matthew Larkin," I said, offering my hand but then withdrawing it when I realized it wouldn't fit through the gap. "I'm an assistant professor. I teach at St. Gustaf College."

"Okaaaay," said the woman, the cigarette still in her mouth. After a beat, she added her own introduction, saying simply, "Bobbi Dodd."

"I, uh, gave Seaver a ride here," I said. "Nice to meet you."

"He's got you conned, huh?" said Bobbi Dodd, almost laughing at me. To Seaver, she said, "Nice one, Stinker." To me, she warned, "Watch your wallet."

"Thanks." I gave her a wry look. "He tried to steal my car but not my wallet."

"Yet," said the woman.

I laughed, but Seaver glared at me as if to remind me that he could report me at any moment. He could claim I kidnapped him. He could claim I was driving drunk. I backed off.

"Shit, kid. What are you up to?" said the woman, flicking her ashes somewhere we couldn't see. The baby was barely tolerating her jiggling. A TV was blaring in the background and there may have been another child in there. "Do I need to call your caseworker?" asked Bobbi.

"No," said Seaver. "I just need to get something out of Mom's apartment. Something for school."

That sounded like a lie and it certainly wasn't what he'd told me. Also, he'd never mentioned a caseworker.

"Sorry, Stinker," said the woman, shaking her head. "I can't do that."

Seaver stomped his foot and the woman shrugged. They were

at an impasse, staring at each other through the gap, with the baby continuing to fuss and TV voices yelling as if even the characters in TV land were unhappy with us.

Finally, Seaver said, "Can I at least come in and use your bathroom. I need to go pee. Please." Seaver grabbed at his crotch and bobbed up and down, really selling it.

The woman watched Seaver shifting around uncomfortably. "Okay, Jesus, don't pee your pants," she said, closing and unlatching the door, then opening it again.

Like a flash, Seaver darted into the apartment. Bobbi and I stood speechless for a beat, as if impressed at how quickly the boy had disappeared into the back. Ignoring me, Bobbi meandered after him, hollering, "Lift the lid!"

There was no response, just a rustling noise, a thump, and we waited. A minute later Seaver appeared; he was holding a key with a blue rabbit's foot for a key chain. "Found it," he said.

"Goddamn it, Stinker." The woman lunged toward him, letting the baby bobble in her arms, but Seaver was already out the door. She called after him, "That's an old key! They probably changed the locks!"

Bobbi was lying too, apparently, because the key worked. Seaver had already unlocked number 7, run inside, and shut the door behind him, leaving me and Ms. Dodd and her crying baby out in the hallway, duped.

"That little shit," said Bobbi and I in unison. Bobbi tried the door, but the kid had locked himself in there. She banged on it, shouting, "Open this door!"

I stood back, wishing I was anywhere else.

Suddenly, the woman handed me her baby. "Here," she said before I'd had a chance to decline.

"No," I said, taking the baby, but Bobbi was already back in her apartment, in her kitchen and dialing the phone. I followed and stood in her chaotic living room, holding her slobbering baby and regretting everything that had led to this point. The place smelled like cigarettes and sour baby food. Or dirty diapers, it was hard to tell. Bobbi held the phone to her ear. I said, "Hey, who are you calling?"

"His caseworker," said Bobbi, frowning and waiting for someone to answer on the other end. "I don't need this shit. His mother has caused enough trouble as it is."

"May I ask: Where is his mother?"

"I'm not gonna tell you nothing. You'll have to ask him." She gave me a look like I was some kind of scumbag. I hated feeling like that. The presumption that I would harm the kid. The lack of trust that I might want to help.

"All right," I ventured. "Since you mentioned foster care, I'll assume the mom is having some kind of trouble. And the dad?"

Same smirk.

"Is not in the picture?" I said.

"What a lucky guess," she said, sarcastically.

Just then Seaver burst out of his mother's apartment and ran down the hallway, into the staircase, and presumably, out the door.

I handed the baby back to Bobbi as carefully as I could, then dashed out and down the stairs, and out the front door. But when I got to the street, Seaver was gone.

And so was my wallet.

I turned back to the apartment building and yanked at the front door, but of course it had locked. I studied the list of names on the buzzer panel and found Bobbi's initials, "B.D.," at number 8. I rang the buzzer.

"Go away," said Bobbi over the intercom. "The little shit stole money from my secret stash," the speaker squawked. "I knew I shouldn't let him in."

"Yeah, he stole my money too. Look, I'm going back to the

college. But if he comes back, will you check on him?" I said into the intercom.

"Why would I do that? Don't you think I have enough kids to watch after? Also, why would Stinker come back here? He got what he wanted," she said, referring to the cash presumably. "Even if he came back, there's no electricity in that place. No food. No heat. His mother's been gone for months. Those utility bills aren't paying themselves."

"Well. In case he does," I said, adding, "I think he's injured. On his left leg."

"Oh? And how would you know that?" she intoned.

There it was again: that ugly assumption. She was intimating that I'd been the one to harm him. Although, in this case, it might have been my fault, I suppose, if he'd been injured while running in that field. "Just leave the accusations to yourself," I said to the intercom. "I saw blood on his pant leg, okay?" At least I thought it was blood. "And he was limping."

"He wasn't limping when he ran outta here with my money," she buzzed back.

"Okay. Well, I don't know what to tell you."

"You don't need to tell me nothing," she said. The intercom went silent.

"Okay, thanks," I said to no one. Turning to the street, I noticed something flapping on the ground. I walked closer. "Oh thank god," I said, bending to pick up my wallet. I opened it. All the cash was gone, but my credit cards were there. Feverishly, I fumbled to check the secret compartment and then pulled out the tiny photos, one of Finn and one of Claire. These were their school photos from day care; each of them had been about eighteen months old, maybe two years old. Their photos featured the same blue background, and their faces shared the same chubby cheeks, doughy eyes. I tucked the precious squares back into the secret spot, careful not to damage the photos' worn edges any further. I wiped my eyes and looked down the street, wondering what to do next. My options were limited, I thought.

The kid was gone, but he had the keys to his mother's apartment. And he had cash, although I wasn't sure how much. I'd only had fifteen or twenty bucks in my wallet. I wasn't sure how much he'd taken from Bobbi. And she had my name. Had I given her my card? I couldn't remember. She was calling the caseworker, which was good. The caseworker would handle things. Everything would be all right for the kid.

I straightened myself up and headed back toward the Shell station. As I walked past the house with the pit bull, I crossed to the other side of the street to avoid any provocation. I checked my watch. Half past three.

I was thinking everything was going to be okay. I'd get back with plenty of time to prepare for my seminar. As I turned the corner, I saw the Shell sign, then the parking lot. Only one problem: My car was gone.

Eighteen

KIRA

I WAS STARING AT THE BLOOD-OIL-PAINT STAIN, WHEN I HEARD Grady's voice behind me.

"Well, look what the cat dragged in," he said. Grady could never hide how he really felt. Maybe he never tried.

I turned and saw the outline of him, backlit and leaning against the doorjamb in the wide entrance to the barn. "Hi, Grady."

"You find Seaver yet?" he said, making it sound like a lost cause.

I shook my head. "That's why I'm here," I said. "I've been checking out his usual spots."

"He won't be around here." Grady stepped into the barn where I could see him better. He looked the same. Gruff. Unshaven. Pushing sixty. He lifted his thermos and pointed it outside, in the direction of the horse pasture. "He's long gone."

"Yeah, it seems," I said.

"My money's on the Cities," said Grady.

I nodded, rubbing my chin as I glanced around the barn.

After a beat, Grady said, "I suppose you already saw my re-modeling job, eh?" He walked past me and I followed him to the room with the bed and the toilet in the corner. He switched on the light again.

"Yes," I said. "Looks great. A studio apartment."

"Almost," he said, sliding his calloused hand along the drywall. "No kitchen."

"You don't need a kitchen out here when you've got June, right?" I nodded in the direction of the big house. June was an amazing cook. I think making food helped calm her when she was anxious. She spent half her waking hours in the kitchen. At least that's how it had seemed when I'd lived there, not that any of her cooking skills rubbed off on me. "Did you do all the work yourself?"

"'Course I did," said Grady, a small frown in his eyes, as if insulted. He switched off the light and we walked back toward the big doors. He stopped and set down his thermos. He picked up a rake and a shovel and some other junk near an empty horse stall.

I wondered who would want to live in a barn. It didn't smell great, and it wasn't exactly warm. I asked, "What's it for? I mean, who's living here?"

"No one, now," he said ominously. I thought of the blood, hoping it was oil or paint. Without speaking about it, we both glanced in the direction of the stain. When I looked up, he was staring at me. He asked, "Why are you asking all these questions? You were never interested in this shit when you were younger."

"First of all, that's not true," I said, and he was pissing me off. He always brought up the past when he sensed he was in trouble. How he and June had taken me in. It was like a debt I owed, and he brought it up any time he needed a boost. "I would have enjoyed learning how to build."

"Nah," he said, shaking his head. He picked up his thermos and took a sip.

"And who knows," I added, "it might have given us something to bond over."

"Pshh," he said, nearly spraying his coffee or whatever he was drinking out of that thermos. "There's enough horseshit around here. Don't need any from you." He turned and walked out of the barn, and I followed. He hadn't given me any clues about the stain, so I decided to pretend I hadn't noticed it. For now. As we approached the back steps to the big house, he stopped and turned around. He said, "You know, you don't need to please everybody all the time."

"I know," I said, taken aback.

"Do you?" His eyes were like lasers and it made me uncomfortable. He added, "Because it's impossible. Even if you try."

I nodded, and he took a sip from his thermos.

"And you try, girl," he said. "You really try."

"Okay, well. Thanks for that advice," I said as we moved up the steps. Opening the back door, which led to the kitchen, I asked, "When did you become such a philosopher, Grady?"

He scoffed, and we let the question dissolve into the aroma of June's pot roast.

"I'm going to clean up," said Grady, disappearing down the hall.

I listened to his footsteps as he climbed the stairs. June had been feverishly gathering apples, butter, and flour, and all the other ingredients for her famous apple crisp. When I heard the water pipes overhead, I knew Grady was out of earshot.

"So can I ask you a question?"

"Before you do that," said June, showing me the apple-peeling contraption she'd set up on the butcher block counter next to the sink, "would you do the peeling?"

"Sure," I said, understanding that June wasn't ready to talk. Or maybe she thought Grady could still hear us somehow. Anyway, I stuck the apple on the pointy end and cranked the handle, removing the skin in a long, snakelike piece that flopped onto the counter like it was alive.

As each apple was peeled, June grabbed it and expertly sliced it into thin wedges. As we worked, we talked. About Seaver, mostly. And how helpless we felt. "So you looked at the campground and park, I suppose?"

I nodded. June tossed the wedges into a large stainless steel bowl.

"And his friends down here. The ones I know of, anyway," I said, listing them. "Michael, Connor, Eli."

"Yes," said June. "Michael is his very best friend. Other than Adrian, of course."

"Yes, and I talked with Adrian this morning."

"Has he heard from him?"

I shook my head. "Not yet." The apples were all peeled, so I picked up a knife and started slicing, adding more wedges to the big bowl. "He'll let me know if he does."

"Good," said June, dumping sugar, cinnamon, and flour into the bowl with the apple slices. "They were so close."

"I know. And they only lived here together for a few months," I said. Usually, there would be three or four other kids in the house at any given time. But after Adrian aged out, it was just Seaver.

"Honestly, I think Seaver was lonely after Adrian left," said June, stirring the ingredients until all the apple slices were coated with the mixture. Then she poured it all into a baking dish, scraping in every last drop with a spatula. "I pray he turns up soon. And can go home."

"That's the goal," I said, watching June make the crumble topping by pressing a fork over three ingredients in a smaller bowl: butter, brown sugar, and oatmeal.

"And if things don't work out with his mom, then what?" June spooned the topping onto the apples, placing the clumps so that they were evenly spaced, covering the whole dish.

"We've been searching for a willing relative, vetting the options," I said. "I found an aunt, but her boyfriend is not on board.

We've been hoping she can turn him around. Apparently, he's not a fan of Nicole."

"Sounds tricky," said June, lifting the finished dish. "Open the oven for me, will you?"

I did, and as I watched her place the dish inside, I said, "In fact, tomorrow I'm visiting the aunt to get an update and check out her house. If they agree to emergency placement, I'm hopeful they'll stick it out for permanent placement."

"If the mom isn't ready, you mean?"

"Yep." I was rooting for Nicole, but I needed to be ready just in case.

"Sounds like a good plan," said June, brushing her hands off like they were sandy. She wiped her sweaty brow with her forearm, then untied her apron and lifted it over her head. "Now," she said, setting down her apron. "What was the big question you wanted to ask?"

From the hallway, we heard footsteps, then a man's voice. He said, "Yeah, what's your big question?"

"Grady! I didn't know you were there!" said June, holding her chest as if startled.

I was startled too. He'd been quick with his shower, and I wondered how long he'd been listening to us, if he'd been listening. Grady stood in the doorway to the kitchen, smirking. Just then, the dogs came running, finding their way around Grady like water around a boulder.

"Saved by the dogs," said Grady, stepping into the kitchen and opening the fridge.

June rinsed her hands under the faucet and said to me, "Let's go for a walk, shall we?"

Nineteen

CLAIRE

AFTER SCHOOL ON MONDAY, NO ONE SAT NEXT TO ME ON THE BUS RIDE home, which was good. I reached in my backpack and pulled out the paper I'd stolen from Evan's file. I unfolded it and looked at his handwriting. So small and weak, so different from Evan himself. If I were a handwriting expert, this sample would cause me to guess completely wrong about him. The truth was Evan was big and strong. He was tough and confident. He had a depth about him that you couldn't see from this paper. You had to see it in his eyes. You had to sit next to him in biology and feel his glowing energy, his power.

I touched the handwriting, then moved my fingertip along the phrases he'd scrawled. At the top of the page, I traced his full name and touched his two phone numbers. I guessed one was his mother's and the other his dad's. He and I had that in common; we both had parents who were divorced. I wondered if his mom had remarried and whether he liked his stepfather. I wondered how much he saw his dad.

As we got close to my stop, I folded the paper and stuck it back in my bag. From the bus stop, Mom and Brian's town house was only two blocks away. As I walked home, I remembered that Mom and Brian were going to a fundraiser after work. I would have to make an early dinner, then drive myself to volleyball practice. No problem. Afterward, I could study for the biology test. Meanwhile, I had biology homework to finish.

I put some breaded chicken strips in the microwave and pulled my homework out of my backpack. When the chicken strips were ready, I put them on a plate with some ketchup and called Becca.

"Hey," I said, as soon as she answered, "is my skin kind of olive-colored or is it more pink?"

"Are you asking if you're a winter or a summer? Because I think you're an autumn."

"I'm not an autumn," I said, although I might be.

"You don't know what you are," said Becca. "No one can decide their own season. We have to see each other's."

"Oh," I said. It made sense.

"Like, that's how I know I'm a winter. My cousin told me. And she works at the Clinique counter. She sees skin types all day long. You, Claire Larkin, are an autumn."

"Okay, but that's not what I'm talking about."

"Oh," said Becca, munching on something. "Then what?"

"I'm doing my traits and genes chart."

"For Biggerstaff?" Becca had had Mrs. Biggerstaff last year and it was definitely the same syllabus. Everyone could see the teacher was just reading her lessons out of an old three-ring binder. Same homework, same tests.

"Yeah," I said. This was a worksheet we'd started in class but were supposed to finish at home. Phenotypes and genotypes. I was completing a chart of recessive and dominant traits, showing the likelihood of inheriting various characteristics like eye color and left-handedness, based on your mother and father and their genes.

"Oh, I did that last year," said Becca.

"Yeah. Anyway." I wanted to ask Becca what she thought my babies would look like if Evan and I got married. Sitting next to Evan while the teacher went on and on about mixing genes together had been kind of exciting and kind of embarrassing. The whole topic implied the sex act without talking about it explicitly. Mrs. Biggerstaff was very matter-of-fact about it, which I found interesting as well. As if human reproduction was just another thing to dissect or examine, like worm guts and single-cell organisms.

"There's no right or wrong answers. Just put in whatever you want," said Becca.

"I know," I said, but I didn't know. Was it a big deal? Sacred, special, magic? Or was it ordinary, instinctive, natural. Just something a species does to survive? Parents acted so weird about it, they probably made it worse for everyone. Some forced their kids to practice putting condoms on bananas, while most ignored the topic altogether. And kids acted like they knew everything and everyone suspected everyone else had done this or that with him or her, but no one knew for sure. I didn't anyway. And I had so many questions that I couldn't ask. I wanted to know, Was there a right way and a wrong way? They said it came naturally but what did that mean?

"It's not like the teacher's gonna check your work. How could she even check it?—go to your mom's and verify her eye and hair color? Your mom gets highlights anyway, doesn't she?"

"Yeah," I said.

"So Biggerstaff wouldn't even know that your mom was a natural blonde."

"I know," I said, and suddenly I was thinking about Finn. "That's not it."

"Then what?"

My little brother had fair skin and pale-yellow hair, which he must have gotten from Mom. Dad has brown eyes and brown hair, like me. And I'm left-handed like Gamma Betty, my dad's mom. I wondered if Finn would have been left-handed too. I said, "I just thought I looked more like my dad."

"Oh. You do," said Becca authoritatively.

"Well, you could have said that."

"I just did."

"No, I did. Whatever."

"Whatever," said Becca and we sat for a moment, thinking. Finally, she asked, "So who are you going to homecoming with?"

"No one," I said, somewhat surprised at the question. The dance was this weekend.

"Why not?"

"No one's asked me."

"So?" said Becca, but I could tell she was playing dumb.

"So," I said slowly, like I was explaining the rules to a first grader, "you have to have a date to go to the dance."

"No, you don't," said Becca, and she sounded sincere. "Really."

"Okay, well, technically, I suppose," I said, but I didn't know because I'd never been. That's why I needed Becca. I asked her, "But I mean, most people have a date, right?"

Becca explained, "That's true, but my point is, you can ask someone to go. You don't have to wait for the guy. And also, I mean, some people go alone. Or just as friends."

I answered quickly. "I'm not gonna do that."

"Yeah, me neither," said Becca.

"I thought you said you were going?"

"I am going," she said.

"With who?"

"With whom," she corrected, then added, "Brad Stevens. He just asked me!"

"Ohhh."

"Yeahhh."

"Isn't he a senior?"

"Yeah," said Becca, like it wasn't a big deal.

"Does he like you?" I asked tentatively.

"I mean, I think so. That's what I heard anyway."

"Do you like him?"

"Obviously," she said. "But I'd go with him as friends even if I didn't like him because, I mean, why not?"

"Yeah," I said. Brad was pretty cute. I'd have to check his student file next time I was in the Counseling Office.

Becca said, "You should go with Evan Lewis."

"Ha!" I said, although I'd been thinking about it during this whole conversation, wondering if he would go. And wondering what would happen after the dance because I'd heard that's when stuff happened. I said, "He won't ask anyone."

"How do you know that?" asked Becca.

"I just know him," I said, and I really thought I did.

"Yeah," said Becca.

"He's not the type," I said, but I was wondering if I was the type.

"You should ask him. You'd make a good couple."

I felt myself blush. I thought about his brown eyes and mine. Dominant genes. I wondered if he thought about it during class like I did. I could never tell what was going on in his head. To Becca, I said, "You think?"

"Definitely."

I exhaled and heard my breath in the phone.

"Gross," said Becca. "Don't breathe so hard."

"Sorry."

"Anyway, I should go," said Becca. There was noise in the background, tousling, arguing. To someone else, Becca said, "Shut up, get out of here."

"Is that your brother?"

"Yeah," said Becca. "Sorry, he's gone now."

"Okay, well, I should finish this. And we have a test tomorrow."

"You'll be fine," said Becca. "But remember: You're an autumn. I'm a winter. Biggerstaff doesn't know what your mom is, so it doesn't matter."

"True," I said. "Thanks."

"You're welcome."

I could hear Becca's brother again in the background and they were kind of screaming at each other and fighting and then Becca hung up and I was smiling because I could imagine how frustrated Becca was and she was just so funny and cool.

But afterward, as I sat there with my homework and the crumbs from my chicken strips, I noticed how quiet it was in my house. I didn't have a little brother to bother me and be annoying and I just felt kind of sad and very . . . alone.

Twenty

SEAVER

APRIL 1992

WHEN THEY TOOK ME FROM MY MOM, SHE WAS CRYING. IT WAS THE middle of the night and I was asleep. Then I heard banging on the door and my mom was screaming at them, calling them pigs and bastards. They came into our apartment with flashlights and their radios were talking on their belts. Mom opened my door and sat on my bed. She told me it wasn't my fault. She promised she'd get me back. I didn't understand and I was sleepy and cold and scared. She said they were taking me to live with another family but it was only for a little while. I said no, I didn't want to go. She cried and hugged me. There was a lady police officer standing in the doorway. The police lady waved a black plastic garbage bag at me and told me to pack some clothes. Mom grabbed the bag from the police officer and told her to fuck off. Then Mom stuffed some of my shirts and pants into the bag. And some of my books. Mom said I had to get dressed. I was crying and I didn't know why this was happening. When the police officer was walking me out of the apartment, my mom came running after us and handed me my Rubik's Cube. I put it in my pocket. It was cold outside. They put me in a van and told me to fasten my seat belt. The lady said I could fall asleep if I wanted to. But the seat was cold and I couldn't sleep.

I watched out the window and cried a little. I didn't want to cry in front of them. I pulled out my Rubik's Cube and rubbed it in my hands because my mom had been touching it so I pretended she was there with me.

It was a long ride and I might have fallen asleep at the end of the drive. When the van slowed down, I woke up again.

They helped me out and carried my garbage bag of clothes into the house. It was a big house with a lady who looked like a grandmother. She was standing there waiting for me. She said, *Welcome to our home. We have a room for you.* The police officer went with us to the room upstairs and put my stuff on the bed.

That's when I met Adrian. I didn't know his name then. He was just an older boy who was standing at the end of the hall watching the police bring me in and he sort of waved at me.

When all the adults finally left, I sat on the bed and cried. There was a knock on the door and I stopped crying. The door opened a little and it was the older boy.

"I'm Adrian," he said. "My room is next to yours."

I looked at him but didn't say anything.

"I just wanted to say that Mrs. Ogletree makes good pancakes. I'll see you at breakfast." Then he said good night and closed the door.

I put my head on the pillow. I watched the moon come through the window and shine on the wall. I held on to my Rubik's Cube and thought about my mom. I wondered if she was looking at that same moon with me. I hoped she was.

Twenty-One

KIRA

MONDAY, SEPTEMBER 28, 1992

"A WALK SOUNDS DELIGHTFUL," I SAID, REACHING FOR MY JACKET from the hook in the back hall. "But it'll have to be quick. I'm going to the college after this. Going to try and talk with the professor."

"If it leads us to finding Seaver, I'm all for it," said June.

"Ask him what he was doing on our land," grumbled Grady, before retreating to the living room.

"I will find out as much as I can," I assured him. Turning to June, I said, "I'm looking forward to seeing the campus again. I always feel at home there."

June smiled as she called for the dogs and they gathered at her feet, their bodies wiggling with excitement. She opened the back door, and we spilled out, down the steps, and into the field behind the house.

The dogs took off on the trail, having traversed it every day, usually twice a day, for their entire lives. The dirt path ran the length of the field, under tall trees and lined with tall grasses. Late-afternoon sunlight lit the fields in all directions. We held hands as we walked. June wore her rain boots because there was always mud somewhere. She let go of my hand and put her arm around me. Our steps were in sync. She smiled and squeezed.

"How are you, really?" she asked.

"I'm good, June. I'm fine."

She bit her lip, as if she didn't quite believe me. She said, "You work too hard."

"I love my work," I said, gesturing to the beauty all around us.

"Well, I wish you had someone special to share it with," added June, as if to clarify.

"I will. Someday," I said, listening to the gentle crunch of our footsteps, a rhythmic patter. "And even if I don't, I'll still be fine."

"Absolutely." June smiled, then let her arm fall to my waist and let me go. She reached down and picked up a long, twiggy stick, periodically waving it at the grass like a whip. After a while, she said, "So what is it you want to ask?"

I took a deep breath. "How do I phrase this?" I said, pausing for a moment before asking, "Is Grady living in the barn?"

June scoffed. "What? No."

"I mean, are you two having trouble?"

"No, Kira." June chuckled. "Why? Were you hoping we were?" She picked up another stick, a short, stocky one, a stick that was good for throwing.

"Of course not," I said. "I mean . . ."

"Are you sure?" said June, chucking the stick. The dogs took off after it. "You haven't exactly been a big fan."

"That was years ago," I said, referring to Grady and myself. When I was first placed with the Ogletrees, I didn't get along with Grady. "He was strict and I was a teenager. We've both grown up since then."

"You certainly have," she replied. One of the dogs retrieved the stick and June tossed it again. After a few turns with the stick, June seemed to be reminiscing, going back in time. She turned to me with compassion in her eyes. "You were only Seaver's age when you came to us, weren't you?"

"Close. I think I was thirteen," I said, slowing down and watching each foot as it landed on the trail: one, then the other. Now I was the one floating back. I was ten when my parents died. A car accident on their way back from supper. At first, I stayed with friends. Then my mom's cousin, but they couldn't keep me long term. Eventually, I was placed into foster care, hopping from one home to another. Finally, I came to live with the Ogletrees and it clicked. I loved the farm, and I actually enjoyed the other kids. "But that was many years ago," I said.

June squeezed my hand. We'd reached the part of the walk where we turn around. We called the dogs and reversed direction. We started heading back.

I said, "So if Grady's not living in the barn, who is?"

"What?"

"Clearly someone's living out there," I said. "Could it be Seaver?"

"Of course not," said June. "I wouldn't let my kids live in a barn."

I loved how she considered them all to be her kids. I wasn't the only social worker who placed children with June; she also got kids from other counties. Whether they stayed a few days or a few years (those were rare), she cared for them the same. She was all in, but it was only temporary. Sometimes her friends and neighbors asked if she was interested in adoption. She'd say no. Fostering was her calling, and it was a perfect fit.

I asked, "So what's the story with the barn bedroom?"

The question hung in the air as we walked several steps in silence. Finally, June said, "It started as a project. Just another idea of Grady's. It was like, what if he finished off a room in the barn?" She went on, "And I said of course, why not? He's good with his hands."

"Right," I said. "And were you going to rent it out or what?"

"No, well, it's hard to explain," she said. "And it's not a topic I enjoy."

"What happened?" I asked carefully, sensing her discomfort.

June appeared to be gathering herself, her thoughts. Finally, she said, "We're not getting younger, Kira. We're getting older."

"I know that. So are we all."

"No, it's not the same," said June. "We're slowing down. Grady is slowing down. He's not as strong as he used to be. I don't want him to wear himself out."

"Of course," I said, trying to be sensitive.

"And yet we have the horses and the fields. Most of it is leased to other farmers, but we have the grazing, the hay. The horses need to be fed several times a day. The labor is just a lot."

"I know, but I mean, he seems fine."

"Exactly. We want to keep it that way. I don't want him getting hurt. And he, miraculously, seems to agree."

"Okay," I said, waiting for more.

"So we thought, well, if we could find someone to help out a bit, in exchange for a nice place to sleep, maybe some meals, that might be a good use for that bedroom."

"I see," I said, holding on to the questions in my head. My hair kept falling in my face, so I pulled it up and tied a scrunchie around it.

"A few weeks back, Grady put the word out. That we were looking for help. A farmhand, a jack-of-all-trades, a handyman. Details to be worked out."

My heart was pounding harder. If June and Grady had planned to hire a live-in, they should have disclosed it. I'd have done a background check on anyone living at the house (or barn).

"June, you should have told me," I said. She glared at me, then we both looked at the trail. It was amazing how different the same path could look when walking in the other direction. Today the difference was particularly stark. "Any residents of the home must be reported to the agency so we can screen them. You know that."

"How can I tell you something if I don't know about it myself?" said June, her jaw tight, her fists clenched.

"Grady hired someone without telling you?"

June nodded stiffly. "I'm sorry, believe me."

"It's okay," I said, rubbing her back. She flinched away, still upset.

"At least there's no one in there now," said June, a bit too defensively.

I was confused. "Well, okay, then what is all that crap in there?"

"There was someone in there, but he's . . ." said June. "Gone."

I sighed. This was not good. "Okay," I said. "So a farmhand was living in the barn bedroom?"

"He was. For two nights, yes."

"And then what?"

"Then he was gone."

"Meaning what, it didn't work out?"

"Apparently not. He disappeared," said June.

"As in, he quit? Or what do you mean, disappeared?"

"Well, that's the thing, honey," said June. "Grady won't tell me."

"Well, that's just bizarre," I said. But on the other hand, Grady definitely had his quirks and could be peculiar about seemingly minor issues.

"He gets grumpy when I ask," said June, her palms up and open, as if she was out of options. "So I've stopped asking. For now."

"I see," I said, not satisfied. "And this was the night before Seaver left?"

"It was the same day," said June.

"What?!" I said, stopping. June stopped walking too. The

dogs swirled around us as if they could detect the tension. "I asked you if anything happened and you said no!"

June seemed to ignore me as she calmly bent down and attended to the dogs, as if she'd rather talk to them than to me. Finally, June stood up, gazed at me with raised eyebrows and stated, "Seaver was at Michael's house all weekend. He didn't even know about the young man in the barn."

We started walking again and I was feeling frustrated. June should have been more forthcoming. Or I should have asked better questions. But if Seaver didn't even know about the farmhand, then it was probably all right, I thought. I took a look around. We were getting close to the house. After a beat, I said, "Okay, I guess."

June put her hand on my arm and it was like an apology and forgiveness mixed into one long touch. When we reached the house, June stopped near the back steps. She turned to me and said, "I truly believe Seaver was missing Adrian."

"Adrian's too young to be a guardian, so Seaver can't live with him even if he tried."

June nodded briefly, then said, "Which brings me to the hardest part, Kira."

"What now?" I braced myself for more bad news.

June's eyes were watery and her voice caught as she spoke. She delivered news that sank into my heart and troubled me after I'd said goodbye and climbed into my VW Rabbit. Even as I left the farm and drove to the college, I replayed her words over and over, words that didn't sound like June. Words that sounded so cold and so final.

"When you find Seaver," she'd said, "Grady doesn't want him back."

Twenty-Two

MATTHEW

MY CAR WAS GONE. *STOLEN?* "MY CAR WAS STOLEN!" I HOLLERED.

Oh my god. I patted my pockets, feeling for my keys. No. My pockets were empty. Had I left the key in the ignition? No! I patted my whole body down, searching for the keys. They weren't on me. I'd left them in the car. My missing, stolen car.

"Help!" I cried to the empty lot. I looked at the gas pumps, the Shell sign, the sky. Anyone anywhere. Please.

I flew into the gas station, nearly ripping the door off. The bell rang and a male voice said, "Can I help you, dude?"

"Oh, sorry," I said, breathing heavily. "Yes, thank you." I made my way to the cash register area, my heart thumping and eyes wide. The young man was sitting behind plexiglass, with a cash register in front of him and rows of cigarettes above. The windows behind him were tinted, but he had a full view of the parking lot.

"What's up?" he said. He was playing with a rubber band and his arms were tattooed.

"My car was stolen," I said, huffing and puffing. "I need to call the police."

"Oh, man," he said, shaking his head. "That sucks."

"Yeah," I said. "You didn't see anything, did you? And, uh, do you guys have any security cameras around here?"

"Nah, sorry," he said. "But wait. What kind of car was it?"

"A Subaru?" I said, pointing to the parking lot. "It was right out there. I, uh, think I left my keys in it and it was just, you know, not a great neighborhood to do that in, I guess."

The cashier looked to be in his midtwenties, about the same age as my graduate students, men and women who asked me to write them recommendation letters as they pursued their adult lives, their future careers. But this man seemed like he was already in his life. Like this auto shop was his future career. He said, "Your car wasn't stolen, man."

I was catching my breath. "What'd you say?" I looked at the man.

He was twirling the rubber band around his fingers, making sort of a churning motion. "I said it wasn't stolen."

"Really?" I gasped. "You mean it? So, it was towed? Oh, thank god. Where? Where'd you tow it?"

"It wasn't towed neither," he said, rising from his perch and opening his shielded plexiglass door. He walked to the back, snapping his rubber band at me as if to get me to follow him, and I did. He opened another door and showed me the garage. There, up on the lift, was my car. "We thought you were dropping it off for service, man. That's your car, ain't it?"

"Yes, that's it," I gulped, staring at the underside of my Subaru. I wiped my brow then leaned over and braced my hands on my knees. I'd never been happier to see my car in an auto shop. "Phew. Thank god."

"Did an oil change. Added fluid. Didn't charge you for the tire rotation. You may need an alignment soon. But she's good to go." The cashier smirked and returned to his post.

I followed him there and he charged me twenty-five dollars, which I happily paid. He tried to sell me on their hail damage removal services, but I passed.

I got in the car and sat for a moment, gathering myself. Something was churned up inside, and I needed to settle. I did a few breathing exercises, then pulled out of the Shell station, following the one-way streets until I reached the closest entry to I-35 South.

As I merged onto the highway, I glanced over at the passenger seat where Seaver had been riding. Something caught my eye on the far edge of the seat and I reached over to touch it. *Oh, for Christ's sake!* He'd left his Rubik's Cube.

"Seaver," I said quietly to the car, shaking my head, "you gotta hang on to your stuff."

Finn was always losing his toys. But he was only a toddler, so it was expected. He left his plastic airplanes, books, and stuffed animals all over the house. Carrying them near and far, leaving them in the strangest places. Teddy bear in the fridge. Cardboard blocks in the dishwasher. Train cars in the toilet. I could still remember the way it made him laugh, to see a toy out of place like that.

I tapped my fingers on the steering wheel, checking off the exits as I passed them: the airport, the new Mall of America, all in my rearview mirror. Traffic was thinning out and it was just me and the other commuters heading to the southern suburbs, the countryside, the smaller towns. When I saw the exit sign, I swerved over and took it. Here was my chance to visit Finn. I'd only skipped it yesterday because of the storm.

I made my way to the cemetery, then to the section that held Finn's grave. I parked on the side of the road and lumbered up the hill to his plot. There was a vase stuck in the ground next to the marker. It held a bouquet of red roses, but I wasn't sure who'd put them there. Tammy? Must have been. But it made me feel I'd missed something. I didn't have flowers and I didn't know who'd been here before me. I didn't like that feeling.

I sat down cross-legged and leaned forward to brush off the leaves. The damp ground seeped into the seat of my khakis, but the coldness of the earth helped me settle into being with my son.

"Finn," I said, leaning to trace the carved letters on the stone. We'd chosen a modest marker, just a smooth granite rectangle, on which was carved:

SWEET BOY, REST NOW IN ETERNAL PEACE
JULY 11, 1980 – JUNE 2, 1984

June 2, 1984. The worst day of my life. Of all our lives. As I sat with the stone and the roses at Finn's grave, I remembered. It was why I came there again and again. I sat and rocked forward and back on the cold ground, my eyes closed, thinking of Finn. And that horrible day.

Our little boy had died on the spot. That's what the doctors told us after. Of course we tried resuscitation. I did. Another parent at the pool party did. And of course, the paramedics. But it was too late. It all happened so quickly. Seemed impossible, too impossible to be true. Couldn't be true. He couldn't be dead. He had to start breathing again. He had to come back.

"Come on," I was crying as I gave him CPR, "come on, buddy. Breathe, please breathe."

I pushed and pushed on his little chest, breathed into his little mouth, and pinched his miniature nostrils, blowing. "Come on!"

The others on the pool deck had gathered around Finn's body, which was limp and droopy. I crouched over him, wouldn't leave his side, and the other parents huddled around us, bent over with concern, watching for any sign of life. The other children were peeking through the legs of the adults, trying to squeeze in for a front-row view, but the other parents were holding them back, telling them to give Finn's daddy some room.

I remember the sound of the children crying with fear, craning to see. Instinctively, the parents divided into groups, with some of them staying to help while others carried their own sons and daughters out of sight, distracting them, telling them it'd be okay. It wasn't okay. Finn's skin was growing blue, and nothing was moving except for me, up and down. I remember someone saying the paramedics were on the way, but I didn't stop. I had to keep going. And no one could reach Tammy, she wasn't home, there was no answer, but I'd begged them to keep trying. Please. I needed her there. I needed her so badly.

The other parents placed their hands on my back, some were crouched beside me, and they continued their encouraging, praying perhaps, until gradually they must have realized that nothing was changing. And as it gradually sank in that this wasn't working, they slowly pulled back and away from me, they straightened up and were leaving me, distancing themselves. They must have known that this was something else, it had become something unimaginable. But I kept on. I had to.

"Hey, Matt," someone said. "Hey, it's okay . . ."

But I didn't stop, and someone else put her hand on my arm, trying to get through to me. Her voice was gentle, she must have said, "Take a rest, slow down. Hey, paramedics are coming."

But I shook her off, crying, "No, no no, no, come on now, come on, buddy."

And when the paramedics arrived, they were swift, moving almost imperceptibly, and they carried my son's small body onto the stretcher, then into the truck. They helped me in too, and closed the doors and we were gone, their lights flashing. Flying through the streets, flashing and flaring, they were still working on my boy. I'd been allowed to ride along, next to Finn, but only to watch and weep, unable to speak, nothing sensical. Where was Tammy? How would she find us?

The back doors to the ER were standing open, as if they'd been waiting for us. There was another transfer to the indoors, the wheels spinning down halls, over clean parchment-colored floors, to that room with the curtain, the stainless steel, and the stiff white sheets. The mechanical bed looked vast as an ocean under Finn's tiny body. Then there was a ballet of people wearing scrubs and badges coming in and out of the room, around the table. The terrible looks on their faces, those nurses and doctors, the helpers and pokers, while they were clipping and connecting, their serious voices, their determination. The movements they made again and again, full force, together, and then no, and stop, finally, no more. Surrender.

They'd said there was nothing more, they were sorry. There was a shift then, to letting go. There was the removal of rubber gloves, snapping and tossing them, the wheeling away, the closing, and retreating, sorrowful, heads down, leaving you alone, someone will come, the pat on the back, the okay, okay? Okay? I'm sorry, I'm sorry, so sorry. And I was alone and spinning, the sting inside, as if my internal organs had collapsed, my legs too, and my mind relentlessly wringing out questions: Where are we? Who are you? What is this? *Okay*, they'd said, *okay, we can wait, okay*. I remember there was a moment when I couldn't feel my face, the soreness and wet of it, my neck was tight with choking and needing air, and water, and I was wiping and crying, not finding answers. Having no direction. And where was Tammy?

Is she here yet? I kept asking. *Has she called?* And then, finally, *Mr. Larkin, we have your wife on the phone, you can take her call over here.* The bobble of the phone in my hands, the far away-ness of her on the other end. And how to get the words out, oh my god, Tammy. I didn't know how to say it. And her voice was so demanding, *What is it? What is it, Matthew?* she kept repeating. She was desperate to know, but I couldn't say it, couldn't until I simply said, *Our son is gone. Finn is gone. Tammy. Tammy, where are you, he's gone*. And the silence, the screams, the full stop of it. Where and how? We were at the pool, the birthday party, and I don't know, and the endless *noooooooooooo*, the struggle to breathe, to say words while weeping, not getting enough air.

And Tammy wailed. She asked again and again, and I answered. She cried *no, no, no, no*, she said, *it can't be, it can't be*, and *I'm coming, I'm coming now*. Then finally after an eternity waiting for her, the door finally slammed, and her footsteps, the sobbing embrace, dropping of everything, this can't be happening, this can't be true. Then the circling around again to what happened, what happened, and the endless why. *Why did you, why didn't, what were you, when, who, how could this be*. And when she got angry, she'd punched me, she said I was the one who'd done this, she was punching at me but I knew she was punching at our fate, at the darkness. I kept saying, *I know* and *I'm sorry*.

And when we got home, we walked in silently then crumpled onto the kitchen floor, weak with despair, run out of words, and we stabbed at violence, reaching for plates and mugs and pens and the phone and we threw them on the floor until we were sitting in a pile of brokenness. And Claire, who was only eight, was terrified of course and was crying and pleading, *Please stop, Mommy, please*. And in the end, we all huddled together on the floor, till darkness and sleep, and then days and then nights, and nights upon nights and the nightmares of nights.

When people ask me what came next, all I can say is it was a flurry. A flurry of decisions, arrangements, and shoulds. Well wishes, opinions, and offers and orders and got-to-be-dones. There were always, and will always be, a multitude of unanswerable questions and blame and sideways glances. There will be doubts forever, and the worst of it came from Tammy. And it was directed at me. Although I had to agree with her. That this was my fault. It was an accident, but I was the one who was there. I was the one who had failed. And Tammy could never forgive me. To be honest, I didn't think I would ever forgive myself either. Not for this.

The experience of losing my son became its own force, a whole world of death, and that loss rolled into a ghost that I believe has followed me ever since. It is with me always and floats past in flashes, popping up inside me without warning. It comes unexpectedly and expectedly. In a sense, I have become comfortable with these swells of feelings and thoughts. They are a part of me now. A paralyzing sting that never goes away, but never lasts too long.

I sat at the grave remembering, just waiting for the pain to subside. I was hugging my knees and rocking, rocking and saying to my boy, *I love you. I love you and I'm sorry.* And when I was settled, I wiped my nose on my sleeve. I stood up to leave and brushed off my pants. I tapped the stone marker, the way I always did, and got back in the car, my face red, my sadness baptized again, and I turned the ignition, grateful to have my car and grateful to have had my dear Finn.

When I got back to campus, I parked behind my apartment building and walked around to the front door. Two figures were sitting on the entry steps. As I got closer, I saw that one of them was Doug. A bit of smoke rose above his head.

Doug and the other person noticed me and stopped talking. They watched me approach. Soon I could see that the other person was a woman. She stood up and brushed off her pants. When I reached the stoop, the woman said, "Whatcha got there?"

"Huh?" I asked. I realized I was staring at the woman. Her eyes were bright. She had an energy about her that was warm and kind. I wondered if she was a new faculty member. Or a friend of Doug's.

"Hey, Matt," said Doug, snapping his fingers at me like I was in a trance. "What's in your hands?"

I looked down to see what he meant. I was holding the Rubik's Cube.

Twenty-Three

SEAVER

MONDAY, SEPTEMBER 28, 1992

I KNEW THAT BOBBI KEPT THE EXTRA KEYS TO THE APARTMENTS IN A shoebox in the bathroom closet. She had the keys because her boyfriend was the handyman, but he wasn't around much. Mom's key still had a blue rabbit's foot on it. I took that and ran into Mom's apartment.

I locked the door behind me. I didn't have much time, so I dashed around. I didn't know what I was looking for. Coins for the pay phone. Dry socks. There wasn't any food in our apartment. Probably because no one was living there. I had to hurry, because Bobbi was banging on the door and yelling. She was saying she would call the police.

Bobbi always called the police any time anything happened in our building. Fights, arguments. I'd heard gunshots before. Seen flashing lights in the parking lot and sick people lying on the steps. Tired, drunk, or high people. Mom worked as a nurse so she knew about these things. She gave people medicine when no one else would. She got in trouble for it sometimes because she would sell medicine cheaper than the other places. I know it was Bobbi who called the police and told them to take me away from Mom. No one told me that, but I bet it was true.

Mom wasn't always nice to me, but that just meant she needed alone time. Like when she was in a bad mood or she was tired from work. Sometimes she didn't pay the bills so they turned off our lights or our heat. We just used flashlights and blankets. If she couldn't buy food, we'd get cans of green beans and boxes of macaroni and cheese from the food shelf. Mom took care of me and I know she loves me because she told me all the time. She would always wink at me and say, *I love you, Doodle Head*. Mom called me Doodle Head because my hair was always messy when I was little. It's still sort of messy now, I guess, but not as messy as it used to be.

I was thinking that if they wouldn't let me live with Mom, then I wanted to live with Adrian. When he left the Ogletrees, he said he was getting an apartment with some other guys in Minneapolis and he said I could stay with them.

But I wanted to live with Mom. That was where I wanted to be. It could be an apartment or a house. It could be a tent or a shelter. I didn't care. I just wanted to be with Mom. And I know she wanted to be with me.

I only saw my dad once but I didn't know it was him. He was just someone in a car in the parking lot in front of our apartment building. Mom was talking to him through the open driver's-side window. He grabbed at her and she shoved him away. Then she gave him something in an envelope and he sped off. I said who was that, and she said, "An old friend." Later she said, *Hey, remember that guy who sped off in the car?* and I said, *Yeah*. She said, *Well, you probably have a right to know that was your father*. I'd said "What?" because she never told me anything about my father and I wished I could have met him. But she said it was too late because he was going to jail soon in Texas. She told me not to worry and promised that I'd meet him when I was a grown-up.

My ankle hurt as I put on the dry socks. There was a red area on my leg, on the side, down by my ankle. It hurt pretty bad. Like a big sliver was under the skin. Bobbi had stopped banging on the door so I figured the coast was clear. I stuffed the coins and the rabbit foot key chain in my pocket. I ran out the door, past Bobbi's apartment, down the steps, and out of the building.

If the police were coming, I didn't want to be there. After I left Mom's apartment building, I turned up the alley, looking for bikes. Bikes in the backyard or just sitting against a garage. I didn't have a cutter with me. I needed a bike that wasn't locked.

I walked as quickly as I could along three blocks of alleys and then I found one. A dusty old three-speed. Black body with huge wheels. It was too big for me. And it was a man's so it had the bar. I reached my leg over it and balanced, taking off down the alley and turning onto Thirty-First Street.

When I was several blocks away, I looked for a pay phone. I needed to call Adrian to get his address.

I put the quarter in and waited for the dial tone. I dialed the number I'd memorized. All the numbers in Minneapolis started with six-one-two, so that was easy. Then it goes: Nine minus one is eight. The rest was a joke about Chicken McNuggets. How many would I like? Twenty four one. While it rang, I wished I had some McDonald's.

"Hello?" someone answered.

"Is Adrian there?" I said.

"He doesn't live here anymore."

"Oh."

There was a pause and I heard the person breathing. He said, "What time is it?"

"I don't know."

"I'm not talking to you," he said. I heard another voice say two thirty. Then I heard him ask that person about Adrian. His new number. Then he said, "You got a pen?"

I looked around the phone booth. There was a phone book on a chain and another chain for a pen but it was broken off.

"Okay, well, here's his number, you ready?"

"Yeah," I said, hoping I could make a math problem again.

He said the number and I said it back. He said, "Yeah," and I said it again. He said, "Yeah, that's right, you got it, okay?" I said it again. He said he was gonna hang up now, and he did.

As fast as I could, I put another quarter in and dialed the new number.

"Hello?" said the new person. They sounded sleepy.

"Is this Adrian's house?" I was watching down the street to see if anyone was looking for me.

"It's not a house, but yeah, he lives here," said the person, yawning. "I mean, I'm his roommate. Why?"

"Is he there?"

"No," said the person.

"Where is he?"

"How would I know?" said the person. "Work, maybe?"

"Where does he work?" I asked.

"Um. Bageletta." He yawned again. A loud groan.

"Which one?"

"South Minneapolis, why?" The roommate sounded annoyed.

"I need to talk to him," I said.

"Who is this?"

"My name is Seaver," I said. "I'm his brother."

Twenty-Four

KIRA

MATTHEW LARKIN LOOKS A BIT LIKE CLARK KENT. THAT IS, HE WEARS glasses and seems to be a bit of a nerd. He also fits the typical professor mold: when I first met him, he was wearing a windbreaker over a tweed blazer, with baggy khakis and brown shoes like Hush Puppies, and his briefcase strap was falling off his shoulder. But in Professor Larkin's case, he was also carrying a Rubik's Cube and he didn't seem to be aware of it. I studied him as he approached the front steps of the apartment building where I'd been sitting and having a lovely conversation with an amazing painter and amateur drummer named Doug.

"So you like doing Rubik's Cubes?" I asked Clark Kent as he finally reached us, stopping and catching his breath from an apparently strenuous walk.

Looking at the Cube, he said, "Oh this, uh. No, it's not mine. I've never solved one without the instruction manual."

"I can do it," said Doug, taking the Cube. He started swirling the rows around, clicking and fussing with it. He was quickly frustrated and handed it back. "Maybe not."

I watched the two men play with the toy, then asked Matthew, "So where'd you get that one?"

"Oh, this, um," he said, looking at the Cube. "Someone left it in my car."

"Lucky you," I said, but if that was Seaver's, I was going to retrieve it.

Matthew made a goofy face, then tucked the Cube into his jacket pocket. When he looked at me again, he was in professor mode. He stuck out his hand. "I'm Matthew Larkin. I teach in the sociology department."

"Nice to meet you." I shook his hand, a nice handshake. "Kira Patterson, I'm a social worker."

"Very cool," he said, pushing his glasses up on the bridge of his nose. "We've got a robust social work program within the sociology department, so I know a bit about the discipline."

"Only a tiny bit, I'm guessing," said Doug, teasing.

"Well, that's fair. They're almost separate disciplines," I said. "At least they were when I went here."

"Oh, you're a Gussie?" asked Matthew, his eyes widening.

"I am," I said, adding the school cheer, "Ygg Dra Dra, Ygg Dra Dra!"

He laughed.

"We're still the Fighting Yggdrasil, right?" I asked, suddenly embarrassed.

"Oh yes," he said emphatically, reassuring me. "We are the St. Gustaf Yggdrasil."

I grinned. "Our mascot is a tree."

"Not any tree," corrected Matthew. "The Norse tree of life."

"Yes." I smiled and pointed at him, acknowledging his accuracy. He seemed proud of the school and earnest. I wanted to get him talking because I had some questions. I continued, "I graduated in '78, then got my MSW in '81."

"I missed you then. I started here in '86," said Matthew.

"We just missed each other," I said, noticing his smiling eyes, the creases at the corners. He was only a few years older than me. "I had Professor Jamieson. Is she still here?"

He nodded. "Oh yes, I was just speaking with Gloria. She's chair of the department now."

"I remember reading that in the alumni magazine," I said.

"We're in capable hands," he said. I liked that he valued the leadership of a woman.

"Welp. Time for me to fly," said Doug. He must have been bored with our conversation, or maybe he was feeling left out.

"I'd love to see that exhibit when it comes to Minneapolis," I said to Doug, referring to the avant-garde photographer he'd been telling me about.

"Cool," said Doug as he sauntered away, ignoring the paths and walking on the grass. He puffed on his pipe as he walked and a trail of smoke rose up around his head, then floated to the sky.

"He's a hoot," I said.

"That's one word for it," said Matthew, grinning. "Are you a friend of his?"

"No," I said, somewhat amused at the implication in his voice. Was he wondering if Doug and I were dating? I explained, "I've never met Doug before. I came down here to meet you, actually."

"Oh?" Matthew seemed nervous and flattered at the same time. We were standing in the shade of a huge tree in front of the apartment building. His briefcase was still hanging on his shoulder. Mine was on the steps.

"Let me come clean," I said finally. "Do you have some time to chat?"

"Who could resist such an intriguing invitation?" said Matthew. "I was going to head over to my office. Wanna walk with me?"

"Sure," I said. As we walked, I admired the beauty of the campus. "The place hasn't changed much since I graduated."

He nodded, surveying the treed lawns that surrounded us, the brownstone buildings and leaded glass. He said, "It's important to have a place to come back to, a familiar place."

"Yes," I said, wondering what he was really talking about. But professors like him very often had their head in the clouds. I'd have to keep us on track if I was going to get any information out of him. I shifted the conversation to my purpose and told him about my work.

When I mentioned the public schools in Hennepin County, he said, "Oh? My daughter goes to South."

"Yes. In fact, I know Claire," I said. "She volunteers in the Counseling Office. You probably knew that."

"Really? Wow," he said, and it seemed like he didn't have a clue about it. Suddenly, he stopped walking as if something had just occurred to him. "Is that why you're here? Is Claire all right?"

"No, she's fine," I said, reassuring him. "It's not about her."

"Good," he said with a sigh. He shook his head as if relieved, and we continued walking. This guy was all over the place. Clueless, maybe, but he cared about his daughter.

"Claire's a great kid," I said, looking up at him. "And I see where she gets her height."

"Ha, I suppose that's me," he said modestly. "She's much more coordinated than I."

"Yes, she's on the volleyball team," I said. "Do you get to many of her games?"

"I have not," said Matthew, lamely adding, "I'm just so busy down here."

"Oh, I bet you could figure out a way to see a game or two," I said, not wanting to let him off the hook with such a weak excuse. I had to be careful though; he was opening up to me and I still needed to find out about Seaver. I smiled and we continued walking, just enjoying the leaves and the crisp autumn air.

"Do you have kids?" he asked suddenly.

"Not of my own," I said, then added my usual line, "but I have hundreds on my caseload. And they're my pride and joy."

"Of course," he said, smiling, "of course."

We reached the library, and I commented how it was my favorite building. We did a quick run-through of all the best buildings on campus, and on the elevator ride up to the third floor, Matthew gave me his pitch for why Sociology should have its own building and not be required to share with Philosophy, History, and Poli-Sci. He seemed quite jealous of Psychology, which had its own building on the quad.

We walked the hall to his office, and Matthew removed the handwritten sign from his door. He explained that he'd had to cancel his office hours, but he also seemed disappointed that there weren't any notes from students who'd been looking for him. Honestly, I thought he shouldn't worry about it so much. If a student needed something, I'm sure they'd track him down. Students had a way of doing that.

Matthew unlocked the door and invited me in. The office was small, very similar to the ones I remembered from fifteen years ago. We crowded in around the oak desk. I moved a stack of papers from the guest chair so I could sit down. "Nice office."

"It does the job," said Matthew, switching on his desk lamp and settling into his chair, ready to listen. "How can I help?"

Clasping my hands, I said, "Okay. I'm here about a boy on my caseload. His name is Seaver Swanson."

Matthew's face fell and he went pale. His shoulders relaxed. He let his head drop into his chest. When he looked up, he said, "Thank goodness you found him."

"So you know who I'm talking about?"

"Of course," he said. "I mean, I didn't know his last name was Swanson. I wasn't even sure his name was Seaver. But it has to be him. And I'm relieved he's all right."

"I'm not sure he's all right," I said, putting up my hands as if to brace him.

"Oh no. What is it?" he said.

"Let's back up," I said. "You must not have gotten my voice-mail."

"Um, no, I'm sorry. I don't always check those in a timely fashion," he admitted.

"Okay," I said, and I repeated what I'd said in the voicemail: that I'd gotten Matthew's name and number from the Ogletrees. That I knew he'd found a boy—probably Seaver—and that he'd tried to take him to the hospital. And that Seaver had run off.

"Right," he said. "But then I drove him to Minneapolis."

"You did what?" I said, trying to stay calm. "Where? I'm sorry. I didn't know that part."

Matthew told me about the big adventure, then simply said, "And now I'm sitting here talking to you. And I'm very glad to be doing so."

"Well, thank you for your candor," I said, and I'd noticed the sincerity in his brown eyes, but I also needed to call this in. "May I, um, use your phone?"

"Sure." Matthew pushed the phone closer to my side of the desk. I picked up the receiver and dialed the number for Family Alternatives.

"Should I leave the room?" asked Matthew.

I shook my head. The line was ringing. I held up my finger and waited for someone at the agency to answer. When they did, I said, "Hi, it's Kira. I have a possible location for Seaver Swanson. Can you ask law enforcement to send a car?"

Matthew stood up and pushed his chair into his desk. He was wringing his hands.

I asked him for the address.

"I don't know," he said, but he gave me the cross streets.

"It's Nicole Swanson's apartment, the address should be in the file," I said to my assistant. I told her to have the cops drive around and check the area and talk to the neighbor.

After the call, I hung up and thanked Matthew.

He said, "I'm not sure if I've hurt or helped the situation."

"We'll find out," I said, inhaling and lifting my eyebrows. "I just want to make sure he's okay."

"Of course," said Matthew. "When do you think they'll go over and look for him?"

"The police? Oh, it could be several hours. Could be tomorrow. Just depends on what else is going on with dispatch. I hope it's soon though." I gathered my things. "I should get going. In case they find him, I want to be near."

"He seemed like a pretty tough kid," said Matthew, watching me.

"Yeah," I said. "On the outside, anyway. He's had to develop a hard shell. He's been through a lot, you know."

Matthew nodded. He seemed to be considering something. Finally, he said, "It would be challenging to be a foster parent, I think."

"It takes a special heart." I flashed him a smile. "Are you thinking about applying? We're always looking for more."

"Me? I don't think I could do it," said Matthew.

"Of course you could," I said. "And you have experience."

"Well, that's true," he said. "I took care of both our children as babies. My wife, I mean ex-wife, was working full-time, so I was home with the kids."

"It can be overwhelming, I'm sure," I said, not that I knew firsthand. "But Claire is perfect in my eyes. You must have done something right."

"Oh, that's nice of you to say," said Matthew, looking down. He mumbled something. It sounded like he said, "You wouldn't want me if you knew."

"Well, then," I said, unsure how to respond. I stood up and scribbled my number on a piece of paper. Handing it to him, I said, "If you change your mind, give me a call. Thank you for your time. And the use of your phone. It was nice to meet you."

"You as well," he said, rising. We walked out the door, down the hall toward the elevator. As we walked, Matthew said, "I'm glad St. Gus has produced a social worker as excellent as you, Ms. Patterson."

"Call me Kira, and thank you, Professor Larkin." I pressed the elevator button.

"Call me Matthew," he said, smiling.

He adjusted his glasses and I smiled back.

The elevator doors opened and we both startled.

"Oh! One more thing," I said, holding the elevator, "I have an idea for your project."

"What project?"

"To improve the standing of the sociology department on campus." The doors attempted to close and I pushed them back.

"Oh yeah? I'd like to hear it," he said.

"Another time," I said, ducking into the elevator and pressing the button.

"Another time," he said, watching the doors close.

Twenty-Five

SEAVER

BAGELETTA WAS KIND OF FAR AWAY, BUT I COULD TAKE LYNDALE AVE-nue. Then over on Fifty-Fourth. The bike pedals were hard to reach so I had to stand up when I needed speed. My left leg was weaker and throbbing where I'd hurt it. The wind was blowing in my face and it made some water come out of my eyes. I didn't want to fall. I wasn't wearing a helmet. When the lights turned yellow, I went through. I went through stop signs because there were no cars around.

Finally, I turned onto Fifty-Fourth and it was only three more blocks. I saw the store from a block away. I coasted into the parking lot and hopped off the bike. I leaned against the window and looked in. He wasn't in the front. I brought the bike around to the back. There were no windows. There was a dumpster and a door marked Employees Only. I knocked on the door. Nothing happened.

I walked to the front and went inside. I stood in front of the glass that protected all the bagel spreads from having us cough on them. I looked at all the bagels behind the counter. I was hungry.

"Can I help you?" asked a person with a Bageletta cap on his head.

"Is Adrian here?" I said.

"Who's Adrian?" said the person.

Another worker overheard us. She said, "Adrian, the baker?"

I nodded. "He works here."

"Yeah," said the second worker. "He comes in later."

"What time?"

"I don't know, midnight?"

"Midnight?" That was late.

"Yeah," said the first worker. "That's when they make the bagels."

"Oh." I turned and walked out. I didn't know what to do next. I would have to wait the whole rest of the day and the night before he would be there. I thought about going back to Mom's, but I was afraid of Bobbi and the police. I thought about calling his roommate again and asking if I could wait there. I went back into the bagel store. The two workers were watching me.

"Can we help you?" they said.

"Could I use your phone?" I asked. I looked at the phone behind the cash register.

They looked at each other and one of them shrugged. "We're not supposed to." But the other one decided it was okay. "I guess."

They motioned for me to come behind the counter and I picked up the phone and dialed. I hoped I was calling the right number.

"Hello?" said the roommate, sounding bored.

"Is this Adrian's roommate?"

"Yeah." He breathed into the phone like he was pissed off. I explained who I was and that Adrian wasn't at work yet and wouldn't be there until midnight. He said, "So what?"

Then I asked him for his address.

"Why?" he asked, sounding angry.

I said, "I only want to wait outside. I won't come in. I just thought he might go home before he goes to work."

A heavy sigh. "I guess," he said, and he gave me directions.

I took a pen that was sitting next to the Bageletta phone and wrote on a paper bag. Adrian's address and new phone number. "Thank you!"

I ran out the door and hopped on the big bike. I pulled out one of the bagels I'd stolen and ate it while I rode. Adrian's new apartment building was on a street that ran next to a highway. There was a tall wall between the road and the highway. There were airplanes flying low and loud above me. I matched the number on the building to the number on the paper I'd scribbled on. This was it.

I parked my bike on the side of the house, behind some bushes. I pushed the doorbell, but no one came down. His roommate must have gone somewhere. I sat on the front steps and waited. After a while, more people started coming in and out of the building. They were looking at me funny. I didn't like it.

A woman came out and asked what I was doing. I said I was waiting for someone. She asked if I wanted to wait inside. She held the door open and I went into the front entry. I said thank you. She left and I sat under the table where the mail was. I ate the other bagels I'd stolen. I was thirsty. It was dark outside.

Finally, I saw Adrian coming up the front walk. I got out from under the table and stood waiting for him to open the door. When he saw me, he stopped.

"Seaver?" he said. His eyes were wide and he was smiling. I was so happy to see him. My eyes started to sting and my stomach hurt. He looked the same as last time I saw him. I was so happy. I ran to him.

"Adrian!" I wrapped my arms around him. I started to cry a little into his stomach. He put his hands on my shoulders and patted my head. I looked up at his face and he was smiling.

"What are you doing here?" He looked around and closed the door. One hand was still on my shoulder.

"I need a place to stay," I said.

"Okay. What's going on?" said Adrian. He looked at my face. It was wet, so he wiped it. I rubbed my nose on my arm. "How long have you been waiting?" he asked.

I tilted my head. I didn't know.

"What is it?"

I explained, "You said I could stay with you if I needed to."

"Yeah, but do the Ogletrees know?"

I nodded. "They said it was okay."

He frowned. "Really? But, uh . . . what about Mrs. June? I thought you were good with the Ogletrees."

"I was. But I had to leave."

"Oh?" he said, like he wanted to know why.

"I can't . . . I just had to go, I . . ."

Adrian said, "It's okay, you can tell me later." He put his arm around me. I put my arm around him. We walked up the stairs and he said to be quiet when we got inside. He explained he had to go to work at midnight, but that I could sleep in his room while he was gone.

He let me use his toothbrush, then he put a sheet and blanket on the floor next to his bed. He gave me one of the pillows off his bed. He promised he'd be back and said I should go to sleep. I was tired but also still hungry. He brought me a bowl of Cheerios.

After I ate, he took the empty bowl and switched off the overhead light. The moon through the window made a glow. I thought about my mom. I could see the outline of Adrian's head. He told me to get some rest and that he'd be back in the morning.

He closed the door and after a while, I fell asleep.

In the morning, Adrian was still gone, and my leg was throbbing. It was hurting bad.

Twenty-Six

CLAIRE

TUESDAY, SEPTEMBER 29, 1992

WHEN I WOKE UP ON TUESDAY, IT WAS QUIET IN THE TOWN HOUSE. Something was wrong. I just knew it. It was like I had a sixth sense and I didn't normally get those. I sprang out of bed and looked out the window. My car was there. Mom's car was there, but not Brian's. Was it in the garage? I ran down the stairs, through the kitchen, and opened the door to the garage. Empty. I turned around and saw the note. On the counter by the coffee maker. Mom's handwriting, overconfident on the front of the page, with large cursive writing, then an arrow to finish on the flip side.

It read, "Claire—Brian and I are in Madison. Last minute asked to testify at Wisconsin Legislature!!! A law that would affect our biz. Fingers crossed. Very exciting!!!! After, will visit Brian's folks. 2–3 nights. Food in fridge. Will call tonight. Xoxo Mom."

"Ugh." I rolled my eyes, letting the note drop. There was a time when I was younger and I would have thought this was cool. My mom being important. Doing big things. But sometimes I just wanted to find her sitting at the kitchen table drinking coffee and reading the paper. I wanted her to ask if I brushed my teeth and wish me luck on my biology exam. She probably didn't even know I had a test today.

When I got to class, Evan was already sitting at our desk. He was jiggling his legs and twirling a pencil. I wanted to tell him to stop it. He was making me nervous.

"Did you study?" I asked him.

"Nah." He scoffed and smirked at me, but then he turned around and looked at the clock behind us. I looked too.

Soon the bell rang and everyone settled down. The teacher gave a few last-minute instructions, then handed out the tests. Four pages, double sided, stapled. I did what I always did before I answer a single question: flip through the entire thing just to get the lay of the land. Once I knew what was ahead of me, I went back to page one, first question. This was going to be a relatively easy test, so I wasn't so concerned about time management. I could take a couple of minutes on each question. No need to rush.

Evan was hunched over his test, flicking his pencil like a cigarette. Was he still reading the question? I tried not to worry about it. I tried to focus on my own paper.

Question two. Question three. Evan was tapping the pencil and bouncing his knees. Somewhat distracting.

"Are you okay?" I whispered.

He glared at me like I'd asked a stupid question.

Another student in front of us turned and looked. I hadn't realized my whisper had been loud enough to hear.

"Quiet, please," said Mrs. Biggerstaff.

I finished the first page and flipped it over. I heard other students flipping their pages too. Just to compare, I glanced at Evan's. He was still on the first page.

God, I wished he would apply himself. Get going. He was never gonna keep up if he didn't speed up.

"Just guess," I whispered. Most of the time, it's better to guess on tests than to leave questions blank.

"Huh?" He looked at me and I could see something in his eyes.

A fear. Clearly, he didn't have a clue. He either didn't study or he couldn't remember the answers or maybe he didn't understand the question. I inhaled and exhaled, thinking about the doctor's reports about Evan and his challenges with reading and comprehension, his need for extra time. I hadn't heard anything about Biggerstaff giving him extra time. I was witnessing with my own eyes how much Evan was struggling.

The teacher was patrolling the classroom, casually walking down the side aisle, arms crossed, looking at each row, then turning around and strolling back up the aisle to the front. At one point, she caught me watching her; she frowned and motioned for me to look at my paper. I did. When she turned away, I glanced at Evan again. He was shifting in his seat. This test was a disaster for him.

I flipped my paper back to the first page and slid it closer to Evan's side of the table. I pretended to drop my pencil and as I bent down, I pushed the paper even closer. I don't know if he saw it or not. I sat back up with my pencil and glanced at Evan's paper to see if he'd copied my answers. He began to write something and I felt so happy.

"Claire Larkin," said Mrs. Biggerstaff. "Evan Lewis."

We both looked up, then at each other.

"Come to the front of the room, please," said the teacher.

"But . . ." I protested, "I'm not done."

"Come to the front, both of you," she said again, "and bring your tests."

Evan groaned but didn't seem in a mood to fight it. He scooted his chair back, making a loud screeching sound, then dramatically scooped up his paper and shuffled to the front. Other kids were sort of giggling and whispering. What was happening? How would I finish my exam?

It was like I was paralyzed. I didn't want to leave my desk. I didn't want to bring my unfinished test to the front.

Evan was already there. He handed his paper to Mrs. Biggerstaff, who indicated for Evan to wait for her in the hall. She stared at me and tapped her foot. Finally, she gestured and said, "Come along, Claire."

"What? What about . . ." I started to rise. "But how will I—"

"—Come on now," she said, beckoning. "Let's go."

"Should I, like, bring my backpack?" I asked.

Students were snickering at me. It was so embarrassing. Mrs. Biggerstaff didn't answer, so I stood up, slung my backpack on my shoulder, and gathered up my test. I pushed in my chair and hurried to the front, hoping to end this humiliation as quickly as possible.

Mrs. Biggerstaff took my incomplete test from my hands and motioned me out to the hallway where Evan was standing. He was shifting from one foot to the other and gently kicking at the bottom of a locker. He had a toothpick in his mouth.

"Go down to the principal's office," our teacher said.

"Both of us?" I said. It didn't seem like I should be in trouble for this.

"Both of you, dear," said Mrs. Biggerstaff. My heart sank.

Evan was already making his way down the hall. It was clear any more pleas to Mrs. Biggerstaff would fall on deaf ears, so I followed him. I was outraged. I was confused. I was scared.

Evan didn't seem to be feeling anything. He just walked and chewed on that toothpick, occasionally banging shut any partially open locker doors as he passed. Obviously, this wasn't his first time.

But it was mine.

"How does this work?" I asked him.

He didn't answer.

"Will we be able to finish our tests?"

"How would I know?" he said dismissively.

We made our way past classrooms full of students, the doors open to allow everyone to see us walking by. The empty halls seemed so much wider, and there was a feeling of both doom and possibility.

We saw students looking bored at their desks or nosily curious about me and Evan walking by. I caught glimpses of teachers mid-lecture, writing on the chalkboard. What were those worlds like, I wondered, and how could I transport myself back into class and out of trouble?

One of the teachers we passed had just posed a question and was waiting for the students to answer. "Anyone?" she'd asked, and I felt sorry for her. No one gave her a single response.

My dad always said that teachers just wanted students to engage. I remembered Gamma Betty saying it wasn't about right or wrong answers, it was a quest to uncover the "absorbent mind."

I had to think about what I would say to the principal. In this case, I wanted to have the right answer.

We passed the bathrooms and Evan stopped at the drinking fountain to take a drink. I waited. Just beyond the fountain was a huge banner advertising homecoming.

I looked at the banner, then I looked at Evan. He was smirking at me. I kept walking.

Finally, we reached the front office. As I entered the space, I noticed everything anew. Were my senses more attuned because I was in trouble? It smelled like brand-new paper and body odor. I wondered if the strong scent was coming from Janice, the school secretary who'd worked there for a million years and probably always would.

There was a giant plant in the corner and a row of guest chairs, just like the Counseling Office. Suddenly I thought of Ms. Patterson.

She would be very surprised to hear about this. I knew that if this incident ended up in my permanent record, I would definitely pull it out and shred it.

"Can I help you?" said Janice.

"Um, yes," I said, "we were told to come here and wait."

"For Ms. Danzer?"

"Yes," I said. Ms. Danzer was the principal.

Evan and I gave Janice our names and she told us to sit and wait, which we did.

Evan started jiggling his legs again, and he was picking at something on his palm. Picking and then biting at it and pulling off bits of skin.

"What are you doing?" I said, but what I wanted to say was *please stop it.*

He frowned at me like it was none of my business and kept on picking. I tried not to watch because it looked painful.

Twenty minutes later, Janice told me to go to Ms. Danzer's office

"Just me?" I asked, standing up. Pointing to Evan, I said, "What about him?"

"They'll be talking to you separately," said Janice, like this was a detective show. She wasn't even looking at me. She had piles of paper on her desk. Her chair squeaked when she moved. She was wiping something off her blouse.

"They? How many people are in there? And who is it?" Of course, they must have needed a witness for whatever questioning was gonna happen. I was hoping it would be Ms. Patterson. She would always take my side. She would understand.

Janice didn't answer. She gave up on her blouse and looked at me with a sympathetic smile. "Don't worry, hon, just go in and face the music. Chin up."

I trudged down the hall, looking for the office that seemed

grand enough for a principal. A secret lair, and naturally, it was the last one. The one with windows. A big desk, two guest chairs facing the desk, plus a row of other chairs behind, sort of like my mom's office. *The principal could hold a staff meeting in here*, I thought.

"Hello?" I knocked on the open door.

"Come in," said the principal.

I walked in and noticed someone standing in the corner looking at the parking lot. My heart sank when he turned around.

It was Mr. Peoples. He was holding a file. I was definitely in trouble.

Twenty-Seven

KIRA

TUESDAY WAS ONE OF THOSE DAYS WHERE I HAD TO THROW OUT MOST of my planned activities and go with the flow. Seaver was requiring most of my attention, so everything else had to wait. Fortunately, I already had an appointment set up with Seaver's aunt, Jen. I'd already gone over the basics with Jen on the phone, but I needed to check out her home in order to know if this would be a good spot for our little man Seaver. And I had to answer any doubts she (or her boyfriend) might have been having.

I'd scribbled the directions on the back of a pink message slip and crossed my fingers as I headed out to Richfield, a suburb very close to Minneapolis. If he lived with Jen, Seaver might be able to return to his previous school district. And it wouldn't be far for visits with Nicole, if that's how it turned out.

When I found the house, Jen was standing outside with a rake. There was a pile of leaves beside her. The house was small, a starter home. A tiny yard. A lovely street. Jen waved when I pulled into the very short driveway.

"Thanks for agreeing to meet in the middle of the day," I said, getting out of the car and shaking her hand.

"I didn't have any appointments this afternoon so it worked great." Jen was a hairdresser at a local salon. She appeared to be my age, maybe a couple of years younger.

I glanced up and down the street, then at Jen's front door. I said, "Cute house."

"Thanks, we like it," said Jen, and she turned to admire it. Blue-gray aluminum siding. Story and a half. Built right after World War II, probably. About eighteen hundred square feet. Detached single-car garage. "They're all about the same in this neighborhood."

"Can I take a look inside?"

"Of course!" Jen tossed the rake in the pile of leaves and brushed off her jeans. She opened the door and invited me in.

The front door led directly to a modest living room. The walls were white and the furniture was dark overstuffed leather, or fake leather—I can never tell.

"Two bedrooms and one bath on the main floor," said Jen, giving me the tour. "And Jeff, my boyfriend, just added a second bathroom, in the basement."

"Great," I said. I needed to do a background check on them both. "Jeff lives here too, right?"

"Yes," said Jen, chuckling. "We both own it. We've been together ten years."

I smiled. There was another world in which this could have been my life.

We checked out the primary bedroom and the small dining area. Off the hall, there was a peach-colored bathroom that needed updating. But it had a tub and shower. It was clean. Jen led me to the guest room at the end of the hall. She flicked on the lights. A large bed filled the room and was covered with an old-fashioned green bedspread.

"This would be Seaver's room," she said.

"Is that a double or a queen bed?"

"Queen," said Jen. "But I guess we could swap it out for, like, a twin, if that would be better."

"Might be nice. It would give him more space."

"Okay, and I have a dresser in the basement I can bring up. And a shelf for toys and books."

"Oh, that would be great." I smiled. "It sounds like you're ready to do this, then, huh?"

"I mean, yes I would. If my sister needed me to," said Jen.

"Or if Seaver needed you."

"Of course," said Jen, scratching her neck. "It's my boyfriend who is not so excited about it."

"Yeah, I remember you telling me that. And Jeff doesn't have any kids, right?"

"No, he doesn't."

"Were you guys planning on having any?" I asked. It was a personal question, but it was important to know.

"Him and me?" said Jen. "Someday, maybe."

"Fostering is a great way to start being parents together."

I smiled and we continued through the house, examining everything along the way. The place was clean enough. It would satisfy the court. Nothing of concern.

"So, how do Jeff and Seaver get along?" I asked.

"Oh, they're great. It's more Nic that Jeff doesn't get on with."

"Okay," I said, making a mental note. Nicole could be prickly, so it would be understandable if Jeff wasn't her biggest fan.

In the kitchen, I opened a few cupboards and then the fridge. I was looking for food, checking the expiration dates. Also hoping not to find any pests or mold. The standards were basic and achievable, but I sometimes wondered if I would pass the test at my own place. "You've got a lot more food in here than I do. So that's good."

"Jeff likes to cook, which is nice," said Jen, patting her belly. "We're not gonna starve, that's for sure."

I was looking at the small backyard. There was a patch of grass and a wooden fence surrounding the property. An alley and small garage in the back. "Can I take a peek out there?"

"Sure," said Jen, opening the back door and guiding me to the small patio. There was a bistro table and chairs. We sat down and admired the beautiful autumn day.

After a beat, I said, "Let's talk about you and Seaver. Are you close? Tell me what you know about him."

"I'd say we're close. He's stayed here a bit. When Nic has needed a night off or whatnot."

"Mm-hmm." I knew what she meant.

"He was a preemie. Did you know that?"

I shook my head.

"He was so small, he looked like a toy. He never really caught up, physically. People always assume he's younger than he is. Like, they'll offer him a glass of milk when he'd rather have a can of Coke, ya know?"

"Yeah. And Seaver's age isn't easy, he's nearing puberty. It takes patience and a thick skin."

"You make it sound so fun," said Jen, teasing. "But Seaver's a good kid."

"They're all good kids," I said, reacting to one of my pet peeves. "Some of them just need different things from us. It's rarely easy."

"I get it," said Jen. "I mean, he had to grow up fast, with Nic's lifestyle and all. I probably should've helped out more. But I mean . . . I dunno . . . It was hard."

"Yeah," I said. A cardinal had landed on the fence. He was close enough that I could see his eye as he tilted his head then lifted off. It seemed he was examining me, or us.

Jen continued, "When Nic was using, she wasn't herself. She was nasty and withdrawn. She thought she had her shit together, but she didn't."

"Uh-huh."

"But when they took Seaver, that destroyed her. Nic was furious, like an animal protecting her young. She was clawing and scratching, she was a mess. I found her in a crying heap in the corner one day, wasted. This was before she went up to Healthy Horizons, thank god for that place."

"Yeah. It's a great facility." I sat up straight, checked my watch. "I'm sorry, but I've got to get going."

Jen smiled and said, "Got a big date?"

I gave her a look. "Yeah, with my paperwork."

She laughed. "I wish I had a social worker like you when I was in high school."

"Aww," I said, and we walked to the front of the house. Before I got in my car, I handed her a folder. "This is information about the process, everything you want to know."

"Great."

"And there's a questionnaire. About your approach to discipline, routines, how you see the child fitting into your lives, et cetera. You'll see. Show it to Jeff."

Jen nodded. "I'll do my best."

Just then, my pager went off. I looked at the number and said, "Uh-oh."

"Who is it?" asked Jen, as if excited by the idea that we were in trouble.

"My supervisor," I said, raising my eyebrows. "Gotta go."

Twenty-Eight

CLAIRE

MS. DANZER STEPPED FROM BEHIND HER DESK AND SHOOK MY HAND. She was dressed like she was running for president or something: a tight pink skirt and matching suit jacket, with a blousy lady-tie around her neck. She said, "Claire, hello."

"Hi," I said.

Mr. Peoples turned and greeted me. I nodded at him.

Ms. Danzer gestured toward one of the guest chairs and I sat. Mr. Peoples sauntered over. He pulled the other guest chair out at an angle and a bit farther away, as if to emphasize just how much he wasn't on my side.

"Did you call my mom? She's in Wisconsin," I said, preemptively explaining her absence. Maybe they'd wait till she got back. Suddenly I really needed her. Or my dad. "My dad is probably teaching." I glanced at Mr. Peoples.

"We've left messages with both your parents," said Ms. Danzer. "But now we'd like to speak with you if that's okay."

"Okay."

"Do you know why you're here?" said the principal. Her voice was gentle and calm, which was annoying.

I nodded slowly, looking from one adult to another. What kind of game was this? I wondered what they would be talking to Evan about. Would his story be different from mine? We hadn't coordinated. I wasn't even sure how much he'd copied from my paper.

"Is this about Evan?" I asked.

"Why don't you tell us?" said Ms. Danzer, coaxing me to confess. She'd folded her hands and placed them on her desk.

Mr. Peoples was sitting back in his chair, his legs crossed in a relaxed pose, with his right ankle balanced on his left knee. He tossed the file onto the edge of Ms. Danzer's desk. I glanced at it. But it wasn't my file; it was Evan's.

"Don't peek," he said, winking.

I glared at Mr. Peoples. He gave me a smirk. So he was gonna bring that whole file cabinet/IEP thing into this, was he?

"Let's start with your test this morning," said Ms. Danzer.

"What about it?" I said.

"Were you helping Evan Lewis cheat on your biology exam?" asked the principal.

"Uh . . ." I said, glancing at the file on the desk. "I don't know what Evan did."

"All right," said Ms. Danzer. "But that wasn't my question."

"He has a learning disability, you know," I blurted out.

"And how do you know that?" asked Mr. Peoples, because he knew exactly how I knew about Evan.

I scowled at him.

"So I'll ask again," said Ms. Danzer. "Why are you here, Claire?"

"Uh . . ." I was debating hard about what to say. Thinking about how my mother would handle a corporate investigation, how my father would analyze a system of rules. And me, feeling more like the victim than the perpetrator of this infraction. Finally, I sat up tall and made eye contact with both Ms. Danzer and Mr. Peoples, looking from one to the other as I spoke loudly and clearly. I said, "I am here because this institution has failed to provide sufficient academic support to a student who struggles with multiple learning differences."

Their expressions suggested a mix of mildly disappointed and moderately amused. Typical teachers.

I added, "I would give this school a D MINUS!"

Very quickly their faces changed. They stopped looking amused. After my outburst, the principal and Mr. Peoples shifted into Discipline Mode. Ms. Danzer got up and closed her door. We waited for her to return to her desk.

"Well," she said, "let's have a chat, shall we?"

Together, they laid out their evidence against me. They gave me a stern warning and some long-winded advice for a young woman like me with so much potential. They told me to think about what I'd said and done. They told me I could think about it in detention for the rest of the day or go home and think about it there, but they were clear that I needed to think.

I was upset and embarrassed, and nothing seemed right, and I thought I might cry. I grabbed my backpack and hurried down the hall and out the front office, past Janice and out into the hallway. I nearly crashed into Evan. He was standing there against the lockers, like he was waiting for me.

"What are you doing?" I said, but I wanted to ask if he was waiting for me.

He took the toothpick out of his mouth. "Got suspended for the rest of the day for cheating," he said. "You?" He put it back in.

"They told me to go home and think about what I've done," I said, hoisting my backpack up.

"Yeah, it's bullshit," said Evan. He looked at me with those coffee-brown eyes. I wondered if that was his way of thanking me.

"Yeah," I said, glancing down the hall to orient myself. I started walking to my locker. "I kinda mouthed off. That didn't help."

He chuckled as he followed me.

"How about you? What did you say?" I stopped at my locker, plopped down my backpack, and started on the combination.

"I just sat there," he said, and I could picture it.

"Well, now I have to sit in detention because I rode the bus and my parents are all out of town and I can't get home." I'd opened my locker and was pulling books out. "And they wouldn't tell me if I could retake the test so I'll probably fail it."

"It's not a big deal," he said, and I turned around to face him. I tried to imagine it not being a big deal. I tilted my head. He smiled at me like he could see me struggling to understand him. He shrugged and smirked. It was like he was trying to teach me something.

I closed my locker.

"Yeah, anyway," he said, "you want a ride?"

"To my house?" I asked, taken aback. I didn't know he had a car. Or whether he was a good driver. Or where he parked. I didn't know how much I'd wanted to be in his car until that moment.

"Sure." He nodded. I zipped up my backpack and grabbed my jacket, lugging my stuff as I followed him down the empty hall. He apparently didn't need a coat. Or any books.

Twenty-Nine

MATTHEW

TUESDAY AFTERNOON

"One of the surest ways to signal professorial openness is to host a group of students in one's home, whether it's for coffee, a potluck supper, or a class discussion. By gaining a peek at the professor at home, students learn that academic pursuits can enrich all aspects of life."

—*The Path to Tenure, a Guidebook for Rising Professors*

ON TUESDAY AFTERNOON, I TAPED A DO NOT DISTURB SIGN TO THE door of my apartment, mostly so Doug wouldn't knock and interrupt my senior seminar. I'd also asked him to keep the music down, but Doug would do whatever Doug wanted. Anyway, on seminar days even Doug couldn't temper my enthusiasm. I loved hosting class in my apartment, small and modest as it was.

I'd set up five folding chairs that I'd retrieved from the storage room in the basement. The other four students could squeeze together on the futon. And I rolled my two dining chairs over as well. At the center was my old coffee table, the one Tammy and I had found on the side of the road one summer, the one I'd stripped and stained to new life.

The bell rang and I buzzed in the students. I propped open my door and placed a store-bought meat-and-cheese tray on the coffee table. Soon the students filed in and took their seats. They knew the drill.

"There's Diet Coke in the fridge," I said. "Help yourself."

As usual, it took one student to start the expedition to the kitchen for free soda, then the others followed. I took note of the leader; it was usually Lanie. Her leadership in social situations, however, didn't always correlate to high grades on papers, and we'd talked about that.

"Come on in, have a seat." I stood near the small dining table, waiting for everyone to settle. "Get the door, would you, Lanie?"

She complied, and I got an idea. "Okay," I said, rubbing my hands together. When I had their full attention, I asked, "Why do you think Lanie just closed the door?"

A few chuckles, then silence. Perhaps they thought I was joking. Someone was still loading a cracker with cheese.

"Yeah, help yourself," I said in the awkwardness, a laugh, then things quieted down again. "But seriously, today's topic is motivation, right? The chapter you were assigned was called 'Motivation, Egoism, and Morality.' So let's apply those concepts here. What do you think was Lanie's motivation to close the door?"

"Egoism?" joked a senior named Maynard, his voice dull and sarcastic.

I smiled at the joke and glanced at Lanie. She was taking it in stride, lifting a can of Diet Coke as if making a toast. We were a good-natured group.

"Well," said one of the students on the futon. "I mean, you asked her to do it, so . . ."

"She was just following instructions?" I said, finishing the student's thought. I made a face that showed it was a plausible answer.

"Yeah," said the student, as if adopting my restatement of his answer.

"And what do we get for following instructions?" I asked.

"We avoid punishment or other negative social consequences," said a voice robotically, as if quoting the textbook verbatim. I spun around to face the speaker. It was Carl, who was perched on a folding chair, his mouth full of grapes.

I pointed at Carl and said, "Exactly! And . . . what if I hadn't asked her? What if she just went ahead and closed the door?"

Blank stares.

"Why would someone do that?" No one answered, so I pointed the question at Lanie. "Lanie, if I hadn't asked you, and you went ahead and closed the door, hypothetically, why would you do such a thing?"

"To be helpful, I guess?" she said, her voice rising like it was a question.

"To be helpful, yes," I repeated. To the group, I asked, "And why do humans wish to be helpful?"

"To be accepted," said Carl.

"To help," said Maynard, unhelpfully.

"To get a good reputation," said another student.

"Mm-hmm," I said, encouraging more.

"For future rewards," said Carl. "You scratch my back, I'll scratch yours."

"Okay," I said. "And all these are types of rewards, aren't they?"

The students nodded or ate cheese or looked at their laps, perhaps hoping not to be called on.

I continued, "According to our reading today, most of human motivation is based on some form of self-interest. Avoiding punishment, seeking reward, for example. Yeah?"

They sat there as they were before, chewing on cheese with blank expressions.

"But," I paused for dramatic effect. "What about altruism? Is there such a thing as a purely selfless act?"

A few students nodded, their eyebrows raised, as if they really wanted to believe it. College-age people were famously idealistic, after all.

"Why do we help the little old lady cross the street?" I asked, using the example from the reading.

"Manners," said Lanie, finally joining in the discussion.

"Kindness," said the student sitting next to Lanie.

"Yeah, we're taught to be helpful and kind," said Maynard, as if he resented it.

"Who teaches us that?" I asked.

"Parents."

"School."

"Church," said Carl. "At least for me, it was in Sunday school."

"Okay," I replied, welcoming all the answers. "So a religious teaching or a family system or other organization influences us. Socializing us, right? And we learn to seek that approval, to gain rewards of acceptance, or some concept of heaven or getting a good grade, right? Of being praised by our parents, right?"

"Yeah, but it doesn't have to be that," said Maynard. "I mean, if you see someone, like, struggling across the street, you'd be a jerk if you didn't help them out."

"Okay," I said, pointing at Maynard. "So we are motivated to avoid negative perceptions, criticism from others, the shame or guilt we might feel if we don't do the right thing?"

"Yeah," he said.

"But it's more automatic," said Lanie. "Like, I'm not thinking, 'Oh, I'm going to avoid shame by closing this door.'"

"Or watching this old lady struggle," added Maynard, and the group chuckled.

"Okay," I said, waiting for the focus to return to the question of motivation. "But you feel good about it afterward, don't you? A little bit, anyway?"

They acquiesced. "Yeah, I guess."

"And that's the self-benefit," I said. There was a natural pause in the discussion while the group absorbed my insight.

After a bit, Lanie said, "But that wasn't the person's goal. It's more like a side effect."

Carl challenged Lanie, asking, "But can you ever know what anyone's true goal is?"

"That is precisely why we study it," I answered, smiling. This was thrilling. "We're scientists, after all."

The students sat quietly and thought about that for a moment, a solidarity in science. A bond.

There was a knock on the door that broke the spell. Who could that be? All students were accounted for. I hadn't buzzed anyone in. Was this Doug, playing with me? Hadn't he seen the sign?

The knocking grew louder, more aggressive. All the students looked at me, waiting for me to take charge. I glanced at Lanie. She shook her head, indicating she hadn't a clue.

The knocking stopped. A woman's voice called, "Matthew Larkin?"

"Yes?" I replied to the closed door.

"Open up," she said. "Police."

Thirty

CLAIRE

EVAN'S CAR WAS JUST AS I WOULD HAVE IMAGINED IT, IF I EVER IMAG-ined I'd have ended up in there. With him. It was a black sedan, with rust around the wheel wells. The passenger-side mirror was broken. The hood was a different color, a dark blue but with a matte finish. There was junk in the back seat, like sweatpants and Burger King bags and Styrofoam containers. There was a dog leash on the floor of the passenger seat. The window wouldn't go all the way up. The muffler didn't work. It was loud.

I held my backpack in my lap. He suggested I put it down, so I shoved it to the floor between my legs. I hoped the seat belt worked.

I gave Evan directions to Mom and Brian's town house. He said he thought I lived on Zenith. I asked him how he knew that. He said his buddy Dom lived over there. I tried to remember which house that was. Anyway, I explained about my dad and how we all used to live in that house and how they were probably gonna sell it when I went to college.

"That sucks," he said.

"I know," I said.

We didn't talk about much else. The radio was going. The windows were down. Evan bobbed his head with the music. He kept his arm hanging halfway out his window and used it to signal his turns.

"Don't the turn signals work?" I asked. He must not have heard me because he didn't answer.

When we got to Mom and Brian's town house, Evan parked a little way down, not in front of the house. He said it was in case my parents got home.

"They're in Wisconsin till Friday," I said.

He shut off the ignition. I unbuckled and lifted my backpack up. It was extra heavy because I had basically all my textbooks in there. I opened the door and pushed my backpack out onto the curb. He asked if he could use our bathroom.

"Really?" I said, struggling out of the car. I stood up and shut the door. "Sure. I guess."

He came around to my side and picked up my backpack.

"Thanks," I said, and he followed me up the street and down the walk, up into the town house. When I got to the door, I needed the key. I motioned for him to turn around so I could dig in the backpack and find my keys. I unzipped the pouch and dug around while he held it. I said, "Hang on, sorry."

He just stood there like a strong statue.

Once inside, I put my keys on the entry table and switched on the lights. I said, "The bathroom's down there, to the left."

He walked as I directed, not quickly. He must not have had to go very badly.

It was strange to have Evan Lewis in my house. Like it made the air change. There was an electricity about us. I tried turning off the lights because they seemed too bright. Then I put them back on. It seemed that something needed adjusting. I just wasn't sure what.

I heard the toilet flush and I waited. When he came back, he was different. He charged toward me. Directly at me. He grabbed my waist and kissed me. I pulled back.

"Whoa," I said. It was so abrupt.

He pulled my jacket down and off me. I watched it fall to the ground. He kissed me again, placing his hands on both sides of my head and pulling.

This wasn't how I'd imagined it. It wasn't like in the movies. There was no slow buildup. There were no gazing eyes. He just planted his face on mine and pushed.

Then he started pushing my whole body.

"Where's your bedroom?" he asked, his hands on my hips.

"Upstairs, b-b-but . . ." I stammered.

He gripped me by the arm, pulling me to the staircase, then up. I yanked back but couldn't get my arm out of his hands. I said, "Hey."

He pulled me all the way upstairs, so hard I almost fell. I couldn't believe how strong he was. I couldn't believe I couldn't get free. He was nearly dragging me. At the top, he said, "Which one's yours?"

I glanced at it, and he pushed us into my room. Before I knew what was happening, I was on the bed. In a flash, he'd undone my jeans and pulled them down. How had he done that so quickly? How hadn't I noticed? His hands were all over me, but I wasn't ready for it. I said no, we shouldn't, but he wouldn't stop. I squirmed and pushed his hands away, but he was stronger. He was pushing me down and kissing me. It was like he had six arms and twenty hands. I was trying so hard, but I couldn't get out.

"We shouldn't," I said.

He kissed me and even his mouth was forceful.

"Please," I said. "Hang on."

He climbed on top of me. He was tugging at my underwear. I was holding it tightly in place, saying, "Hey, come on."

He was kissing me and touching me everywhere. He pulled on my hair to keep my head down. Suddenly I realized he didn't get it; he wasn't going to stop. A cold truth descended: Evan was in control, and I couldn't contain him.

"Hey," I said, trying a new tactic, "I can't. I can't. My aunt Flow is here. Aunt Flow!"

Finally, he heard my words. It registered: I was having my period. I wasn't, but it was a good lie. It worked. He flashed a look of disappointment and immediately let go of my undies. I pulled them back into place and felt a moment of relief.

Then quickly he pivoted. He unfastened his fly and pushed his jeans down. Everything to that point had already been too much. Too fast. Too harsh. But this I really wasn't ready for: his penis. I'd never seen one in person before. Only illustrations in sex ed. This was real and erect. It was large and oddly shaped, and the skin was darker than the rest of Evan's body.

He kneeled next to me on the bed, positioning his penis near my face. I stared at it, not knowing what to do.

"Come on," he ordered. "Kiss it."

I didn't understand. He was so upset with me. I moved toward it and kissed it.

"Ugh," he said, disgusted. "Not like that."

His penis was only an inch away from my face. I had no idea what to do. I tried again, and he pushed me away. He complained, "Don't bite it."

I felt so stupid. He was getting more agitated. Clearly this was not what he was expecting at all. Finally, he flipped into a seated position and pulled my head toward his crotch.

I was so confused. I felt trapped and panicky. I was a prisoner. How had I gotten myself into this situation?

He pushed my head down.

"Open your mouth," he said impatiently. He was acting like

I should have known what to do. Like this was such an ordinary thing to do, like changing the channel or playing a CD.

I didn't want to. Nothing about this was natural or pleasant for me. I couldn't understand how he hadn't noticed my lack of enjoyment. He hadn't noticed my resistance.

Finally, he released my head. Annoyed, he said, "Forget it."

I exhaled. Relief. But as soon as I sat up, he pushed my shoulders down so that I was on my back.

"No, wait," I said, reaching for my underwear but his body was blocking me, and I couldn't get hold of them. I pressed my legs together and wriggled but he pinned me down.

Evan covered my mouth with his own, slobbering on my face as he climbed on top. I turned my head to the side and gasped for air, then tried to push Evan up and off of me, but he was too heavy, too powerful. I pressed my legs tightly together and slid my hips side to side as much as I could, trying to keep away from his penis.

Suddenly the doorbell rang, and we both froze.

"Someone's at the door!" I said.

"Ignore it," said Evan, pinning me down.

The doorbell rang again and again. Then loud knocking.

"No! I gotta get it!" I shouted and Evan relaxed, giving up. He rolled over and I got up.

He sat on the bed, looking pissed, exasperated.

I was focused on the door. I hurried to get dressed and ran down the steps as quickly as I could. I shouted, "Coming! Hold on!"

I reached the door, stopped for a moment to get my breath; I smoothed my hair, then I opened it.

The person standing on the other side of the storm door said, "Hi, Claire."

I just about fainted.

Thirty-One

MATTHEW

THE POLICE WERE AT THE DOOR. DURING MY SENIOR SEMINAR. WHY? And how? I was sure Doug had let them in. Maybe he'd called them? But that didn't make sense; he was the one with all the marijuana pipes.

The knocking continued. It was unnerving.

"I'm coming," I hollered, willing the police to quiet down. I apologized to the students and scooted to the door. I opened it a crack. There was no need to invite the police in. I stuck my face and shoulder in the opening. A large, uniformed woman stood in the hallway, with another officer behind her. They had badges on their chests, guns on their hips. I inhaled deeply, wanting to protect the students. And my seminar. And myself. Through the crack, I said, "Can I help you?"

"I'm Deputy Vasquez, Rice County Sheriff's Department," said the woman. She was at least six feet tall, confident and imposing. Tilting her head to the man behind her, she said, "This is Officer Goan."

Compared to Vasquez, Officer Goan was petite and wiry. He was so much smaller than her, he almost looked frightened. As if to explain himself, he held up his notepad and said, "I'm a trainee."

I nodded and returned my attention to Deputy Vasquez.

"Can we come inside?" she asked. The walkie-talkie on her hip squawked and she switched it off without looking.

I glanced back at the students still seated in a circle in my living room. To the officers, I said, "Well, I have a class going on in here."

"We don't mind," said Deputy Vasquez, pushing into the apartment, with Goan behind her. "This won't take long."

I stepped back to allow them in, and I could feel the intensity of the students' curiosity like a sunburn on my neck. "Everyone," I said, "this is Deputy Vasquez and Officer . . ."

"Goan," said Goan.

I nodded my apology. "From the Rice County—"

"—Sheriff's Department, yeah. Sorry to disturb you," said Vasquez, looking around the living room, glancing to the kitchen, the dining table, the open doorway to my bedroom, the bathroom. She seemed to take in the entire apartment in one or two seconds. At the flick of her chin, Goan, who was still holding his notepad, began snooping around every nook and cranny while the students remained still and silent in their seats. "We're looking for a runaway child, a boy, aged twelve. We understand you might know where he is."

At this revelation, the students murmured and wiggled. The room was suddenly very warm.

"All right," I said, extending my arms to settle the students. As I watched Goan enter my bathroom, I said, "Uh. Forgive me, but do you have a search warrant?"

Deputy Vasquez smiled slyly, then replied, "We could come back, but do you mind if we look around?"

The students were following this exchange like it was a tennis match.

"No, it's fine, go ahead," I said, waving my permission to the trainee in the bathroom.

"Professor?" said Lanie. "Is everything all right?"

"Yeah. We should go," said Carl. A few of the students stood up. There was murmuring. Clearly something strange was happening.

"Mr. Larkin," said Deputy Vasquez, "when did you last see Seaver Swanson?"

The students quieted and turned to look at me. They had frozen, midstream in their packing up, as if waiting to exhale. Their books were still on the table, the futon. Their jackets were still strewn on the backs of chairs, backpacks half on. Their faces were open, concerned. For me. And I didn't want them to leave. I wanted to continue the seminar.

I held up my hands, palms facing the students.

"Monday night," I said to Deputy Vasquez. The students gasped. I turned to them and said, "It's all right. You are witnessing the marriage of our legal system with the state's interest in child welfare and family systems."

There was no reaction. The students merely watched, their mouths hanging open.

"Okay," said Deputy Vasquez.

Suddenly I had a brilliant idea. "Sit down, everyone. Sit down, please." Turning to the officers, I said, "I will tell you everything I know." To the students, I said, "Listen to my story, which is a real-life sociological dilemma."

The students sat down.

The trainee sat down too, like it was story time, his eyes wide, pen and paper poised. Vasquez rolled her eyes and remained standing. She said to me, "All right, Professor. Tell us what you did."

When it was quiet, I began, "There is a child—out there somewhere—who has been taken out of his home. Ostensibly, for his own good."

Deputy Vasquez shifted her weight.

I continued, "He was placed with a foster care family."

Maynard raised his hand. When I called on him, he said, "I was in foster care for about two weeks when I was a baby."

"Wow," said Lanie. "That's intense."

"How has it impacted you?" asked Carl.

"I don't know," said Maynard. "I don't remember."

"Shh," I said, attempting to regain control of the room. I thought of Granger and his tips on nonverbal communication. I stretched out my arms and leaned forward, telegraphing earnestness. I said, "So let's say you found a child . . . on the side of the road . . . in the middle of a storm . . . in the middle of nowhere. And you have no idea how he got there . . . and no identifying information . . . He might be hypothermic . . . What do you do?" I glanced at Deputy Vasquez and nodded as if to reassure her. To the students, I said, "Huh? Anyone? What should I have done?"

The students took turns guessing.

"Nothing?" said the first student brave enough to answer.

"Leave him there," said another.

"Yeah, don't kidnap him." The students were all joining in, certain of their answers.

"Don't be a creep?" said someone.

"Call the police," said another.

I snapped my fingers and pointed to the student who mentioned the police. I didn't want to mention the alcohol aspect of the story—it might have unnecessarily complicated the hypothetical—so I simply said, "But what if the child doesn't want you to call the police?"

A different student answered, "Do it anyway. Kids don't know what's best for them."

"Yeah."

"Kids are stupid."

I clapped my hands together, only once. "Let's say you honored his request? And you put him in your car, intending to go the hospital, okay?"

I paused, nodding at each student, making sure they were tracking. The trainee was taking copious notes. I continued but spoke slowly to emphasize the drama. "But the child didn't want to go to the hospital and begged you not to, so you took him to your apartment."

Gasps from the students.

"Eww, no," they said.

"Perv!"

"Bad idea."

"Just no."

"Fascinating!" I said. "And what does that tell you about our society?"

"Mr. Larkin, uh, Professor," said Deputy Vasquez, apparently unimpressed by the discussion. "Can you tell us where you took Seaver Swanson and where he is now?"

"Absolutely." I looked at the students. They were horrified. To the students, I said, "Okay, good. Let's stop there. We'll pick this up next week."

The students gathered their backpacks and hustled to leave, quickly forming a traffic jam at the door. The trainee was still seated on the futon near the door. He swiveled his body to the side so his knees wouldn't block the exiting students. The class members pressed awkwardly through the door, as if they couldn't get out of there quickly enough. But of course, they were curious, and some of them were ogling and whispering.

"Excuse us," said one.

"Bye," said another. "Thanks."

"Thank you."

"See ya." To which someone added, faintly, "Wouldn't wanna be ya."

I stood and waved at the students, trying to project confidence with good posture and a smile. After the students were gone, I took a deep breath and rubbed my forehead. Gossip about professors was rampant among college kids, particularly in the social sciences.

When it was just me and the two officers, their questioning was much more efficient, and as promised, I gave them all the pertinent information.

At the end of the interview, Deputy Vasquez said, "You should have called us. We know how to handle these things."

"I realize that now," I said, but of course I couldn't tell them why I didn't call. "I thought I was doing what was best."

The trainee handed me a small card.

Vasquez explained, "We've assigned an incident number to this case. It's circled there on the card. And our phone number is there too. If you have any more information, call us."

"I will, I will," I said, looking at the card. "An incident number, huh? Will I be charged with something? Because I didn't do anything wrong."

No comment. The officers ignored my question. Then, poker-faced, Deputy Vasquez said, "You don't have any plans to leave the state, do you?"

"No, none."

"Good." She put on her hat. The trainee popped his notepad into his back pocket, and they left.

I watched them switch back on their walkie-talkies, squawking as they made their way down the hall. As they pressed the elevator button, I lingered outside my apartment. Finally, I went back inside and closed the door.

The seminar could not have gone better.

Thirty-Two

CLAIRE

"WHY ARE YOU HERE?" I ASKED, ALTHOUGH I DIDN'T REALLY CARE. I was just so grateful that Adrian had rung the doorbell and I was standing there with him at the front door and not still pinned to my bed upstairs with Evan. In the back of my mind, I wondered what Evan was doing up there. But it didn't matter now that I was on the main level of the town house and the front door was wide open. If I'd wanted to, I could have run outside. I was free. And safe. "How did you get this address?"

Adrian smiled sheepishly. He said, "Bageletta."

"Oh," I said, and I admired that.

"How did you know I was home?" Suddenly I was embarrassed.

"Mr. Peoples told me you'd gone home early," he said. "Sorry. Are you sick?"

"Um, no, I'm not. Not really. But it's fine," I said, and there was something ironic in all that, but I didn't care because Adrian's arrival had given me the means to escape. And as if to emphasize that, Evan had started to stumble around upstairs, and I could hear his heavy footsteps. "I'm just surprised."

"I actually have a favor to ask," said Adrian.

"Uh-huh," I said, not really listening. I was distracted, wondering what Evan would do next. And just like that, he came thundering down the stairs. His shoes were untied, and he looked a mess, but he stormed past me, barged through the door, and nearly knocked Adrian over as he blazed down the sidewalk, across the lawn, to the street and into his car.

"Hey!" said Adrian, but Evan hadn't reacted.

Before he got in his car, Evan shouted something I didn't understand, and I wasn't even sure it was for me. Something angry. Probably an insult.

I might have blushed. I might have teared up. I wanted to disappear.

"Are you okay?" asked Adrian.

"Yeah," I lied. What could I say about this? Wasn't it obvious to Adrian what had happened? "Um . . . Evan was just bringing me his, uh, notes from biology. We have biology together and, uh, there was a test."

"Oh," said Adrian. He turned and we both watched Evan's car race down the street, his taillights flashing briefly at the corner. And then he was gone. "Was that the same guy from—"

"—Friday night, yeah," I said, looking at the ground.

"Okay, well, he's kind of a jerk, if you ask me," said Adrian.

"Yeah," I said. "That was weird. Sorry about that."

"You don't have to apologize, Claire."

"Okay, yeah. You're right," I said. "Anyway."

"Maybe this isn't a good time."

"No, it's fine." I stepped outside to join Adrian on the front sidewalk. I wanted the fresh air. I wanted to be out of that town house. "I'm sort of in trouble."

"Oh?"

"Yeah. They, um, sent me home today. For cheating," I said. I hated the way it sounded. It was so unfair.

"Okay," said Adrian. "Well, that sucks."

"I know," I said. "What is the favor you wanted to ask?"

He looked at his car. I hadn't realized it until then, but there was someone else in the car. A smaller person. Adrian motioned for the person to come out, and the car door opened. A little blond kid climbed out.

"This is Seaver," said Adrian. "He's like a brother to me."

"Oh, okay," I said, not sure what was going on. All of us should have been in school. What time was it? There were probably two more hours of classes before the end of the day.

The boy walked slowly toward Adrian and stood next to him. We nodded at each other, but I could sense the skepticism.

"Seaver showed up last night and needed a place to stay," explained Adrian.

"Uh-huh," I said.

"I left him alone this morning when I went to my morning class, and . . ."

The boy squirmed a bit.

"I don't want to leave him alone again if possible."

"Yeah," I said, getting a terrible feeling about what Adrian was gonna ask me.

He continued, "I have an interview at four o'clock. It's with a chef who might write me a recommendation. For when I apply to culinary school. Or college. Anyway, it's someone who can help me. And it's important."

"That's so cool. Congratulations," I said.

"Well, I haven't applied yet," said Adrian. "This is just an interview. So . . . I was wondering if you could babysit, I guess. Since you're home."

"Oh, uh-huh," I said, confirming my suspicions. "Well . . . I mean, I'm actually a terrible babysitter."

It was true. Once I'd lost a toddler I was supposed to be watching at the playland at the mall. Someone eventually found her and it was fine. But I hated babysitting. That's why I'd quit as soon as I turned sixteen. Also, I'd been fired from my main babysitting job because the kid had some cuts on his hands and arms. Apparently, I wasn't supposed to let him play with knives even though the kid insisted his parents let him do it. And I didn't think I could stop him, not without getting stabbed.

And then there was Finn. I hated to remember this, but I'd had a scare with him once at the playground. We were playing on the tire swing. He kept jumping on my back while I was swinging, and I'd asked him to stop. I asked and asked but he wouldn't get off my back, so finally I sort of flung my arm back to shake him off me. He fell onto the wood chips pretty hard and didn't move. I was so scared. I said his name over and over. I slapped his face, lightly. I jiggled his shoulders. Nothing worked. And then he sort of just woke up and shook his head. He was fine. But I was a terrible sister that day.

I looked at Seaver. He seemed absolutely miserable, and he was stuck to Adrian like Velcro. There was no way he wanted to hang out with me willingly, even if I'd said yes. I could see it in his face. Besides, I was feeling pretty miserable too. What I really wanted was Becca. I needed her advice about what had just happened with Evan. I didn't even know what to call it. I just knew I needed to talk. I had questions that only Becca could answer.

I looked at Adrian. He had a hopeful expression, and it was going to be hard to break the bad news to him. I mean, I would have liked to help him, but I just couldn't. Not today.

"Actually," I said, "I'm supposed to be somewhere."

"Oh?" he said, sounding surprised, almost like he didn't believe me. "Okay."

"Yeah, I was just leaving," I lied, but it became true because I had just decided to leave. I had to get out of that house, and I had to see Becca. "You understand?"

"Sure."

"Maybe you can take Seaver with you to the interview?" I suggested. "He could, like, sit in the car and wait?" I'd certainly done that plenty of times with my parents in various situations where they didn't want to deal with me.

"Yeah, I guess I could," said Adrian. "Thanks anyway, Claire."

"Sorry," I said. I felt awful as Adrian and Seaver turned and walked slowly toward their car. I would have liked to have helped Adrian. He'd helped me so much already.

But I would find a way to pay him back another time. I turned and went back into the town house. I locked the front door, grabbed my things, and dashed out the back to the garage. We had two cars in there: one was Brian's BMW, which he only took out in the summer. The other was "my car," which had been my grandmother's old car that my dad gave to me when I turned sixteen. I'd named the car Betty after Gamma, and the name really suited the vehicle. Very retro looking. Pale pink. Couldn't go fast. Guzzled gas, but it had cushy seats. And I loved her.

Normally I parked Betty on the street because Mom and Brian used the two allotted stalls in the garage. But since they'd taken Mom's car to Wisconsin, I'd moved Betty to the open spot for safekeeping.

I turned the key in the ignition and coaxed, "Come on, Betty."

The engine turned over and I pulled out onto the street.

I drove slowly through the neighborhood and across town, toward my friend's house. It was only a five-minute drive, but I noticed my hands were kind of shaking on the wheel. I gave myself a little pep talk like my dad always does. I said, "You're fine. You're doing great. Just keep breathing."

When I got to Becca's, I parked on the street. No one was home yet. School wouldn't be out for another hour, so I decided to wait in Betty. I pulled out my spiral notebook and flipped around the pages. My hands were still a bit shaky, and I couldn't focus on the words I was reading. "Come on, Claire, just relax. Becca will be home soon."

A car drove past, and I slouched down in the seat. I didn't want anyone to see me, not that they would recognize me or be out looking for me or anything. I just wanted to be invisible.

I felt different but I didn't know why. I didn't want anyone to think that anything was wrong with me. Did I look the same? I knew what had happened, but also, I didn't know. I was there, but nothing made sense. I knew what Evan had been saying, how he'd acted, and how I'd felt, but none of those things matched. They were like three different species in three separate columns and no scientific theory could explain them. And yet, that is what happened.

I imagined what I would say to Becca. I didn't even know what to call it. The event? The misunderstanding? *The Thing with Evan.* I needed to ask Becca. Why was it like that? Was it normal? What did I do wrong? Would everyone at school find out? Had Becca heard anything? What should I do now? Had Evan gone back to school this afternoon? What would he tell his friends?

Someone knocked on the window and I jumped so fast and hard, I hit the horn. I screamed. The horn was blaring, and it wouldn't stop.

"Oh my god," said Becca, standing beside my window. "What are you doing?"

I opened the door and got out. When I shut the door, the horn finally stopped.

I collapsed into Becca's arms.

Thirty-Three

SEAVER

ADRIAN TOOK ME TO HIS MEETING WITH THE CHEF. MY LEG WAS HURTing worse and worse, but I didn't tell Adrian about it because I was afraid he wouldn't take me with him.

Each time I looked at my leg, it was redder and I could see a dark line under the skin. I knew when it had happened. It was that night I was running in the field. It was dark and the crops had been cut. The stalks were short like sharp sticks. I stepped on them wrong and they poked into my skin. I remember the feeling like a stab but I had to keep running. I was watching the professor's car. When he drove into the Ogletrees' driveway, I ran close enough to listen. I needed to know if they were talking about me. Then I snuck into the back of the professor's car and hid. I had to get far from that farm. But my leg was throbbing. The sliver had gone in too far.

Today my leg was aching as I sat in Adrian's car. He left the keys in the car so I could listen to the radio and work the heater. The heater was on, but I had the chills.

I watched the windows of the building where Adrian had gone. It was all glass, like an office place. People were coming and going. I wished I had my Rubik's Cube.

I lifted the bottom of my pants to see if my leg was worse. It was swollen and red. The redness was longer. It went up the side of my leg. My head hurt too, and I rubbed my forehead. I looked at myself in the mirror. My eyes were puffy. I looked fuzzy. My forehead was hot.

I checked my leg again. I wondered if I could pick at the sliver and get it out from under the skin. I could see it in there and it seemed like I should be able to pull it out. But it hurt really bad when I tugged on it, so I stopped. It was like a small branch and it was stuck to the inside of my skin, like it had grown attached.

I didn't want to listen to the radio anymore. Adrian was taking a long time. Lots of people had gone into the building and already come out. But not Adrian. He was still in there. I had to pee. I was hungry. I switched off the ignition and pulled out the keys. I got out of the car and limped to the front. There was a stone bench on the wide front sidewalk. I sat there.

Grown-ups stared at me as they passed. They said things like "Can I help you?" and "Are you waiting for your mom or dad?"

I ignored them. I was breathing hard, trying to think about anything besides my leg. I rocked back and forth. I rubbed my hands together. Where was Adrian?

Finally, I decided to go inside and get him. I pushed myself up. I was dizzy but I took a step toward the front door. It hurt to put weight on my left leg. I dragged it. My eyes were weak. It was hard to see.

"Oh my god, help!" said someone, a woman.

Thirty-Four

CLAIRE

"YOU SCARED ME TO DEATH!" I CRIED TO BECCA.

"Okay, weirdo, relax," said Becca. "You'd better come inside and get a grip on yourself."

I laughed and felt better when Becca teased me. This was something familiar. I felt safe with this.

We walked up the driveway to her house.

"What are you doing? I didn't know you were coming over," said Becca.

"I need to talk to you."

"Obviously," said Becca. She opened the front door and hollered, "Honey, I'm home!"

There wasn't anyone inside; it was just what Becca did every time she walked in.

Turning to me, she said, "You're lucky I didn't go to the Depot today."

"Yeah. For sure." The Depot was a frozen yogurt shop where a lot of the kids went after school to hang out. Becca was a frequent Depot-goer. "So glad."

"Come on," said Becca. "Let's talk in my room."

We zigzagged through the hallway till we got there. I'd always considered Becca's to be the perfect bedroom. The walls were covered in posters upon posters, sprinkled with cute snapshots of

Becca and various friends. Her bed wasn't made and there were piles of clothes all over the floor. We literally had to step on the clothes to get to the mattress.

Becca quickly made her bed, pulling up the duvet and clearing a space for us to sit. She flopped into position, crossed her legs, and patted the spot next to her. "Here ya go."

I sat on the side of the bed as if it were a chair, with my legs over the edge and my feet on the ground.

"Come all the way up here, why don't ya?" said Becca.

"No, this is good," I said.

"What's going on with you? You're being so weird right now." Becca leaned forward and stared, trying to figure me out. She studied my face so closely it was like there were clues in the pores of my skin or something.

"Yeah," I said. "Something happened . . . and I don't feel right."

"So just tell me. I'm, like, your best friend."

Slowly, I spit out the words. In small chunks. I added my doubts as I went. Like I wasn't even sure. It was all very painful and embarrassing to eke out. I gave her the basic outline. She seemed to understand, so I didn't give her all the tiny, gross details.

"Okay," said Becca, holding out her palms, as if she'd instantly recognized this. She went ahead and named it. "So you blew him. What's the big deal? You had to do it sometime."

"I guess," I said, but really? Was it a blow job? If so, was I supposed to be relieved, like this was a necessary experience? A milestone? Mostly I felt ashamed. It was clear I hadn't done what Evan wanted. I wasn't good at it. I didn't even know what was going on. It was humiliating. I didn't know how to explain that to Becca.

Also, I felt angry. And scared. I couldn't believe Evan—or any boy—could be so much stronger than me and that he would fight me like that. He'd frightened me. He'd made me feel helpless. He'd made me feel awful about myself and I don't know why. I said, "But I didn't know how to do it."

"So what?" said Becca. "No one does, really."

"Well. Evan acted like everyone knew but me."

"Gross. That's just stupid," said Becca.

"I didn't want to," I admitted. Nothing about it was enjoyable. No one had warned me that it could be like that.

"Yeah," said Becca. "I don't like giving blow jobs either."

"But he was acting like . . . I dunno. Like I should want to."

"Yuck," said Becca. "I'm sorry, Claire. It sounds gross."

"It was," I said. "Please don't tell anyone."

"I mean, I won't but . . ."

"But what?"

"I mean . . . He probably will," said Becca. "Tell someone. Everyone maybe. At least his friends. For sure his friends."

"Oh my god."

"They always talk about that shit. Most of it is lies. But he'll probably say something."

"But why? I mean, it was a disaster."

"Oh, he'll tell it in a way that makes him look like a hero," said Becca. "Sorry."

"Arrrgggh," I said, clenching my fists. My face was red. I stood up and paced, marching over her clothes. "I don't know what to do."

"Yeah," said Becca. "Not much you can do."

I needed to escape. I had to hide. I said, "I can't go to school tomorrow. I can't ever go back."

Becca scooted off the bed and stood next to me, following me around her room and rubbing my back. "Shh. No, you can. You can."

I started crying. "What will they say? I can't . . ."

"Shh," said Becca. She rummaged around her desk and found

some Kleenex. She handed me some tissue. "Sit down here and just breathe."

I did as she said.

"Put your head between your knees. I don't want you fainting."

I was starting to feel better.

"Listen." She sat next to me. "He's gonna tell his friends about this. I don't know what he'll say. He'll say whatever, who knows what, about today, about you. And he's gonna make himself look good—"

"—but—"

"—no matter what. He'll tell lies all day long, if he has to, okay? And his friends are going to believe him. They'll rally around and cheer him on. They'll probably think it's funny because that's the kind of thing they think is funny."

"Oh my god. Biology! How can I see him now? Or any of his friends," I cried.

"Look," said Becca, taking my shoulders in her hands. "Those guys are assholes, okay?"

I nodded.

"They're like sharks and they're basically slinking around in the scum of the scum, okay, looking for something to take a bite of. And they'll probably talk about you and laugh among themselves. It'll be a topic for a while. And they'll be watching you for signs of weakness, okay, because they feed on that. That's what we're deal-ing with, Claire. They're assholes in high school. And we have to coexist with them because they don't start to grow up until college or grad school when at least some of them become decent guys. Okay?"

I was crying and nodding as I listened to Becca, and what she said reminded me of something my dad was always talking about at our family dinners, and I wanted to tell Becca, but my voice was shaky, and my eyes were wet.

I plowed ahead and blurted it out, through my tears. "Yeah, that's true . . ." I sobbed, choking and breaking for air as I went along, "On average . . . boys are bigger than girls . . . physically throughout, like . . . adolescence, but . . . on average . . . girls are more . . . advanced and, like . . . surpassing boys in major . . . developmental milestones . . . mentally . . . and emotionally . . . . and psychologically . . ."

"That's right," said Becca, rubbing my back. "You don't have to talk right now."

I relaxed and my body calmed down. "It felt good to get that out."

Becca listened like the best friend in the world. Then she said, "Your dad is one hundred percent right, Claire. So here's what we're gonna do . . ."

I nodded, ready.

"You are going to go to school tomorrow, okay?" she said. "Tomorrow and the next day and the next day."

"Oh, Becks," I whined and twisted away, hiding my face.

She uncovered my face and stroked my hair. She took me by the wrists. She said, "You have to. And you have to act normal, like nothing happened. Nothing happened, okay?"

I nodded, but I didn't understand. Something did happen. But I trusted Becca. I said, "Okay, I'll try."

"Fuck those fuckers," she said. "You go to school and you act normal."

"I don't know if I can," I said. "I don't feel normal."

"Listen. Those sharks are gonna be sniffing for blood. If you give them anything to work with, anything at all, they'll annihilate you. And we don't want that, right?"

"Right."

"So you give them zero. It's just another day, okay? It's the only way."

I was nodding, absorbing the advice, steeling myself for battle. "Just another day."

Becca nodded, then said emphatically, "Fuck those fuckers."

"Fuck 'em," I said, but my voice was softer than hers.

"Here," said Becca, leaping off the bed. She rummaged through a pile of clothes, then another, tromping around her messy room until she found it. A cream-colored finely ribbed ultraluxe long-sleeve shirt from The Limited. She held it up for me to see. "Take this."

"Take it? You mean like . . ."

"You can have it," said Becca, handing it to me. "I know how much you love it."

"I LOVE this shirt," I said, holding it to my face. "It's the softest!"

"It's good with your brown hair, the contrast."

"But you love it too. Are you sure?"

"Yeah," said Becca brightly. "Try it on."

I put the shirt on and slid my hands over it, rubbing my arms and shoulders and tummy. I wanted to see how I looked, so I hopped over a pile on the floor to get to the full-length mirror in the corner. I smiled and twirled at my reflection. "It's perfect."

"It's so good on you," said Becca, almost with a hint of jealousy.

I raced back to Becca on the bed and hugged her.

"Aw," said Becca. "Are you crying? Don't cry, Clarinetta, it's just a shirt."

"I know," I said. I was crying but I smiled because I loved it when she called me Clarinetta, her silly nickname for me.

"Wear it tomorrow," she said, nodding at the shirt.

"You think?" I said, trying to imagine it.

"Yeah, it'll be, like, your shield against the sharks."

I looked down at the shirt on me. I did feel good in it. It was a type of armor. I liked being wrapped in the luxe fabric, sort of stretchy but also extremely soft. I said, "Okay, I will."

"Good," said Becca, beaming. "Now, I'm sorry to say this, but I gotta go."

"Oh, okay."

"I gotta take my stupid cat to the vet. She's throwing up all over the place and my mom made this appointment and asked me to take her since she's my cat technically. Anyway, do you wanna come? It's only two or three blocks."

I thought about it. "No, I should get back to my mom's. I actually have a volleyball game tonight, although I don't know if they'll let me play or if I'm still being punished. Anyway, I should go to support the team, right?"

"Right," said Becca, pleased. "Just go about your life."

"Okay. And I have to make up that test somehow." I took off the shirt and put my regular clothes on.

We walked through the house to the front door. Becca picked up the cat and held her like a baby. The cat meowed.

"Shush, Dinky. We're going to the vet," said Becca, stroking the cat.

"She purrs so loudly," I said, wishing Mom and Brian would finally let me get a pet. It seemed nice.

"She's a good girl." Becca kissed the cat's belly and the cat batted at Becca's head, fake-biting her hair. Becca put the cat down and said, "Okay. Remember what I said."

"Thanks, Becks," I said, hugging her then walking out the door.

"Anytime, Clarinetta," she said, watching me go. "I'll see you tomorrow. At school."

"Yes," I said, holding the cream-colored shirt, lifting it. "Thanks for this."

"Wear it tomorrow. Remember," Becca mouthed the words, *fuck the fuckers.*

I smiled and she closed the door.

At the bottom of her driveway, I stopped and glanced around the neighborhood. It was nicer than mine. It was quieter. There were more trees, and the houses were farther apart.

I walked up to Betty, tossed the shirt in the front, then swung myself into the driver's seat.

Thirty-Five

KIRA

AFTER I LEFT JEN SWANSON'S HOUSE IN RICHFIELD, I DROVE TO THE agency office. My supervisor had paged me, and if I was in trouble, it would be better to take the medicine face-to-face. I was gathering my thoughts as I pulled into the parking lot at Family Alternatives in Minneapolis. I was supposed to spend half my week here, but I rarely did.

"Is Cindy in?" I asked when I got inside. My colleagues nodded toward her door, which was open; she was on the phone.

When she saw me in her doorway, she waved me in and gave me the "just a minute" signal.

I walked in and took a seat as quietly as I could. The person on the other line must have had a lot to say, because Cindy was nodding and saying "uh-huh, uh-huh" over and over.

Cindy Garcia was a powerful woman. Smart, direct, and kind. She was a large person with a booming laugh. She'd seen it all and she didn't suffer fools. I thought she should run for office. But she was too real for that.

Finally, she said to her caller, "I've got another meeting, can we pick this up later?" She smiled at me, ended the call, and hung up.

I took a deep breath.

"So," she said, slapping her thighs. "What are we talking about?"

"You paged me," I said. "It's Seaver Swanson, right?"

Cindy got up and walked to the door, shut it, and returned to her desk. "Yeah, it's Seaver Swanson."

"I'm sorry I didn't tell you—"

"—I just don't think you should confess before you know what you're confessing to," said my supervisor.

"Oh," I said, sitting up straighter. "What am I confessing to?"

"Law enforcement notified us they went to look for him at his mom's apartment."

"Good, I called that in as soon as I—"

"—Uh uh uh," she said, holding up her hand. "You really need to cool it."

"Sorry," I said. "I'll just listen."

She bit her lip and stared at me for a moment, as if I were a giant human puzzle but also an intriguing piece of art. Then her face relaxed and she was back to business. "He wasn't there or anywhere near there."

"Shit," I said, deflated.

"Not last night. And they went again this morning. No luck," said Cindy as she picked up a pen and opened a file on her desk. "So I've got a couple of questions."

"Go ahead," I said, wringing my hands.

"The neighbor talked about a man who'd apparently driven him there," she said, checking something on her pad. I stayed quiet because I could tell I wasn't meant to answer yet. "A professor from St. Gustaf. Did you know about that?"

"Yes, I actually went to talk with him—"

"When was this?"

"Yesterday."

"And?"

"That was about it," I said.

Cindy considered this. "So why is Seaver running? Is everything hunky-dory at the farm?"

I nodded, although something did seem off. "We think he went to find Adrian."

"And?"

"I saw Adrian at school on Monday and he hadn't heard anything."

"Okay, but send someone over to check it out. And keep me informed, please. As soon as my caseworkers know, I should know." She pointed at me, and I felt the sting.

"Yes, ma'am," I said. "And I'm sorry."

"You don't have to call me 'ma'am.' Just follow the protocol. That's all I ask."

"I understand," I said, shifting in my seat.

"All right. Let's move on." Cindy turned the page in the file. She held up a memo that looked like my recommendation for kinship care. "What's the status with the aunt?"

"Yes, I just came from there," I said. "Jen Swanson, Nicole's sister. I think she's a go."

"Well, that's some good news." She initialed the memo and put it back in the folder. "What are the odds on reunification with the mom?"

"Optimistically, I'd say fifty-fifty. She hasn't found a job and she hasn't been going to parenting classes."

"Is she clean?"

"As long as she's in rehab," I said. "Once she's out, I'm unsure. But she's very motivated to get Seaver back."

"Sometimes that's not enough."

"Yeah. That's the reality," I said, and we sat with that uncomfortable truth for a moment. "I've set up a visit with Seaver, his mom, and the aunt, Jen. We're going to go to the Mall of America."

"Oh goody," said Cindy unhumorously. "Now you just have to find him."

"Right," I said, and I was wondering how to bring up the problem with the Ogletrees. "And there's another thing."

She gazed at me with an expression that said, *Bring it*.

"Grady Ogletree—" I started.

"—doesn't want any more kids," she said. "I know."

"What? Wait, I mean, I knew he didn't want Seaver back, but—"

"—he doesn't want anyone."

"Oh," I said, surprised and disappointed. "I hadn't heard that."

"Well," she said, "sometimes I hear things before you, if you can believe it."

"Okay," I said, ignoring the dig. I knew not to tread on Cindy's ego at the moment.

"It's a loss, obviously," she said. "But I figure, you find Seaver, he goes to his aunt's on emergency placement, then we get the court's decision on Mom. If she's a no, then we seek approval for permanent kinship care for the aunt and we're off to the races."

"Yes, that's the plan," I said.

"Good," said Cindy, as if satisfied we'd reached agreement on one thing anyway. Then she added, "Too bad about June and Grady calling it quits."

My throat got tight. It was the end of something big, and something was stirring in my chest. "I don't understand that, but I'll try to find out."

"Hey," she said, as if snapping me out of a trance. "Don't poke this bear. It's the Ogletrees' decision and that's that."

"Okay," I said. Cindy was the boss and she didn't seem bothered by Grady's decision, but I was struggling.

"I know you've placed a lot of kids with them. They're your

people, I get it. But this might open other horizons for you. Try to see it that way. As the start to something new," she said.

Just then, there was a knock on the door. An administrative assistant opened the door and stepped in. She was holding a message slip.

"Sorry to interrupt," she said. "We just got a call from Children's Hospital. They have Seaver Swanson in the ER. They're asking for his medical history."

"What?!" I said, standing up.

"Yeah," said the assistant. "They wanna know, has he had a tetanus shot in the last five years?"

Thirty-Six

MATTHEW

I THOUGHT MY SEMINAR HAD BEEN A SUCCESS, BUT APPARENTLY NOT everyone agreed. As evidenced by the phone call I received Tuesday evening. It was Gloria Jamieson, and she was angry. Not an explosive anger, but worse: a calm, controlled concern.

"I understand the police made an appearance at your seminar today," she said.

"Yes," I said, matching her demeanor. "In fact, it was Deputy Vasquez from the County Sheriff's Department. As well as her trainee."

I heard Gloria take a deep breath, then she asked, "And why, pray tell, didn't you notify me? This seems like something that would have warranted a heads-up."

"I'm sorry," I said. "I guess I didn't see it that way."

"Matthew, I thought it was clear from our earlier conversation that I had to protect the college—and this department—from liability, from damage to our reputation, from whatever else might flow from this. I thought you understood. And now this?"

I paused. "You mean the police? Don't worry about the police. It was great, actually. I transformed the police interrogation into a teaching moment."

"Impressive," she said, not at all sounding impressed.

"Well," I said, ignoring her sarcasm, "the students seemed to enjoy it."

"Not all of them, apparently," she said.

"What? What are you talking about?"

"There's been a complaint," she said, completely composed.

"A complaint?!" I cried. "About me?"

"About you. It's informal at this stage. But it's something I have to disclose to the P&T Committee."

"Oh Christ, Gloria, no." I groaned. I'd been sitting, but now I stood up. I paced my tiny kitchen. "A complaint from whom? About what?"

"A student," she said. "To be fair, I haven't yet seen the written—

"It's a written complaint?"

"—complaint," she said, "but I'm told it has to do with the seminar."

"Oh, what a load of—"

"Matthew, we must take this seriously," she cut me off.

"—absolute crap." I cleaned up my language but I was furious. "Are you kidding me?"

"No, this isn't a joke," she said. I thought I heard a tinge of superiority in her voice, a bit of *I told you so*, similar to the way Tammy used to talk to me.

"I know it's not a joke," I said, almost losing my temper. "It's a figure of speech."

"Matthew," said Gloria.

"And you haven't even read it yet," I said, mystified. "Who told you about it?"

"My assistant," said Gloria. "All right? So can we please—"

"Do I need a lawyer? I mean, Jesus." I thought about calling my brother-in-law, Hal, although he was only a real estate attorney. "Are you doing an investigation?"

"I simply want to talk to you about the seminar and understand what happened," she said.

"Well, okay, fine, let's talk," I said, "but please don't tell the committee. Gloria, come on. That'll jeopardize the vote!"

"Matthew, let's take one step at a time. But you've got to cooperate. At best, this is a distraction."

"At worst, it could tank the vote."

"Right," she said. "So we've got to nip this in the bud."

"Okay," I said, sitting down again. "I'll do whatever you suggest."

As Gloria asked questions, I answered them. She gave me her observations and insights, and I jotted them down. She challenged me to design my own solution, and she committed to supporting me but that I would be responsible for taking steps to remedy whatever damage might have been done to the committee's view of my application, my credibility, my judgment.

I told her all about that stormy night when I picked up Seaver. The one thing I didn't tell Gloria—or the police—was that I'd been drinking. And of course, I hadn't told the students either.

As soon as I hung up with Gloria, the phone rang again and I jumped. When I answered, I assumed it was Gloria calling with another suggestion or task for me to complete.

"Yes?" I'd answered, exasperated.

"Hi, Matthew? It's Kira. Am I catching you at a bad time?"

The answer was yes, it was a terrible time, but the truth was I was glad to hear Kira's voice. I said, "This is a perfect time."

With relief, Kira explained they'd found Seaver. He'd landed in the hospital, which was the place I'd been trying to take him in the first place.

"Excellent news," I said. And I should have been relieved, I supposed, but actually I was harboring a bit of resentment. Or regret. I couldn't place it. All I knew was that kid was lucky and I was feeling very unlucky and suddenly I didn't know how I felt about anything.

"Yes, but he's got an infection in his leg and may need surgery," she said.

"Dear god," I said, and my mind went straight to Gloria and the P&T Committee and what they would think, and I remembered Hal's story of the Good Samaritan law and his friend with the exploding car. If this kid was having surgery, I feared I would be held responsible somehow. "I hope they can clear everything up."

"Well, he's on antibiotics and they're watching him closely," said Kira. "He's had his tetanus shots, so that's good. I mean, technically I shouldn't be telling you about his medical condition, but I know you're a good person."

"Thank you," I said, feeling a warmth at her trust in me. I needed that, and it had been a while since I'd heard words like those from a woman like her, a woman who I hoped could see the integrity in me. "And I hope the infection clears up," I said, thinking of my brother the doctor. Perhaps I should have called and asked for his medical advice. "Tell Seaver to hang in there."

"I will. He's a little fighter," said Kira. I wondered if she knew he'd tried to hot-wire my car. Or about the money he'd stolen. "He's strong," she said, her voice admiring.

"Yeah, I picked up on that," I said, a mix of caring and despair suddenly filling my chest. As if a child could magically survive if only they were strong, and enough of a fighter. I cleared my throat and glanced at my briefcase. I'd been carrying around the Rubik's Cube in there for no reason. It wasn't like I thought I'd see the kid again. I just didn't know what else to do with it. I decided to tell Kira. "Hey, I have his Rubik's Cube. Maybe he'd like to have it."

"Oh, I'm sure he would," she said. "I'm glad you're finally fessing up to that."

"Yeah, I'm sorry. I should have given it to you when you were here."

"Don't worry," she said. "Even if you hadn't offered to surrender the Cube voluntarily, I would definitely come down there and confiscate it."

"Okay." I chuckled at the absurd image. "But seriously, how can I get this thing to you?"

"Oh, I'm sure we'll see each other again."

"We will?" I said, enjoying her certainty.

She teased, "Maybe there's an alumni brunch or something."

"Well, sure," I said, "but I'm not an alum. And wouldn't Seaver like to have it back soon?"

"Aww, that's sweet," said Kira. "Okay, let's figure something out. I come down to Northwood pretty often."

"And I'm up in the Cities on weekends," I said, and a feeling like hope stung in my throat.

"Okaaay," she said, holding out the vowel, and suddenly I felt awkward for suggesting a weekend.

"Hey, I've got it!" I said. "Didn't you say you had ideas for me?"

"I've always got ideas," she said, and it felt like she was smiling.

"Well, I mean. I thought you had a proposal for improving the sociology department, remember?" I was smiling too.

"Oh yes, I do. But I must warn you, they're bold ideas."

"I'm up for bold," I said, and I was enjoying our back-and-forth. Plus I actually needed some creative options to present to Gloria and the P&T Committee.

"But I'm not going to share my thoughts with you until I get that Cube back into the hands of its rightful owner."

"I see. The Cube for your ideas."

"Yes," said Kira. "Like a hostage exchange."

"Ha, no. Please don't make kidnapping jokes. I already feel bad enough about putting Seaver in my car."

"Sorry. Gallows humor. Jokes in poor taste sometimes leak out with a job like mine. You understand?"

"I do."

"Matthew, for what it's worth," said Kira, returning to her serious side, "I don't think you did anything wrong. You were trying to help."

"Yeah, but."

"No, listen," she said. "I have a pretty good bullshit detector. But even I double-check my instincts when it comes to my kids. And you're okay."

"Wait," I said, "does that mean you checked up on me?"

She sounded like she was half-teasing, half-serious when she said, "I sure did."

"Wow. All right," I said, impressed. But she still didn't know the whole story, and in that moment, I wanted her to. "Look, can I tell you something?"

"I'm all ears."

"Okay, here goes," I said, and I could feel her bracing herself on the other end of the line. I was taking a chance, but I needed to talk about it. I needed someone else to know the truth. I wasn't proud of it, but Kira seemed like a person who wasn't shocked by other people's flaws and failures. So I told her I'd been drinking that night.

"Oh," she said somberly.

"And I couldn't take the risk of the police finding out, which meant the college finding out. It was weak of me and wrong and I regret it. But it's the truth."

There was silence on the line and I felt all the buoyancy of our previous conversation dissipate.

"Matthew, that's not good."

"I know," I said. "But I thought I was fine, I really did."

"Oh, you think you can tell when you're fine to drive?"

"I did, yes."

"No, you absolutely cannot tell that. And you could hurt someone," she said. I didn't like how the conversation had turned so serious and I didn't know how to turn it back. After a few tense beats, Kira finally confessed, "Um, that's how my parents died, actually. They were hit by a drunk driver."

"Oh my god. Kira, I'm so sorry. Oh, I'm such an ass."

A pause, then she said, "Well, you didn't do it."

"Yeah," I said, wishing this conversation was happening in person so I could have shown her my sincerity. "But you're right: I could have hurt someone. I mean, I don't think I was impaired but still."

"That's what they all say, right?"

"Right," I said sheepishly. God, I felt stupid.

"Look, I should go," she said.

"I'm really sorry, and I'm sorry about your parents."

"Well, thank you," she said, "and let's pick up this conversation another time."

"All right," I said, grateful for her grace.

After a moment, she said, "Meanwhile, I'm still willing to trade you my ideas for that Rubik's Cube."

"Thank god," I said.

"Well, it's for the betterment of the local community, I hope," said Kira, referring to her ideas. "I'm thinking the college can serve the foster needs of local kids and families."

"I love it," I said. "Public engagement. Gloria is going to eat it up. Thank you so much."

"Well, I need that Rubik's Cube."

"You're funny."

"I am funny, yes," said Kira, feigning modesty.

"And smart. I admire you, Kira Patterson," I said.

"Thank you. You're not so bad yourself," she said warmly. She added, "You could definitely improve in a few areas, but overall, not bad."

I laughed. "Maybe I'll ask you to write me a letter of recommendation."

She said, "I'd be happy to."

We both knew we were kidding. Academia humor. We said good night, and I sat on the futon for a long time. I had a lot to think about.

Thirty-Seven

MATTHEW

WEDNESDAY, SEPTEMBER 30, 1992

THE NEXT MORNING, I WOKE UP FEELING RESOLVED, NOT EXACTLY back to my old self, but better, newer, like a cicada fresh out of the shell. I arrived at Lindberg Hall a full fifteen minutes early. Plenty of time to write on the board, "George Herbert Meade" and "Symbolic Interaction." Ample opportunity to observe the students as they entered and took their seats. As I watched from the well, I wondered why they looked so different to me.

It occurred to me: *Do I look different to them?*

Or was this simply the nature of autumn, my favorite season? The weather was perfect today, but it could change dramatically and I liked that. There was comfort in knowing that Seaver had been found, although I was waiting to hear from Kira about the results of his surgery. And of course, there was my conversation with Gloria and the ways to address the student complaint against me. And hopefully save my tenure file.

All these things combined into a pretty powerful engine inside me, there at the base of Lindberg Hall. That conversation with Kira had stirred things in me I hadn't felt in years. I was excited to see her again and hear her ideas. I liked the way Kira's mind worked and the way she advocated for the kids on her caseload.

And she'd said nice things about Claire that had me thinking. It made me feel that, against all odds, I'd done a decent job raising my daughter. And perhaps I wasn't a terrible dad. I hadn't failed her, but I had work to do.

A hypothesis was jelling. Something about the resilience of children. The importance of believing in them. I hadn't quite articulated it. Something about kids growing into adults and adults returning to kids. I'd been noodling some ideas as I walked to class, inhaling the autumn air and thinking about risk and renewal. There was something about the leaves falling to the ground, drying underfoot and becoming part of the earth, making room for new growth in the spring.

I set out my overheads for the day's lecture. When I glanced up, the students seemed to be staring at me more than usual. Had they heard about the complaint? Sometimes I thought they could read my mind. Other times, it seemed nothing was going on in their heads. The thought made me smile. I pushed up my glasses and I paced back and forth. At the top of the hour, I began, "Humans. Form identity. Through interaction."

I let those words ring in the room. The chattering ended. The students were paying attention. I said it again.

"Humans. Form. Identity. Through. Interaction."

I paused, then said, "Let me ask you this: Are you influenced by your peers?"

"Yeah," said one student.

"Obviously," said another.

I nodded; my hands were clasped. I said, "All right. Now: *In what ways* are you influenced by your peers?"

Students were glancing down. It wasn't as easy a question. Finally, someone said, "Lots of ways."

I pointed to my head and asked, "Are we aware of it? Perhaps. Are we *always* aware of it?"

No response.

I bounced along the well, gesturing, making eye contact as I continued, "The clothes we wear, the food we eat, how we talk, what we think is good or bad, all of it, is influenced by those around us. How? *Through interactions with others*. Why? Because we are *social beings*."

I paused. I was having fun. I said, "We need human interaction. Without interaction, we get sick. Or die."

I returned to the lectern, opened my notebook, and flipped the page. "How does change happen, in a society? Through interactions. Change is built into the system. Society is interaction. Self is interaction. We are a constantly swinging pendulum of conformity and individuation. Are you a conformist?"

I looked at the audience, waiting for someone to volunteer. Some of the students were shy, shaking their heads. I asked, "No? Okay. I bet you can name something that was cool last year but isn't anymore. Right?"

Some heads nodded.

"How did that change occur?" A pause. "Through *interactions*."

I picked up the chalk and wrote a few key words on the board. I tapped the words as I spoke. "Exogenous—or external—influences are constantly shaping us. We learn which behaviors elicit a positive response from others. We are all, every one of us, seeking a Positive Sense of Self."

I put down the chalk and wiped my hands together. Then, to indicate that we were all the same, I walked up the steps and stood in the aisle, close to where students were sitting. Turning in a three-sixty as I spoke, I decided I wanted to talk about it. I said, "I am up for tenure this year. You may know that. I don't know how much you follow the internal workings of academia."

There were chuckles and murmurs. Clearly, I was making them somewhat uncomfortable.

"I have completed all the requirements. I have performed all the positive behaviors. This is reflected in my letters of recommendation and in my evaluations."

I walked down the steps as I continued. "You, the students have evaluated me, judged me, and rated the effectiveness and quality of my teaching. And of course, I am aware of that, and I have taught you in a way that will earn me high marks. Symbolic interaction. I am a social being. A human being."

At the bottom, I paused for dramatic effect. Looking up to the students, I counted on my fingers as I listed the criteria in response to my own question: "What are those behaviors? I am prepared. I deliver the material in a dynamic way. I do not read from my notes. I am respectful. I do not argue with you. I am accessible. I have conformed to the so-called 'rules.'"

And then, from the middle of the audience, a voice rang out. "That's not what the police said."

I stopped short and swallowed. There was a smattering of laughter. Heads were turning. There were whispers and murmurs. Students loved a drama. A mystery.

"Aha, the police," I said, squinting at the class, overhead lights in my eyes. The student who had spoken had not identified himself, so I didn't know who to focus on. I asked the room in general, "Are you referring to the police who visited my seminar yesterday?"

No response. Some looked at their papers, as if wishing to disappear. Others were nodding. A few held their chins high, as if they were entitled to an explanation.

"So, you've heard about it," I said. "Okay. Word travels fast, doesn't it?"

"Is it true?" someone asked. There was a hush in the crowd, an anticipation, as if awaiting an implosion. Something important.

I nodded, signaling I would answer their questions, but I was biting my lip as I considered how. Gloria and I had come up with a plan, but this was not a part of it. I could go a bit further, I decided.

"Curious thing, gossip," I said, looking down. When I raised my eyes again, I said, "Okay, quick detour. Have you ever wondered why we gossip? This is a bit of anthropology, but I told you there'd be some overlap. The answer is: It's evolutionary. We are wired to notice weakness in others, for survival, as early humans traveled in clans. When one member was weak, it threatened the safety and survival of the whole clan. Therefore, the weak one must be helped or abandoned, saved or left behind.

"Today, perhaps I am the weak one. You are perceiving this incident, with the child, as a weakness in me, perhaps. You may worry there is a target on my back."

I stopped talking as if I suddenly realized I'd been going on and on and needed to shut up, the way I sometimes snored so loudly that I startled myself awake in the middle of the night. And in the silence, an uncertainty wafted in the air like an odor.

Finally, a student boldly asked, "Did you kidnap a little boy?"

The question rang out like a bell, an accusation deserving an answer. Every single student was paying attention. There were coos and nervous shushing, quiet, then someone cleared her throat. In response, the class snickered. The tension was thick.

"Kidnap?" I said, looking down and pinching my nose. I was gathering my thoughts. "Did I kidnap him? Well . . . yes. Probably, technically the answer is yes."

The room gasped.

"But we're getting ahead of the syllabus," I said. "Nevertheless, it makes sense to touch on it here." I resumed pacing. It helped me think, and it was more interesting to look at. I walked slowly, with my hands behind my back. I said, "Kidnapping is a crime. It is defined in the law. Who writes the laws of a society? For what purpose? And who decides when the law has been violated?"

"Rich people," said a student.

"The government," offered another

"The people of the society," said a third.

Acknowledging those answers, I said, "But consider, if you will, how one action, when looked at through a certain lens, constitutes a crime, the crime of kidnapping, for example. But when examined through another lens, is not a crime at all. In fact, is a desired action, the act of helping an injured child." I stopped pacing and waited for a reaction. Nothing.

"So let me ask you," I said, "was it reckless? What I did?"

The class erupted in chatter, as if they were instantly answering and debating among themselves, as if I were an alleged criminal and the students were the judge and jury. I assumed the class was chattering at the provocative questions I'd posed, but soon I realized there was another disruption.

A person was trotting down the steps of the center aisle, all the way from the top of the hall to the front. It was a student, but not a student of mine. She came all the way to where I was standing. This had never happened to me before.

"I'm sorry," she said, handing me a note. "But they told me to bring you this."

I took the note and thanked her. The class was buzzing. Here was another test. They were giddy to watch me try to handle another drama.

I read the note, then started packing my bag.

"I have to go," I said to the class. "Something, a personal matter, has come up." A hush fell across the room. "Please use the rest of the hour to review your notes," I said, slinging my briefcase onto my shoulder and dashing out of the hall.

Thirty-Eight

CLAIRE

I WORE MY ARMOR TO SCHOOL ON WEDNESDAY: BECCA'S CREAM-colored finely ribbed shirt from The Limited, plus the steely re-solve to not give the fuckers any ammunition. I'd gone over it in my mind the night before. And I'd done something I hadn't done since junior high: I laid out my outfit for the next day and smoothed out each piece so they'd be perfect. When I rolled out of bed, I immediately put on the shirt. It gave me strength. It gave me focus.

I drove myself and parked in the student lot. I'd arrived precisely on time. I waited for Becca inside the side door; she'd promised to walk with me to every class.

"Hey!" called Becca from halfway down the hall.

I hurried to meet her, and we hugged. Nothing out of the ordi-nary so far.

"Cute shirt," she said, stroking my arm and winking. "Re-member what I said."

I nodded, and we put the plan into action, walking without shame. Projecting an air of confidence. Not taking any shit. The Limited shirt—and Becca's presence—were holding me together.

When biology rolled around, I felt a twinge of trepidation. I took my spot in the last row. Evan wasn't there yet, which was both a relief and a mystery. Would he be late or was he skipping? If he was skipping, why? Did it have anything to do with yesterday?

The teacher walked down through the rows of desks, a pile of graded tests in her arms. At each student's desk, Mrs. Biggerstaff slapped down the news, a clump of stapled pages with a big red mark on the front. There were as many groans as smiles as everyone took in their grades.

The mood was tense. The sound of flipping pages, murmurs, and the scootching of chairs. Still no Evan. I was hoping he wouldn't show up today, but I had a sinking feeling he would. There was a tightness in my throat, a giant rock in my gut when I thought about it. So humiliating. How would I look at him now? What would I say? I listened for Becca's voice in my head: Pretend he doesn't exist. If he showed up, I resolved to focus only on biology.

Mrs. Biggerstaff returned to the front of the room and was writing on the board. The class was moving on. Next chapter. I reached into my backpack for my textbook. Then I sensed it, Evan's presence, his shadow. The thump of his backpack on the floor behind me. When I looked up, he had fallen into his chair.

His eyes caught mine. I didn't say anything. Did I smile?

"Hey," he said, his deep voice gravelly and barely audible. He'd flicked his chin as he spoke, but his eyes were cast downward.

I couldn't think of a single thing to say. But that was good because we weren't supposed to be talking and I had to keep my focus on the blackboard.

Still, I couldn't help notice that sitting next to Evan felt different today. His body seemed larger, closer to mine. His smell was off, like something he'd eaten was rotten and emanating from his pores, trying to escape. Like he hadn't washed his T-shirt. Like he'd rolled around in something with his dog. Something about him stunk.

Ignore him, I thought. Was he ignoring me?

He wasn't taking notes, like I was. His hands rested on the

desk. No pen. No paper. He was shifting in his seat and breathing heavily. I thought about his attention deficit disorder. He caught me looking at him and I looked away fast. He sort of scoffed and pushed a hand through his thick hair. Maybe it was his hair that smelled bad. Whatever it was, I needed to forget about it. Evan clearly hated me now.

Mrs. Biggerstaff was lecturing, and half the students were taking notes. I was hyperaware of the sound of their pens scratching paper. And the occasional cough or sneeze. Bodily sounds seemed much more apparent today, everything felt exposed, everything was embarrassing. Why was Jason's cough so phlegmy? Was Tara faking that high-pitched sneeze?

At one point late in the hour, I looked at the clock. The red second hand was moving lethargically, as if forcing itself to shift just a tiny bit forward, tick by tock. *Come on, now, you can do it*, I thought. I thought of Becca and her urging me to hang in there. Tick tock tick. *Hang in there*, I told myself.

Finally, the bell rang, and Evan pushed himself away from the desk. He stomped off with his useless backpack dragging at his side.

I watched him go. Becca's shirt was working. For now, at least. But I wondered what tomorrow would be like. Would it be any easier? Would it ever feel easier?

After lunch, Becca and I were walking toward our lockers. We didn't even talk about homecoming anymore. Homecoming was irrelevant, stupid. But for everyone else, it was still the buzzy topic, and I could imagine what everyone was thinking as they filled the halls, walking past us. Traffic flowed in both directions, students walking in clusters of three or four, clutching books to their chests, holding on to backpack straps, or swinging arms blithely, weaving their bodies in and out of the stream to avoid collisions. Being high schoolers, we were somehow able to navigate crowded hallways while talking, identify cliques without looking, avoid foes without seeming to care, and still get to class on time. Multiple times a day, five days a week. We were superheroes.

As Becca and I rounded the corner past the gym, we spotted four friends of Evan's. They were walking abreast, casually filling the hall, moving toward us. All four were football players. All four were looking at me.

I lowered my head, but Becca was maintaining eye contact with the guys as they got closer, like she was daring them to keep gawking, like she was about to say, *Hey, whataya looking at?*

As they got closer, we moved to the side to make room. I felt their eyes on me as they passed, like I was a car crash they couldn't help but stare at. After they were gone, Becca whispered to me, "Sharks."

I smiled, relieved they'd passed, happy my best friend was with me. But I was worried. "They were definitely looking at me weird."

"Assholes," she said, glancing back at them.

"What were they saying, did you hear?" I asked, but I didn't really want to know.

Becca shook her head.

"It seemed they were talking about us. Do you think they were?"

"Maybe," said Becca, squeezing my hand. "Who cares?"

I lowered my voice and asked, "Were they laughing?"

"Fuck them."

I nodded tentatively then turned around to check if I could still see them, but they were far down the hallway, going in the opposite direction.

Becca pulled me back in the forward direction, toward our lockers. When we got to mine, I'd never been so glad to see a dented locker door in my entire life. I fussed with my combination and opened it. I leaned into the tall skinny space and inhaled, letting the gray metal door block me from view. This stupid locker was just a locker, but it was my space and I wished I could crawl in there and stay for the rest of the day.

Becca was haphazardly putting her notebooks away and expertly pulling other books out, then she slammed her locker and spun the combination lock. "Don't worry about it, okay? Ignore them. I'll see you after French."

I nodded, then crammed my entire backpack in there. I was hanging on to the open door, deciding what to do. When I closed the door, I turned to Becca and said, "Actually, I think I'm gonna go home early. I'm not feeling well."

"Really?" said Becca, sounding disappointed.

"I think it's a migraine," I said, scrunching up my face.

"All right," she said, hoisting her backpack. "I'll call you later?"

"Yeah. Thanks, Becks." I watched her bullet down the hall, then she punched her fist in the air, turned and gave me a smile, then disappeared into a classroom.

I sighed and walked the other way, toward the Counseling Office. It wasn't my time to work there; I just hoped I might catch Ms. Patterson.

Before I got there, however, I saw two of the same guys from before. Evan's friends. They were hanging around outside the boys' bathroom.

I gulped. Something inside me froze, but I kept walking. They stared at me again as I passed, and said something to each other, but it was unintelligible. I kept my head down, taking steps as quickly as I could. Was I imagining this? I kept moving. I knew where I wanted to be.

When I got to the Counseling Office, I closed the door behind me and breathed as if I'd escaped something. I sat in one of the guest chairs and closed my eyes.

No one was around and no one bothered me. I don't know how long I sat there, but when I heard Ms. Patterson's voice, I leapt from the chair.

"Claire, are you all right?" she said, checking her watch. "I mean, I'm happy to see you, but it's early, right?"

I felt my eyes start to water, but I fought the urge, pressed it down. My voice caught as I answered, "Yeah. No, I just needed a break. Sorry."

"It's all right," she said. "I'm glad you thought to come here."

"Thanks," I said.

"We missed you yesterday." Ms. Patterson winked. "I heard Mr. Peoples wrote you up."

"Yeah," I said. "So embarrassing."

"Hold your head high," she said. "You've learned from this, I know."

"Yeah, I guess," I said. "Actually, I'm not feeling well. I think I might have a migraine."

"Oh no," said Ms. Patterson. "What can I do? How about a glass of water?"

"Um, sure, but, um, do you think I could go home early?" I said. I wanted to say more, and I wished I could tell her about Evan's friends who were laughing at me, I thought. I wanted to ask her about stuff, but I didn't feel I could talk about any of that now. I said, "My heart's beating kinda fast. I feel like I might throw up."

"Uh-oh, okay. Let's get you to the nurse," she said, putting her arm around me.

Ms. Patterson escorted me to the front office, watching my face and slowly rubbing my back as we walked. As we passed the open classrooms, I kept my head down and shaded my eyes. I wanted to hide but I didn't know from what. In some ways, it was like déjà vu from yesterday. But it was different. Everything felt exaggerated. Exposed.

As we turned the corner, I saw the plate glass windows of the front office, with Janice at her desk. She'd probably think I was in trouble again. And there was someone else. Sitting in the waiting room. A blond woman who looked, from behind, a lot like my mom. But it couldn't be her. My mom (a) never came to my school and (b) was currently in Wisconsin.

Ms. Patterson and I walked into the front office and nodded at Janice, who was watching me with the knowing eyes and fake smile of an older woman who knew too many secrets. She pointed to the guest chair, and when I turned to look, I gasped.

"Mom," I blurted. "What are you doing here?"

She'd been sitting with her legs crossed at the ankles, reading a magazine that was really just a quarterly report from the superintendent of schools. She set down the report and stood up, dusting off her skirt. "I'm here to pick you up. Isn't that why you're out of class? Didn't they just come and get you?"

"No," I said. "They didn't tell me. And I drove today anyway."

"Oh, you drove," she said, pretending to be impressed. "Well, all right. Nice shirt, by the way."

"Thanks," I said, looking at my armor from Becks.

My mom continued, "But if they didn't come get you, then why are you here?"

I sighed and looked at Janice in case she was eavesdropping.

Ms. Patterson spoke up. "Hi, Ms. Larkin, I'm the school social worker, Kira Patterson."

"Nice to meet you," said Mom.

"Yes, same," said Ms. Patterson. "Um, so Claire here wasn't feeling well. We were just going to see the nurse."

"Yeah," I said, "I want to go home."

"Oh no. Honey, what is it?" My mom placed her palm on my forehead, like she was checking for a fever.

"Don't." I shrunk away. I didn't like the feel of her hand. "Don't touch me. I'm not a baby."

Ms. Patterson said, "Well, Claire, I'll leave you here." To Mom, she said, "It was nice to meet you."

"You as well," said Mom.

We watched Ms. Patterson walk out the door and away from view. I'd been hoping Ms. Patterson would have explained everything to the nurse. Now it was just me and Mom, and in that moment, I didn't want to explain anything to my mother.

She said, "I'm sorry you're feeling punky, Bear."

I rolled my eyes. I shifted my weight and said, "I thought you were testifying in Wisconsin."

"We were," she lowered her voice and said, "but we came home early, honey, because something's come up."

"What now?" I quipped. God, she was so annoying.

She leaned so close to me I could smell her doughy breath. She whispered, "It's your grandma, honey."

"Gamma Betty?" I said.

"The nursing home called, Bear. Apparently, they've called the immediate family, including your dad of course. They're saying we should all come now, and . . . say goodbye."

Thirty-Nine

KIRA

ON WEDNESDAY, I WENT TO THE HOSPITAL AGAIN TO SEE SEAVER. Adrian was in the room with him when I got there, just like he was last night. Apparently, a kind stranger had seen Seaver fall at the building where Adrian was doing an informational interview to get a letter of recommendation. Adrian was a go-getter. But he'd left Seaver alone and hadn't known the poor guy was in so much pain.

Anyway, last night the doctor had informed us they'd been concerned about the extent of the infection in his leg. Organic material in the wound, bacteria from the plant causing infection, fungi, possibly chemicals from the field he'd been running in. His body had been trying to isolate and reject it, but the infection was there, something about the lymph vessels. A red streak ran up his leg. They were very concerned. Luckily, the doctors were able to surgically extract the plant stalk or whatever it was, and they'd given Seaver a tetanus shot and started a full antibiotic regimen. He was going to be fine. But I'd been racked with guilt.

To apologize, I brought Seaver a box of donuts and a new Lego set. He was thrilled, but he was also somewhat loopy from his medical procedure.

Adrian looked tired. I wondered if he'd spent the night there even though he wasn't immediate family; my kids were geniuses at finding cracks in the rules to get what they needed.

"Did you sleep here?" I asked Adrian, setting down my jacket on the windowsill.

He smiled and I understood that was a sneaky yes.

I gave him a thumbs-up. To Seaver, I said, "How's our boy?"

He murmured, "I'm good."

"You've been through a lot," I said, rubbing his arm gently. "Just rest."

Adrian eyed the door, as if he wanted to speak to me out of Seaver's earshot.

"Hey, pal, Ade and I are gonna get some coffee. We'll be right back, okay?" I said.

Seaver nodded and closed his eyes. Adrian and I walked down the hall so we were a few rooms away from Seaver's. When we were out of range, I asked, "What's up?"

Adrian inhaled deeply. "First of all, Seaver's been asking if I can be his guardian."

"What a sweetheart."

"But would I be allowed to do that?" asked Adrian.

"No, Ade, you have to be twenty-one," I said, not mentioning all the other requirements that go along with guardianship.

"Okay," he said, and I detected relief.

"Plus, you're going to culinary school and maybe college. You've got a lot to think about there."

"Yeah."

"But it's okay," I said, putting my hand on his shoulder. "You're not letting him down. We have a good spot for him if Nicole doesn't come through."

"Okay," said Adrian. "I was worried."

"It's gonna be fine," I said, and I believed it. "He can live with his aunt. I really like her. In fact, we'll take Seaver over there when he's ready to leave the hospital, okay? It's all set up."

"Okay, but I know he wants to see his mom," said Adrian. "He said she's coming home soon. Is that true?"

"Sort of," I said. "She'll be moved to a sober house later this week. And if Seaver is well enough, I've set up a visit for him and Nicole, along with the aunt and me. We're going to the Mall of America."

"Oh, that's cool."

"Yeah," I said, closing the topic for the moment. Turning my focus to Adrian's own situation, I asked, "And how did your chef interview go?"

"Very well," said Adrian, unable to suppress a giant smile. "Except for this part with Seaver, it was a fantastic meeting."

"I'm so pleased," I said, squeezing his elbow.

"Yes, but if I get in, I'll be busy, and I won't be able to spend much time with him."

"That's okay! You have to do this, Ade. We'll take care of Seaver," I said. "You'll always be in his life no matter what. Whether or not it's 'legal,' right?"

"Right," he said, and there was a twinkle in his eye. After a moment, he let out a sigh.

"Was there something else?" I said, sensing there was more. I'd spotted a free coffee station and began helping myself. Adrian stood beside me and watched. The coffee machine hissed, and steam came out of the top. It was probably horrible coffee, but I was desperate. I poured myself a cup and searched for creamer. "You want one?"

He shook his head. "I need to tell you something, but I don't know what it is exactly."

"Uh-oh," I said, gesturing for him to keep walking. There had to be a sitting area nearby. We turned the corner and found a tiny room for guests. Vinyl padded chairs. A lamp. Magazines on an end table. We moved in and sat. I set down my coffee and leaned forward toward Adrian, ready to hear this.

"I think something happened," he said. "At the farm."

"Okay," I said tentatively, hoping he'd say more but dreading what it might be. Of course I had my own questions about Grady but I couldn't share that with Adrian. "Can you expand on that?"

"Last night Seaver was, sort of, talking in his sleep," said Adrian. "Like he was having nightmares."

"What did he say? Could you tell what it was about?" I took a sip.

Adrian shook his head. "But I asked him about it this morning."

"Okay," I said, bracing myself.

"He seemed afraid, Ms. Patterson. Really afraid." Adrian's eyes were welling up. "Then finally he told me."

"What is it?" I asked.

"He said something happened in the barn. Something bad."

Forty

CLAIRE

I DIDN'T WANT TO LEAVE MY CAR IN THE SCHOOL PARKING LOT. I DON'T know why. I just felt like I wanted to protect her, like she would be vulnerable there overnight without me. Kids were stupid and did stupid things. So I told Mom I would meet her at home, and we could get in the same car. Mom reluctantly agreed.

On the way to the nursing home, I made Mom tell me everything she knew, which wasn't much. I already knew Gamma was in hospice care. I knew they'd called Dad and his two siblings. I knew she was not like herself and might not recognize us. I wasn't a little kid, I kept telling my mother as she drove.

"She's on morphine, I imagine. She might be goofy or groggy. I just want you to be prepared."

"I know, I know."

"And it's okay to leave the room if you're uncomfortable."

"Mom, please."

"Just remember, it's not your grandma, really. It's a different version of her." Mom's hands were tight on the steering wheel. "And the nurse said it probably wouldn't be long."

"How long?"

"They can't say, but I'm guessing it'll be quick. That's why we're hurrying."

I checked the speedometer. Mom was driving fast.

"I just hope your father makes it," she said, giving me a pathetic look. I knew what she was thinking. She didn't want Dad to miss it, the way Mom had missed Finn's death.

"Dad'll show up," I said, hoping I was right. "He's probably already there."

But when we arrived, the nurse said we were the only ones so far. We rushed to the room, and it was true. There was Gamma, alone in a big room, under a white sheet on a metal bed. Mom walked right up to her and leaned down and talked to her. I couldn't tell if Gamma understood. She looked asleep.

I stood farther away, not sure what to do.

Mom squeezed Gamma's hand, then let it go. She came over and stood by me, stroking my hair.

"I don't want to talk to her," I said.

"You don't have to," Mom whispered.

We stood there watching for half an hour before anyone else arrived. I heard my boy cousins running down the hall. I knew it was them. Who else would bring their children to this depressing place?

"I hear Jake and Caleb," I said.

"Hmm?" said Mom, snapping to attention. "Oh. Good."

Soon enough, in walked Uncle Hal and Aunt Audrey. We made eye contact, and they came toward us with outstretched arms. Hugs all around. Then Aunt Audrey went over to be near Gamma. Uncle Hal stood beside her, his head bowed, his hand on her back.

Jake and Caleb appeared in the doorway, out of breath and squirrelly, as usual.

"Where's my dad?" said Jake.

"Shh," said my mom, pointing to Hal and Audrey.

Jake approached his parents and tugged on the back of their shirts.

Hal turned around.

"Can I have a dollar?" asked Jake, his palm outstretched for the money.

Hal shushed him and escorted him out of the room, smiling apologetically at us as they left. Out in the hallway, he gave the boys some money and some hushed instructions.

At that moment, Uncle Greg walked in. He was holding hands with a beautiful woman who looked a lot younger. I knew he'd gotten married recently, but I wasn't invited to the wedding. No kids were.

"Hello, everyone," he said. Gesturing to his wife, he said, "You remember Darcie."

She smiled and everyone greeted them. Mom kissed Gregory on the cheek and said, "Matt will be here soon."

I tugged on Mom's shirt the same way Jake had done. "When is Dad getting here?"

"Soon," she said. "Don't worry."

It was excruciating to be there without Dad. He needed to get here, and now. Mom kept saying he was on his way, but I knew Mom was nervous too.

Finally, there was a shadow at the door, blocking the light. I looked over and saw Dad.

I ran to him and buried my head in his chest. He hugged me and kissed my head, then pushed me away so he could take off his coat. He handed it to me. Or I took it. It was nice to have something to do.

The siblings all greeted one another. Jake and Caleb ran in and out of the room. Apparently, buying snacks from the vending machines was very exciting for them. Mom kept saying it was okay, because they were little kids, and they didn't know what was happening. I thought it was annoying. And disrespectful.

But the adults were preoccupied with Gamma. They stood in a half circle around her bed. Staring at her as she fidgeted in her thin nightgown under that white sheet. Gamma was making sounds, but she wasn't talking. She didn't seem to know where she was or who was with her.

Finally, I joined the half circle. I was the oldest grandchild, and I didn't know what else to do. We were just standing around Gamma, watching for death. Sometimes when she moved, the sheet would slide off and her bare skin would be exposed. Her nightgown didn't cover her whole body, so it wasn't very discreet. I thought Gamma probably wouldn't like having everyone see her like that.

"Should we put a blanket on her or something?" I asked, but no one answered. No one seemed to be in charge. No one was giving any clear directions. They'd ignored my questions. They were, like, frozen in place, gaping at Gamma. Maybe they were in shock.

What were we witnessing exactly? It didn't seem right. Seven of us and one of her. With no way to ensure Gamma knew what was happening, that she was dying. On the other hand, Gamma was the one dying, so she knew more than any of us what was going on. She was the one traveling to the other side or whatever. We living people could only guess.

I'd never been at a death before. What were the rules? There were no rules. I figured I should be quiet and keep watch. It didn't matter that Gamma's nightgown was loose and sliding up. No one minded about her old body, her messy, thin hair, not even her slurred words. None of it mattered. That stuff only mattered *before*. Now, it was important to just be there, together, and to be with Gamma, so she wouldn't die alone, I guess.

No one wanted to leave the room, even after an hour when nothing had changed. No one wanted to miss the moment of death, and it seemed like it could come any time. That definitive moment. I wanted to see it too. But why? So I could say that I was there? So I could know it was real? I wasn't sure.

Even Jake and Caleb were mesmerized. They'd calmed down and had stayed in the room, huddled around Aunt Audrey. Their eyes were glued on the old woman on the bed. I wondered if it was appropriate for them to see death—they were only nine and seven—but apparently, their parents were fine with it.

To be honest, I wasn't sure I was fine with it. Maybe I was too young for this. Had anyone thought about that? Maybe for my own protection my parents shouldn't have allowed me in the room. It might have been too upsetting.

It was like we were being let in on something many people never saw, at least not until they were older, and it was their elderly parents or maybe their spouse, thrashing around and dying on that nursing home bed under that sheet. And then I thought about Finn because most people who die are old like Gamma. But I hadn't seen my brother die. Only Dad had been there. I looked at Dad's face and wondered if he was remembering it.

I stood between my parents, and they put their arms around me. It was like we were all stronger when we stood like that. And I realized that I was watching something sacred, that I should pay attention, because this was something I'd need to know about in the future. And I had to be brave.

Once or twice a nurse came in and checked on everything, the monitor and Gamma's position. She'd nearly flailed off the bed at one point, so the nurse put up the guardrails. But that was all. The nurse didn't say anything to the family. Was this normal? How long would it take? Was she in pain?

And then something shifted and suddenly the squirming and moaning became something else. It looked like she was fighting with someone invisible on the bed, like she was pushing someone or something away from her, causing her to thrash around. She groaned again and again, saying, "No . . . no, Morris . . . no . . ."

Mom and Audrey looked at each other, as if they recognized what was going on. Even Darcie had a knowing look on her face, a look of sorrow, of rage, and Darcie had spent hardly any time at all with Gamma because she was so new to the family. The room was filled with pity, but no words were spoken.

Finally, I asked my mother what was going on. "Why is she writhing like that?"

"Shh," said Mom.

"Who is Morris?" I whispered. "Is she fighting against death?"

"Morris was her brother," whispered Mom.

Darcie must have heard us because she caught my eye and shook her head somberly. Then she leaned over to Uncle Greg and said something.

Aunt Audrey was standing at the foot of the bed. There were tears in her eyes. She touched Gamma's ankle and said, "I love you, Mom. You're okay. Everything's okay."

Uncle Greg also seemed to be crying a little. He stepped closer, lowered himself to the bed, and said, "It's all right, Mom. You're safe now, you can let go."

I watched as people took turns talking to Gamma. I whispered to Mom, "But the nurse said she can't hear us."

"It depends what you believe," said Mom, squeezing my arm and releasing. "I believe she can."

I thought about that. I decided I believed the same. I asked Mom, "Why did Uncle Greg tell Gamma she was safe?"

Compassion flashed across my mother's face and she whispered back, "Because it looks like Gamma is reliving something scary."

Suddenly my hands were hot, and my forehead started sweating. I didn't like what my mom had said, but I could see it with my own eyes. It seemed true.

Aunt Audrey might have been eavesdropping. She looked at us with a sad face. Then she moved closer and whispered, her face still sad, "Oh, you guys. It's so hard to watch."

Aunt Audrey turned away, but I looked closer at my grandmother. What was hard to watch? Something scary she was reliving, Mom had said. I looked at Darcie. Mom. Audrey. Then back at Gamma.

It looked like someone we couldn't see—her brother, Morris, apparently—was attacking her. And she was trying to squirm or run away. It was like watching her nightmare, but it was real. Something she couldn't get away from, she couldn't stop.

"Oh!" I gasped, slowly stepping backward, finally understanding.

Mom moved to my side and put her arm around my waist, containing my arms. Gently, she said, "You okay?"

I nodded, tears in my eyes. "I get it now," I said. "And I don't think we should watch this."

Mom nodded and I extracted myself from her embrace. "Hey," she said.

"I'm gonna take a break," I said. "I'll be in the hall."

"Okay," she said. "Want me to come with you?"

I shook my head. I wanted to be alone.

Forty-One

MATTHEW

FRIDAY, OCTOBER 2, 1992

IT HAD RAINED HARD THE NIGHT BEFORE MY MOTHER'S FUNERAL, A wicked storm with thunder and lightning. Claire and I stayed at the Zenith house, which felt particularly empty. We watched the storm out the back window. The tree branches were bowing and bouncing like dancers, and all the deck furniture huddled together as if cowering from something awful. Appropriate for a funeral, I thought, like the rain was urging us to join, showing us all how to grieve. But in the morning the sun was shining again as we drove in procession to the cemetery for the burial.

Audrey had made most of the arrangements. She'd chosen Hilldale Cemetery because it already held several of our ancestors on Mom's side, so it only made sense. Hilldale was also where we'd laid Finn to rest, so I certainly knew my way around the place. I remembered how, at Finn's funeral, Tammy had cried her makeup off, so when we reached our son's burial, her face was blotchy, her nose was red and raw, and her whole body was weak. For some reason, I hadn't cried at Finn's funeral. Certainly, I'd been in shock and perhaps I was stepping back, making room for Tammy's grief, trusting there'd be time for my own later on.

At Finn's funeral, people were talking to me and shaking my

hand, and I'd resorted to repeating the same phrases over and over: *Thank you for coming, Our hearts are broken, He was a sweet boy.* I would have traded places with Finn in a second. How I wished I could go back in time. I would skip the stupid pool party. I would never take my eyes off him. I would make him wear a life vest. I would have never left his side.

Over the years since, I've had flashbacks whenever I saw a pool or a lake, or children running through a hose, or a grocery store display of kids' water toys next to the charcoal and patio umbrellas. I've learned to avoid anything involving kids and water.

Now, on a cold Friday morning, I was standing at my mother's grave, not far from Finn's, and my thoughts were wandering. My tears were not only for Mom; they were for my son too, finally. It was as if I had a second chance at mourning. I watched the men lower the urn of Mom's ashes, and I remembered Finn's tiny casket. Today it was Betty's priest saying the prayers, but in my head, I heard Finn's minister. When I looked at Claire today, somehow I saw her as an eight-year-old girl, confused and lost. My mind was flashing back and forth; all the past was here in the present.

But this time, with my mother, the death we were grieving was not my fault. It wasn't my fault, and I was still devastated. Something about that allowed me to loosen my grip. Allowed me to let it go.

And I began to cry. We were forty yards from Finn's grave, eight years after his death, and I was finally crying. Hal was standing next to me, and he patted my back. "I feel for ya, Matt."

Audrey squeezed my hand and said, "You've been holding it together for a long time, big brother."

"Yeah," I sniffled, as I removed my glasses and rubbed my eyes. I choked out the words, "It still hurts."

"It always will," said Audrey, dabbing a Kleenex to her face.

"Would the family like to say anything?" The priest had finished his reading of the scripture, his brief blessing, and he was now focused on the family members. He held out an open palm, inviting any of us to speak.

We looked at one another. Audrey and I shook our heads. Gregory, as the oldest, stepped forward. "We'd just like to thank everyone. Our mother was a complicated person, but a special one."

"And now, if you would." The priest gestured to the mound of perfect black dirt.

Reluctantly, Gregory took a handful and tossed it into the grave. Then Audrey followed suit, and Hal, then Tammy, and Claire, then Darcie. Finally, I bent down and scooped up the dirt, sobbing as I stood over the grave and opened my hand, letting the soil fall, enough for both Mom and my boy.

I turned around and Claire was there. She hugged me tight, and I rested my head on hers. Soon Audrey joined us. I looked up and caught Tammy's eye. When she saw me, she shook her head. She turned and briskly walked away, toward Finn's grave. The pain of Tammy's scorn was unbearable. Her distance. Was she still blaming me? I wanted to follow her, to beg forgiveness. It was too much.

Audrey and Claire released their hug and looked up at me. I saw the sympathy in their gaze. I wanted to tell Claire that I was so glad she would outlive me, that she would toss dirt on my casket, the way it was meant to be. That children should bury their parents, not the other way around.

"I love you, Claire," I said, my voice catching.

Claire straightened up, as if alarmed. "I know, Dad."

"I'm sorry," I said, and there were probably several things I should have been sorry for. Usually it was about Finn and what I'd done wrong that day. But today, in this moment, I felt the need to clarify. "I'm sorry I haven't been . . . there for you. I haven't—"

I let out a single sob, then caught it. I squeezed my face and blinked, shook my head, trying to stop it, but it burst out and I cried, "I haven't . . . been a . . . very good . . . father."

"Oh, Matty," said Audrey, consoling me. "Come on now, that's not true."

Whether it was true or not, Claire hugged me and said, "I love you, Dad."

I hugged her and Audrey both, squeezing my eyes and sniffling. We were holding one another up. Or they were holding me.

Hal had taken the boys to the car. Gregory and Darcie were mingling with the other mourners, Betty's friends from way back, colleagues and neighbors. Darcie's long black hair blended into her dark sunglasses and hat; her entire ensemble was black, except for her bright red lipstick. We weren't sure she was going to fit in to the family just yet, but she was clinging to Gregory and nodding at everything he said, as if she shared his sentiments one hundred percent.

"Are we ready?" asked Audrey.

I nodded. Claire and I had been standing with linked arms, helping each other walk and not wanting to let go. I glanced around for Tammy, but she hadn't returned. I asked Claire, "Where's your mother?"

Claire said, "I dunno."

"Anyone seen Tammy?" I asked the straggling guests.

No one spoke. Some shook their heads.

"Her car's still there," said Audrey, pointing.

"Okay. She's here somewhere," I said, pulling my arm from the tangle with Claire's. "Go ahead and ride with Aud. I'll catch up."

Claire nodded and walked away. Everyone had been invited to a gathering at Hal and Audrey's.

I loitered a bit, hoping I'd find Tammy. I wandered among the folding chairs, the mound of dirt, the small, tented structure the priest had been standing under. I meandered past the tombstones, making my way to Finn's.

"I'm here," said Tammy, stepping out from behind a giant tombstone. Her face was red with patches of white, a stark contrast.

"What, are you trying to scare me?" I said, cupping my chest with my hand.

Tammy's tone was serious. "Can we talk?"

Forty-Two

SEAVER

SUNDAY, SEPTEMBER 27, 1992, THE NIGHT I RAN AWAY

THERE WAS A MAN IN THE BARN, BUT I DIDN'T KNOW IT. I'D BEEN AT A sleepover at Michael's and I'd just gotten home. June was going to make me a grilled cheese sandwich. I said I wanted to check on the horses first. Especially Bucky because she was my favorite and she was probably missing me.

I went to the back fence and called for the horses. Bucky came over and I gave her an apple. Then I led her to the barn and opened her stall. I switched on the faucet and put some fresh water in her trough. She was thirsty. I pulled some hay into the feeding net and stood on the bottom rung one stall over, watching while she ate.

I heard noises from behind me. Sounded like it was coming from the side room that Grady built. Sometimes Grady left a radio on in there so he could listen to the Twins games. But this wasn't a radio.

First, it was a shuffling noise. Then a man's voice. He said, "Where you been, kid?"

"Huh?" I turned around.

"Hey, Seaver," said the man, "I got some nice pictures of you."

I saw him then. He was sitting on the bed in that small room. He was sitting in the dark and I couldn't see his face. Then he stood up and walked slowly toward the door opening. He leaned on the doorway, chewing on a piece of hay. He said, "Recognize me?"

I squinted to see better. I realized who it was. The guy from summer. With the scarred head and the long thin ponytail. The Bomb Pops guy.

"You do remember me." He had a big grin. Like a clown.

I nodded.

"So this is where you live, huh? With Grady and June." He said it like it was a great accomplishment. Like I'd won some kind of award.

I wanted to get out of there. I glanced back at Bucky. She shook her head and huffed.

"You feeding them horses, huh?" he said.

"Just Bucky," I said. Just then, the horse stomped and snorted, like she knew we were talking about her. "But she's done eating," I said, unlatching her stall.

"Hey, that's my job!" he said, like he was kidding around and only pretending to be angry.

"No, it's not," I said.

"Yes, it is!" he yelled, like he was angry for real. Then he calmed down and smiled a fake smile. Slowly he said, "I work here. As a farmhand."

"Oh," I said. That was news to me. There hadn't been any farmhand living here before I went to Michael's for the weekend. "Since when?"

"Since when?" he said, imitating me. "Since when? Since Grady hired me, that's when."

"Okay." I looked at Bucky. She was just standing there, biting at her chest.

"Why you keep looking at the horse? She don't speak English, you know." He stepped closer to me and I stepped back. My back was against the stall, the one next to Bucky.

"Don't be scared," he said. "You don't gotta be scared of me."

"I'm not," I said, shaking my head. But I was scared, and I wanted to get away. I wanted Bucky and me to both leave. But the horse was just standing there. So I stood beside her.

"I wanna show you something," he said. He motioned to the room. "Come here."

I shook my head. "No thanks."

"Yeah. I wanna show you the pictures I took," he said. "Of you and your friends, remember?"

I shook my head again. I said, "I should get back."

"Come on, kid," he said, annoyed, his teeth gritted. He lurched toward me and put his hands on my shoulders. His hands were big, and he squeezed. He started pushing me toward his room.

"Hey," I said, tugging at my arm, "that hurts."

Just then, Bucky stomped and bucked a little, like she does when she first gets outside.

"Get back," the guy said to the horse, pushing at her chest.

She bobbed her head down and bit him. Not hard, just a quick bite.

"Ow!" he cried, holding his bitten hand with the other. To the horse, he said, "Get!"

She went running.

The guy turned to me, madder than before.

I started to move for the exit, but he caught me. I felt his hands on my shoulders again, then he wrapped one arm around my neck.

"Hey!" I screamed, frantic, squirming, trying to get away. I slugged my elbows into him and he grunted. I stomped on his feet and spit at him. His arm tightened around my neck. I twisted and twisted.

Whack! He fell to the ground with a thud.

I put my hands to my neck and rubbed. When I turned to see, the guy was on the floor, not moving. His head was in a clump of hay, his eyes were closed. His hat had fallen off, and there was blood near the scarred part.

I looked up. Grady was there. Holding a shovel. His face was red. He looked angrier than I'd ever seen him. He had come in through the wide door. He said, "Go, Seaver. Now!"

"But—"

"Just get the hell outta here," said Grady. The sky was wild and dark behind him.

And that's when I ran.

Forty-Three

MATTHEW

FRIDAY, OCTOBER 2, 1992

"SURE, WE CAN TALK," I SAID TO MY EX-WIFE. WE WERE ALONE IN THE cemetery; the rest of my family and friends were already on their way to Hal and Audrey's. I was standing next to a giant granite headstone that said NELSON. "Nobody can hear us."

"Ha ha," said Tammy. She'd never liked my sense of humor.

I braced myself. There were very few topics that could be important enough for her to raise them on a day like this, I thought. "What's up?"

"First of all . . ." She inhaled as if gathering courage. Her hands were facing down, fingers spread, and she bounced them gently, as if tamping down something in the air between them. "About the alimony."

"Oh, geez, Tamara, can't that wait?" I said. The last thing I wanted to talk about was money. Tammy paid me about seven hundred a month in spousal support, but every year she and Brian tried to reduce it. It was the perennial sob story. "I mean, I got your attorney's letter."

"I think it's time to phase out the alimony," she said. "Since you're getting tenure this year."

"I don't have it yet. It's not guaranteed." I walked around

the NELSON marker, dragging my fingertips along the top of it. I wasn't sure. There was the student complaint I still hadn't seen. I'd worked on a tentative response, a series of efforts including an open forum to listen to concerns, a written apology, and—thanks to Kira—a possible new initiative with the foster care community. Gloria had suggested that the vote might be delayed, especially now with my brief bereavement leave, but she had also prepared me for worse. It was possible the committee might vote no based on the mood on campus, the chatter. A loss of confidence, that kind of thing. But I wasn't going to tell Tammy about any of that.

"Yeah, but you know you'll get it," she said.

"I guess, but I mean . . . ." I really didn't want to talk about it. "I can't believe you're bringing this up now."

"I know. It's just that I hardly see you. And we've been away. And—"

"What?"

"I mean, I'm still paying the mortgage on the Zenith house. The truth is, I need that extra money, Matthew," said Tammy, stepping forward, closer to me. "I can't afford the alimony."

"Yes, you can," I said, turning away. "Brian makes plenty of money, Tam."

"This is not about Brian. This is about me." Her voice sounded pleading.

"Is it?" I turned to face her. "Because according to what I see, you are living with Brian—"

"—We're married—" she interjected.

"—Yes, I'm aware that you're married. And Brian is getting a big corporate paycheck. And you—and this is about you, apparently—you are also getting a big corporate paycheck. So according to what I see, you are getting two big corporate paychecks." I was facing her, hands on my hips.

"And I paid for your grad school," she said, her voice ringing out through the graveyard. "Don't forget about that."

I kicked at the ground, clearing away a space. Finally, I said, in a low voice, "How could I forget that? When you keep reminding me."

And it was true, of course. She'd been the breadwinner when I was in grad school and hopping between teaching jobs. Her income kept us afloat when I didn't get tenure at Macalester, which—as I'd explained many times—was all based on a minor misstep. I'd used a graduate student's summary of our research and hadn't given her proper authorial credit in a departmental colloquium. It was easily remedied, and easily contained, but the dean had had concerns. So I decided to resign. It was a low point. But Tammy's high salary gave us security.

"Here's the thing," said Tammy, finally getting to the point. "I quit my job."

"What?" I couldn't believe it. She loved her work. She was a compliance genius, a master at corporate ethics training. She was a lion tamer.

"This is confidential," she said. "So please don't say anything. But I'm opening my own consulting business."

This was something we'd talked about when we were married. I always said she should go into business for herself. But Tammy had been reluctant to leave the safety of the corporate infrastructure. She didn't want to give up the benefits. Insurance, office space, support staff. I told her all that could be replicated as a freelancer. She'd been skeptical. Risk averse. Apparently now she'd come around to my way of thinking. Probably had something to do with Brian.

"Wow. Congrats."

"Thanks," she said.

"Did Brian convince you to take the leap?" I said, adding, "I know I never could."

She made a face. Had I crossed the line? Then she admitted, "I mean, it's been difficult for Brian to truly advance as a senior attorney at Bodewell Industries when, you know, he's married to the VP of Compliance."

"Uh-huh," I said, because I'd been right: this was about Brian.

"And Bodewell could be my first consulting client, so it's a win-win-win."

"That's great, I guess." I bent to pick up a crusty dead leaf. I stood up and studied it, twisting the stem between my finger and thumb.

"There's something else," said Tammy.

"What is it?" I moaned. "I have to get to Hal and Audrey's at some point."

"The thing is, Bodewell is in discussions with a major corporation, and if the merger goes through, they'll be headquartered in Milwaukee and . . . well, they'd want Brian to be there, so . . . we'd be moving."

"To Wisconsin?" My eyes were wide.

She nodded. "It wouldn't be until next year."

I grimaced and shook my head. I leaned on NELSON and took a deep breath. "What about Claire? You're just gonna take her to Wisconsin?"

Tammy shook her head. There were tears in her eyes. "No, not necessarily."

"So you're gonna just, what, let her live alone?"

"No, Matthew. She could live with you," said Tammy, reaching in her purse.

I scoffed again. "In Northwood? She wouldn't want that."

"You could live in the Cities, at Zenith."

"What? I mean, I don't know." I felt like the cemetery had turned into a maze, a house of mirrors, and I was getting dizzy. "And anyway, what about you? Wouldn't you miss her? Don't you care that she needs you?"

"I'll visit. It's only five hours."

Five hours? That sounded like a lot to me. "I don't understand."

Tammy stepped closer. She put her hand on my arm. Softly, she said, "Matthew, I need to move on. Brian and I need a fresh start. I need a fresh start. . . . Everything here reminds me of, you know, the past."

"The past? You mean Finn?" I pulled my arm away from her, as if it were contagious, this agony, as if she might infect me with her need to flee. I said, "Everything *should* remind you of him. We need to remember. To honor him."

"I know that," she said with a tone of indignation.

"It's the least we can do." My voice was cracking. "That's the least . . . *I* can do."

"Matthew," she said, taking hold of me again. "Don't do this."

I was looking at the ground. Where Finn was. And now my mother too. Or maybe they were both somewhere else.

"Listen," said Tammy, "hey, listen."

"What?" I said, turning away, tears on my face. I didn't want to hear anything more. I wanted to get myself together and go to be with my sister and brother. And Claire.

"Matty, I need to apologize," said Tammy, using my nickname again for the first time in years. She handed me a tissue.

"No, you don't," I said, wearily. "Apologize for what?"

"For the way I've been blaming you," she said, ". . . all these years . . . for Finn's death."

"Tammy, come on," I said, wanting this to stop.

"I blamed you," she cried.

"Yeah, well, you should blame me because I was the one who took our son to a pool party. I was the one who was there. I was the one who wasn't . . . watching him . . ." I said, choking back the sobs.

"No. Listen to me." Tammy took me by the shoulders, she moved her hands to my cheeks. "Listen."

My arms went limp. I looked down at her, suddenly so sad and meek, this woman who was, after all, the mother of my children. Her face was pleading with me. My eyes were all water.

She said, "I'm sorry that I've been holding this over you."

I shook my head and she let me go. The leaves were brown and broken. The grass was matted and cold.

She said, "Because I'm at fault too."

I wiped my face with both hands. I walked a couple steps away as if the air would be easier to breathe over there.

"For everything." Tammy followed me. "For our marriage falling apart, okay?"

I looked at her.

She continued, "And for Finn too."

I shook my head.

"No, I am," she said. "It wasn't only you."

"Come on, Tam," I said, begging her. "I don't want to go over this again."

But she wouldn't stop. She asked, "Do you know the reason the hotel couldn't reach me that day?"

I furrowed my eyebrows. Whatever she was about to say, I didn't want to hear it. I mumbled, "You were at the conference. You were giving a presentation."

"No," said Tammy. "I wasn't at that conference."

I inhaled, bracing.

"Matthew," she said. "I was with Brian."

"What?" My head was suddenly empty, dizzy with despair.

Crying, Tammy said, "I was with Brian on the day our son died."

"No, that can't be," I said. My stomach lurched. "You said you'd ended it."

"I did," she cried. "But then it started again."

"No," I moaned.

"I was with him that weekend," she sobbed. "That's why I didn't go to the pool party. That's why you were there alone. That's why . . ."

I was dazed. I walked in circles, grasping at tombstones to keep my balance. I didn't want to look at her. I didn't want to be near her. I said, "I can't even believe this."

"I'm sorry," she said, following me.

"We just buried my mom," I said. This was too much.

"I know."

"Right over there." I pointed twenty yards away, to the hole in the ground, the pile of dirt, the priest's table. "And you tell me this now? *Why?*"

"I shouldn't have," she said. "I'm sorry."

"You just needed to get this off your chest?" I said. I started pacing. "So you could move on. To *Wisconsin*?!"

"Matty," said Tammy.

"Don't call me that," I said angrily.

She held her tongue. After a beat, she explained, "Brian's family is in Milwaukee. He wants to be closer to them. He wants to, um . . . try for another child."

That was the final punch. I bent over, unable to stand or speak, feeling I might vomit. When I regained my composure, I straightened. I held out my hands, keeping her away from me. I wanted my distance from her. Shaking my head, I said, "Okay, okay. I get it."

"Please forgive me," she said.

I scoffed. "Forgive you? Why should I forgive you? I've been apologizing for eight years, and you've never forgiven me."

"I know," she said.

I started walking to my car, stomping on leaves, kicking them out of my way. "You've been torturing me with this. Letting me suffer."

"I forgive you, Matthew. I forgave you a long time ago. It wasn't your fault."

"And now you're gonna just start over." I stopped moving and she nearly crashed into me.

"It's not like that."

"You know what?" I said, waving my hands in the air as if wiping it all away. "I'm gonna pretend we never had this conversation."

"I'm sorry," said Tammy, tears running down her face.

"No," I said. "And please don't come to Hal and Audrey's."

She nodded. She was frozen in place, standing between two graves.

I arrived at my car, then turned around and shouted, "You know what else? You can't stop the alimony without my approval. It's in the final decree . . . that you got, after spending Claire's college fund . . . to pay your damned divorce attorney."

She stood there, taking it.

"And I won't agree to it," I said. "You know why?"

She shook her head.

"Because I've been saving those payments. For Claire to go to college. So you can take your lawyer's letter and shove it!" I opened the car door and got in.

"Matthew, please!" Tammy fell to her knees, sobbing.

I slammed the door and took off. I didn't look back. When I left the cemetery, I was driving fast.

Forty-Four

CLAIRE

SATURDAY, OCTOBER 3, 1992

AFTER MY GRANDMA'S FUNERAL, I SPENT THE WHOLE WEEKEND WITH my dad at the Zenith house. People brought us food and cards and flowers. I'd never seen my dad be so social. He seemed really happy to see his old friends. And of course, my aunts and uncles and cousins were there. It was chaos. We kept running out of decaf and I kept having to make more. Dad made a giant batch of wild rice soup. Jake and Caleb were dashing around in the backyard like puppies. They were making friends with neighborhood kids that I hadn't even met yet.

Ms. Patterson came by on Saturday. She brought a book about grief and an empty journal. She said writing was a good way to express feelings, especially about hard things. Dad put all the gifts on the entry table, except perishables, which went in the fridge. There were flowers and framed photos of Betty everywhere, the ones from the funeral. We tried to get other people to take the flowers, but they wouldn't. The ceremony was very sad, but I didn't cry. I felt very self-conscious about it. I wished I could have cried, but I couldn't.

I've been on bereavement leave from school. They give you three days off when a close relative dies. Ms. Patterson was helping me keep track of my homework and whatever else I had to make up. To be honest, I wasn't looking forward to going back. But also, in some ways I was glad Gamma died when she did, because it gave me more time away from biology class and Mrs. Biggerstaff and Evan.

Ms. Patterson had given me her home phone and told me it was okay to call her anytime. She also said she could meet me somewhere if I needed a break or wanted to talk.

Saturday was the homecoming dance. I almost forgot, but then I remembered. Dad and I were cleaning up after dinner. Everyone had been there all day but then they went home and it was just us. He asked if I wanted to watch TV, but I didn't know what to watch. He started reading and I was pacing around. Restless. Finally, I stood in front of him. He was sitting in his chair. I asked why Mom hadn't come by, and he said she was busy.

"That's such a lie," I said.

"No, it's not," he said.

"You don't want her here," I said. "Just say it."

"Well, I mean, it's complicated."

"It's complicated? She's my mother. And Finn's mother. Why do you hate her so much?"

"Claire, I don't hate your mother."'

"I can tell when you're lying. I'm not stupid."

"Where is all this coming from? We've been having such a lovely time. Not lovely, but close. I thought we were close."

"Dad. We're not close," I said.

"Stop it now, please," he said. He had that begging look on his face. I almost felt sorry for him.

"We're not, Dad. You don't know anything about me."

"I know everything about you. I'm your father," he said. "I may have to catch up with some of the more recent developments, but I—"

"You haven't come to a single volleyball game," I said, feeling the list coming on. "You don't care about meteorology—"

"—Yes, I do—"

"—You couldn't be bothered to teach me how to drive, so Mom had to. And Brian," I said, my voice catching.

"I'm sorry," he said.

"You never visited me at Bageletta. Did you even know I worked at Bageletta, Dad?"

"Yes, you told me all about it," he said.

"No, I haven't," I said. Not everything. I wished I could tell him everything. My voice started getting thin. I said, "And every Sunday, you rush the hell out of here, like, as fast as you can go."

"You know why, Bear," he said. "It's the—"

"Don't say it!" I didn't want to hear about tenure, not this weekend. I was holding my finger up to his face, trying to stop him from saying the *T* word. "I don't need to hear you explain it again. I know all about it."

"Well, that's the truth," he said, clenching his jaw.

"It seems like you want to get away from me, Dad," I said, choking back tears. I really didn't want to cry. "Like you can't . . . stand . . . being with me . . . Like, our family basically fell apart and then you just decided to . . . move on."

"What?!" He truly seemed confused and that made me angry. He was supposed to be smart.

But I was on a roll. Finally, I said, "Is it Finn? Is that why you hate it up here? Because we remind you of Finn? Do you wish I was Finn? Is that why you hate me?"

"I don't hate you, Claire. I love you," he said. "I'm not perfect, but I love you. I cherish you."

I stared hard at him. Finally, I said it. I said, "I think you wish that Finn had lived and that I'd been the one who drowned."

He stood up. "No, stop it."

But I couldn't stop. Stuff was rolling out of me, and it was like I had no control over it. An ocean, a gush. "Is it because I'm a girl?"

"What? No, of course not!" He moved toward me.

I moved away. "And you don't know how to handle a daughter? You wish you had a son? Would a son be more fun for you? Or easier? Easier to understand?"

"No. Honey," he said, "what on earth would give you that idea?"

I didn't know. I didn't know what to say, so I stopped. I paused. I breathed. And I sat down. I was tired. "We never talk about it," I said.

"About Finn?" He sat down next to me.

"Yes. About how he died. About Mom and Brian. It's all just fake pretend we get along and fake pretend we're over it," I said. "But I can tell you're not over it."

He looked at his shoes. "No, I guess I'm not."

"Right," I said, relieved. "That's all I'm asking."

"Okay," he said. "I can admit it. I guess I didn't want to bring sadness into our time together."

We were just sitting on the sofa and thinking about things. I didn't know if I should bring it up or not, but then I said, "And why didn't anyone talk about Gamma Betty?"

"What do you mean? The past few days we've been talking nonstop about her, about her life, the kind of woman she was, her teaching career, everything," said Dad.

"No," I said. "No one talked about the way she died."

"What?" He seemed mystified. Like he was trying to keep up with me but couldn't. "She had cancer with complications of pneumonia. It was in the paper. The donations went to the American Cancer Society."

I stood up. "I'm talking about the way she looked when she died. What was happening to her. What happened to her, Dad?"

"I don't know what you mean."

"See, you're lying again. You don't think I can handle it, but I can, Dad. I can handle more than you think."

He was quiet. He looked at me. "You're right," he said.

I relaxed and took a deep breath. "Thank you."

"It was hard to watch that, Claire," he said gently. He was leaning forward, his hands pressed together like he was praying. He let them drop between his knees. I was afraid he was going to cry. "It was very hard to watch."

I scooted closer to Dad. I said, "Yeah, I mean, yeah, it was."

He let his head fall into his hand, and he was shaking his head. "You're an amazing person, Claire. I hope you know that."

I felt a sting behind my eyes, the thorn of his love, his recognizing me, my need to hear those words. To be sitting and talking like this. I leaned over and rubbed his back. He reached over and rubbed mine, and we laughed because our arms were kind of tangled.

"I just wish people would have talked about it more."

"Yeah," said Dad. "Maybe they're talking about it privately. Maybe it was too private to discuss in a group."

"Yeah," I said, exhaling again. The back rubs were over. I leaned back on the couch and let my whole body drape. I was staring at the ceiling.

After a bit, Dad said, "I'm sorry I haven't come to your volleyball games."

"That's okay."

"No, it isn't," he said. "And I'd like to."

I smiled at the ceiling.

"Are there any more coming up?"

"Tons," I said, sitting up. "The season just started."

"Good," he said.

We sat thinking about that for a while.

Finally, I said, "Did you know that tonight is actually the homecoming dance?"

He said, "Uh, I think you'll probably not be surprised to hear that I did not know that, no. I was not aware."

"Yeah." I laughed because my dad talked funny sometimes, and I had to laugh.

"Is the dance a big deal?" he asked. "To you, I mean?"

"No," I said, but I wasn't really sure. "I wasn't planning to go or anything, I mean no one asked me and I didn't ask anyone or want to go. But, I mean, I was thinking about going with my friends or whatever, but Becca is going with a senior so she'll be there but—"

"—Well, then, why don't you go?" he said.

"What? I mean, no. We just had the funeral and, I mean, I haven't been at school." I didn't know how I felt. Finally, I said, "Besides, it probably already started. I don't know, what time is it?"

"Seven," he said, looking at his watch. "What time does it start?"

"Like eight, I think," I said. "But I mean, I don't have anything to wear, really."

"You have the dress from your mother's wedding? Would that work?"

"I mean, maybe, but it's at Mom and Brian's, I think."

"Okay, we could go get it," he said. "Or does it have to be a dress?"

"I mean, no, probably." I didn't know how I felt about this idea. I wanted to go, but I didn't want to go.

"Well, if you ask me," said my dad, "high school is but a fleeting experience and there are certain moments that only occur during these short years—"

"—Okay, Dad," I said, because I didn't want to hear a lecture about cultural rites of passage and if I was gonna find something to wear, I'd have to hurry.

I stood up and he stood up and hugged me. We hugged for a longish time, longer than a normal goodbye hug.

"Can you drive me?" I asked when the hug was over. "Because Betty—I mean, my car—is at Mom's." It felt weird to call my car Betty now that Gamma had died.

"That's okay, you can call it Betty," said Dad. "I kind of like it. I like hearing her name."

I mumbled, "We should have done that with Finn."

He glanced at me, and we exchanged a smile. He said, "You're right."

"Yeah, I know," I said, before running upstairs. I didn't know what I was doing. So last-minute. Who would be there? Becca, for sure. I would find her, and everything would be all right. I thought about wearing the shirt she gave me and some fancy pants. But then I found the perfect outfit.

When I came downstairs, my dad was in the kitchen. He was looking through the fridge.

"Whataya think?" I said, twirling. I was wearing a maxi skirt with chunky black shoes, a sleeveless summer top, and a jean jacket. I'd put on a bit of makeup, but not much. I thought I looked okay.

He said, "Beautiful."

"Thanks," I said. "What are you looking for in the fridge?"

"I thought we had some chocolate milk."

"Aww," I said, because that was our father-daughter drink back from the old days. After he'd pick me up from school, we'd stop at the gas station mini-mart and buy two containers of chocolate milk: a pint for me and a quart for dad. Sometimes, when the store only sold chocolate milk in quart-size containers, we'd each get a quart. Then we'd sit in the car and drink them. Those were some of my most special memories of me and Dad from back in the day. I said, "I think we ran out. Caleb, probably?"

"I see," said Dad, disappointed. "Maybe I'll pick some up after I drop you off. You ready?"

"I guess," I said. It was seven forty-five. "Can I have thirty dollars?"

"Let me see if I have the cash," he said, digging in his wallet. "Tickets are expensive."

"Yeah," I said, holding out my hand.

He gave me three ten-dollar bills and I tucked them in my shoe.

In the car, I flipped down the mirror and looked at myself. Dad had said I looked grown-up and I wanted to know what he meant.

The dance was being held in a grand ballroom of a hotel next to the Y. As we entered the parking lot, I saw other parents dropping off their kids. The ballroom had its own entrance, and I instructed Dad to pull up near that. I saw kids roaming around, in and out of the double doors. They'd put down a red carpet and there were sparkly lights just inside the lobby.

"Okay," I said, just before getting out. "Wish me luck."

"You'll be fine. Just have fun. I'll pick you up when?"

"Ten?" I said. The dance ended at midnight, but I knew I didn't want to stay long.

"Roger that," said Dad, adding, "I'll wait here for a bit."

"No, you can go," I said.

"Okay," he said. "Proud of you."

I got out and walked into the lobby. I was constantly glancing around to see if I knew anyone. I saw some girls from my French class, so I joined them. They complimented me on my outfit, and I felt happy. Together, we went to the ticket table and stood in line. I reached into my shoe and pulled out the cash.

"Tickets," said one of the two students sitting at a folding table that had been draped with a white cloth. "Tickets."

The girls from French handed over their tickets, oversize-purple paper tickets with the name of our school and our logo and the theme of the dance professionally printed on them. There was a perforated edge where the bored ticket taker tore off the end and then handed them back to my friends.

"Ticket?" they said to me.

I handed them the thirty dollars. "One, please," I said.

"No, where's your ticket?" said the first student volunteer.

"Yeah, we're not selling tickets at the door," said the other student volunteer.

They were members of the planning committee that must have been staffing the event. These two were dressed for the party and had probably volunteered for an early shift because they planned to spike the punch after a while. Just a guess.

"We only take tickets," said the first one.

"We can't take your money or whatever. It was on the poster," said the other.

"Yeah, and, like, it was in the reminders that were sent home," said the first one, her voice trailing off like she was losing energy with this.

"Oh, I . . . I didn't know . . ." I said, scanning for my French-class friends. They were hovering near the next set of doors, ready to push through into the party. They had looks on their faces like they felt really bad about it but they really wanted to get going.

"Do you need us to stay?" one of the girls from French class asked me.

"No, I'm . . . I'm good," I said, glancing out at the parking lot. I didn't want anyone to see me in this situation. I wanted to disappear.

The first ticket taker was still holding my ten-dollar bills in her limp, uncaring hands, waiting for me to take them back. The bills looked so pathetic and unwanted, which was exactly how I felt. I grabbed the money and turned around. I busted through the doors and back out to the parking lot, tears starting to fall, sobs rising in my throat. I searched for my dad, but I'd told him not to wait. Suddenly, there was my dad! Waving at me from his car on the far side of the lot. I picked up my skirt and clunkily ran across the pavement toward him. I let myself cry as I ran to his car and got in.

He rubbed my back as I reached for the seat belt. I said, "Just go."

He put the car in gear and took us out of there.

"Well, that was a bad idea," I said.

"I'm sorry," he said. "What happened?"

I was crying so much I felt like I couldn't stop, and I wondered, later after I'd calmed down, if I'd been making up for the noncrying at the funeral. Maybe I'd had all these tears stored up in my brain or my neck or wherever the source of tears was, and the switch got flipped and all the tears got released at once. I couldn't speak and I didn't know what to say; it just felt so good to have my dad there when I was looking for him. After I got in the car, Dad just drove calmly and slowly through town, stopping at yellow lights and slowly proceeding through green ones.

After a while, I told him about the ticket situation.

He said something I don't remember.

Then, finally, he said, "Hey. Wanna get some chocolate milk?"

And I felt like I'd never wanted anything so badly before in my entire life and I said, "Yes, please!"

Forty-Five

KIRA

SUNDAY, OCTOBER 4, 1992

WHEN I ARRIVED AT THE MALL OF AMERICA ON SUNDAY EVENING, Jen and Seaver were already seated at a table in the food court on the fourth level. I approached their table with a big smile, waving hello.

"Hi, guys," I said, genuinely happy to see them.

Jen stood up and greeted me.

"Hi," said Seaver, glancing up from his book.

"Whatcha reading?" I asked.

He held it up, showing me the cover.

"Ooh. *Goosebumps*?" I said. "Sounds fun."

"He loves this book," said Jen, sitting down again and lightly touching Seaver's back.

Seaver read me the full title. Looking at the front cover, he said, "*Welcome to Dead House*."

"Scary," I said, my eyes wide. I tousled Seaver's hair. "How you doing, sport?"

"Fine," he said, his head back in the book.

To Jen, I said, "How are you? How's everything?"

"All's good. Just waiting on Nic," said Jen, sitting up straight and peering around the food court.

"This place is huge," I said, hoping we'd see Seaver's mom appear soon. It had taken me a few minutes to find the food court area, which was past the movie theater and overlooking an indoor amusement park.

"Yeah, I hope Nic's not lost," said Jen, chuckling, but also possibly not joking.

"She'll find us," said Seaver, still reading.

"Is this your first time here?" Jen asked me.

"To the Mall of America? Yes," I said, adding, "I don't get out much."

"Oh come on," said Jen. "I was teasing. It just opened a few weeks ago."

I smiled. To Seaver, I said, "So, what's new? How's your leg? How's school?"

Jen looked at Seaver as if he might speak, but he kept reading. Jen answered for him, "Everything seems fine."

"Good," I said. "That's what we like to hear."

Suddenly I remembered the Rubik's Cube Matthew had returned to me. I dug in my purse and proudly held it up like I'd caught a baseball. To Seaver, I said, "Hey, look what I've got."

He glanced up, saw the Cube, and grabbed it. The thing disappeared into his lap.

"What do you say, Seaver?" said Jen, reminding him of his manners.

"Thanks," he grumbled.

"It's fine," I said to Jen. I didn't need thanks. I knew Seaver was happy to have his beloved Rubik's Cube back again.

Jen looked at her watch. Nicole was only a few minutes late. "Oh! Here she comes," said Jen, spotting her sister in the oncoming crowd. Nicole was recognizable from a distance because of her bright pink hair and rocker-style attire.

Her eyes widened when she spotted us, and she picked up the

pace. Making a beeline to Seaver, she cooed, "There's my baby. Hi there, Doodle Head."

He dropped his book and stood up. She hugged him and covered his head in kisses.

"You look like Cyndi Lauper," said Jen, standing to greet her sister.

"Thanks," said Nicole, hugging Jen briefly. Turning to me, she said, "Hey, Kira. How're you?"

"I'm great," I said. "It's good to see you."

"This place is nuts, huh? Did you see that giant Snoopy?" said Nicole. To Seaver, she said, "Hey, babe, we should go to the Lego place. You still like Legos, right?"

"Yeah," he said, glancing at me quickly. I looked away, smiling.

"And the roller coaster?" said Nicole. She was acting like she'd forgotten we had planned to see a movie today.

"Sure." Seaver returned to his seat. He picked up his book, like it was a safe place to be, and turned to the page where he'd left off.

"God. He loves that book, huh?" said Nicole, tilting her head, studying her son.

"I know." Jen beamed.

"Christ. Maybe I should read it," said Nicole.

Seaver flashed her a look.

"Just kidding," she said.

"So, Nicole," I said. "Any updates on the job front?"

"Jesus. You get straight to business, don't you?" said Nicole.

"Might as well." I shrugged. *The sooner the better*, I thought. "But I'm curious. How's it going?"

"It's going," said Nicole. "I've been applying places. Just waiting for the phone to ring."

"Okay. Like where, what are some of the places?" I asked. "Did you try that company I mentioned?"

"The manufacturing plant? No, not yet," said Nicole, not seeming particularly excited about that opportunity. To Jen, she said, "Should we eat or what? I know we can't drink."

"Yes," said her sister, smiling nervously. "If we're gonna catch that movie, we'd better eat."

Seaver lowered his book and perked up. "I want pizza."

"Pizza, huh?" said Nicole, looking around. "Okay, Doodle, you got it. They must have pizza here. They got everything else."

We were surveying the assortment of fast-food restaurants as if whoever found the pizza place first would win a prize.

"There!" Nicole pointed to a spot and started walking toward it. Seaver got up and followed her.

"Should I wait here? Save the table?" Jen asked me.

"You go with them. I'll stay here. Just get me a slice of whatever. Meat," I said. "No onions."

"Okay." Jen was smiling as she ran to catch up to her sister and nephew.

As I sat, I watched the people flowing past. Seaver's book was on the table. I picked it up and flipped around the pages, trying to get a feel for it. Eventually I set it down. Other families arrived, their trays overflowing with fries, their chairs pushing in and out from the tables. Kids were hollering. Parents were wiping things up. I peered through the crowd, watching for Nicole's pink head.

They were taking forever. Was the line that long?

Finally, it was Seaver who emerged, running toward me with a tray in his hands and a straw in his mouth; he was heading right for me. His feet slapped the floor loudly, and it occurred to me that Seaver was in that awkward growth phase when the feet grow faster than the body, and it was like he was wearing clown shoes.

"There you are," I said as he flopped down in his seat, his tray clattering on the table. He didn't answer, just glanced at me as he bit into a huge slice of pepperoni pizza. "Looks yummy."

He pulled his chin away from his plate in an attempt to break off the gooey cheese.

"Are those new shoes?" I asked, peering under the table. They looked new. And big.

"Nikes," he said, smiling wide, his open mouth full of pizza. He tipped his head up as if trying to keep the food in while he talked. "Jeff got them for me."

"Jeff, huh? How nice," I said. It had only been a few days, but the previously skeptical Jeff was apparently rising to the occasion.

Soon the sisters arrived, smiling and chatting. "Sorry it took so long."

"No problem," I said, putting my hand on my chest, relieved.

Nicole set down her tray, then dispersed the slices and drinks for the three grown-ups. Seaver was practically done with his.

We were quiet for a while as we ate; just like at every meal, there was that period of ten seconds or so when no one says a thing, and everyone is happy because they're eating. And they're together.

After a few minutes, Nicole reached in her purse and pulled out a pack of cigarettes. She held them in the air, waving them at Seaver, as if this was her sign for *I'm gonna go and smoke*. He nodded, grabbed another piece, and kept chewing.

The sound of Nicole's chair screeching out from the table gave me a chill. I said, casually, "Where're you going, Nic?"

"Nic? You never call me that," she said to me. Not in a friendly way.

"Sorry," I said. "Nicole."

"Gonna smoke," said Nicole, pointing to the exit, like it was so obvious, so not a big deal.

"Oh, okay," I said. "What about the movie? Aren't you all trying to catch the next showing?"

"I'll be quick," said Nicole.

Jen gave me a look. "It's fine. We'll wait here."

Nicole shuffled away, flashing them the peace sign, a cigarette already dangling from her lips.

I checked on Seaver, as if he might be upset. He was eating Nicole's leftovers. I asked, "Are you sure she was done?"

He just looked at me. "She never eats after she smokes."

"Oh," I said, nodding.

"He's right," said Jen.

And we sat there waiting. And waiting. I had a terrible feeling.

Finally, about twenty minutes later, I spotted her sauntering toward us. In no hurry.

I stood when I saw her, hoping it would encourage her to speed it up.

"There she is," I said. "Your mom's coming."

As Nicole got closer, I caught a whiff of the smoke on her. The scent triggered memories, the way certain smells do; perhaps it was the brand of cigarette, or the combination with pizza crusts, but it sent me on a time travel, to past lives, previous homes, former families.

I waited for Nicole to sit, but she never did. I studied her face, her glassy eyes.

She stood there with her hand on her hip and delivered the news I'd been dreading. "Guys," she said. "I'm sorry but I can't go to the movie with you."

"Oh," said Jen, disappointed but not terribly surprised. It was as if we all should have known this was coming.

Seaver didn't react at all.

"Yeah, I know, it's too bad," said Nicole. "But I'll see you soon, Doodle, okay? Promise."

Seaver barely moved his chin in acknowledgment.

I asked Jen, "Do you guys have any plans next weekend? Maybe we can arrange another visit."

"Yeah," said Jen, "we're free."

"We'll see," said Nicole. "Not sure."

I looked at Seaver. He seemed to be barely tolerating this conversation. He seemed checked out.

"Okay, guys. I'll see you," said Nicole. She slung her purple purse onto her shoulder, then opened her arms. "Come here, baby. Can I get a hug?"

Seaver stood up and moved slowly toward her. When he was close enough, he leaned in, arms at his sides, and let himself be hugged, like he was surrendering to a Venus flytrap.

She wrapped her arms around him and swiveled a bit, side to side, saying, "My boy, my boy."

Jen got up and started picking up the dirty paper plates and napkins, dutifully putting trays away.

Nicole kept Seaver close, still swaying. She kissed the top of his head. Then she pulled away and looked at him. "I swear you're taller every time I see you."

He shrugged. "I guess."

They were inches apart, facing each other. She held his chin in her hand. She said, "I gotta go now, okay, baby?"

He nodded, looking up, never losing eye contact with her. There seemed to be a silent conversation going on between them. Finally, she said, "Okay. See ya."

He nodded, his eyes still locked on her.

She kissed his head quickly, like a punctuation mark. Then she swirled away and began to blend into the crowd, if that were truly possible. And we simply watched her walk her loopy walk, and then she turned briefly and blew a kiss. And she was gone.

Jen was holding Seaver's book and his jacket, her purse and her remaining Diet Coke. She took a sip but it was only ice. Another slurp. She shook the cup and the ice rattled.

Seaver asked Jen, "Can I have my book?"

"Of course," said Jen, giving it to him, as if she'd forgotten it was in her hands. "Hey, Seaver, do you still wanna see the movie?"

"Yeah," he said flatly.

"Let's do it," said Jen, as if trying to stir up enthusiasm.

"Have fun, you two," I said.

I smiled and watched them walk to the movie theater on the other end of the food court. Jen was carrying everything and Seaver was walking beside her. They were one or two feet apart. In the last few seconds before they disappeared from view, Jen reached out to Seaver, and he stepped closer and allowed her to put her arm around him. Jen was saying something to him, and he was looking up at her.

Forty-Six

KIRA

MONDAY, OCTOBER 5, 1992

ON MONDAY, CLAIRE CAME TO SEE ME, JUST AS SHE HAD PROMISED she would. She wasn't going to classes yet, but I wanted her to come in for a chat. She agreed. And she showed up. Early.

But as usual, I was running late. I hustled in the door to the Counseling Office and there she was, waiting in the guest chair.

"Sorry!" I said, waving her to follow me into my office. "It's so funny seeing you in the guest chair instead of behind the desk."

"Yeah," she said, getting up and carrying her jacket. "I hope you let me have my job back."

"Oh, well, that's not up to me," I said, unlocking my office door. "But if it were, I guess I would want to know about why you felt the need to go looking in the files in the first place. What was going on there?"

"Yeah, I'm pretty embarrassed," she said. "It's hard to explain."

"We can talk about it another time, if you like, when you're back." Inside my office, I set down my purse and briefcase and travel coffee mug. I hung my coat on the tree. I closed the door.

"No, I guess I want to talk about it now," she said.

"Okay, if you're sure. I know you've been through a lot with your grandma dying."

"Yeah," she said, starting to cry. "About that."

"Ohhh," I said, feeling sorry for her. I was surprised her tears had come so quickly.

"You have a way of talking that makes people sad, you know that?" she said, teasing me while also crying.

"I'll take that as a compliment," I said, coming around to sit next to her. I rubbed her back and listened. She started slowly, tentatively, and I listened.

I listened as Claire unloaded her burden. At first, her words were like a song, high and plaintive, and then they were an avalanche. She poured it all out, everything, about her grandma, her brother, her dad. She talked about school, about her shame at being punished, about biology class, and she got stuck there and sobbed.

I knew there was something more, and I was putting the pieces of her story together.

After a while, I asked, "Is this about Evan?"

She nodded, but then asked, "How did you know?"

"Because you were looking in his file," I said gently. "And also from what Adrian said."

"What did Adrian say?" she asked, sounding panicky.

I reassured her, "No, it was when you were there. Remember? We were all standing in the waiting area?" I pointed to the spot near the front desk where Adrian had been standing. "You said you worked together and Adrian mentioned the bagel-throwing thing."

"Oh yeah," said Claire, clearly relieved.

"Throwing bagels at you wasn't very nice," I said. "Sounds terrible. And confusing from a boy you maybe liked?"

"It was," Claire was nodding, holding back sobs.

It broke my heart, this knowing. And I thought about the number of times I'd had this conversation with a girlfriend or a student or a family on my caseload . . . it was a lot. And I wished I could share that with Claire. But of course, there was only so far I could go.

"Claire, I work with a lot of kids and I can tell you that whatever you're struggling with, you are not alone, okay? There are other kids out there struggling with the same or similar things."

"Okay," said Claire through tears.

"And it helps to talk about it. It helps."

Claire was wiping her eyes.

After a beat, I said, "So I want to suggest two things, okay, Claire?"

"Okay." She took a deep breath.

"Number one, I want to suggest for you to see a counselor, a therapist that I can refer you to, who is outside of the school, a psychologist, that you can talk to about all the things you are feeling, not just about school or your grandma or Evan, but about everything that's going on in your heart, in your head, all the things you're worrying and wondering about. And this person can help you. When you're ready. To talk about it."

She gazed at me like she was taking that all in. Finally, she said, "Okay. What's the other thing?"

"The other thing is for our school."

"What is it?" Claire's eyes looked somewhat panicked.

I considered how to start this. I said, "You know how we teach kids about sex education and preventing pregnancy, STDs, etc.?"

"Yeah," said Claire, leaning away, as if highly suspicious.

"Well, I think we should be teaching kids about how to prevent other things, including assault. Like what happened with your grandmother. So kids can know what it is, what it isn't. So we can help kids not get hurt. And not do the hurting. What to do about it, how to get help. You know what I'm saying?"

She nodded. "Like training?"

"Yes, exactly," I said. "Like your mother does. But with schools, not corporations."

Claire looked horrified. "Okay, but . . . I mean, what does that have to do with me?"

"Oh, you wouldn't be involved. I just thought I'd run the idea by you. What do you think?"

She shook her head, like she was trying to shake the whole topic out of her mind. "Fine, I guess."

"Good." I waited a beat. "And can you come back tomorrow?"

"I guess. Why?" said Claire.

I smiled. "I'm going to find a few therapist options for you. I want to help you find one that you like."

She smiled. "Okay."

We got up and hugged, then I walked her to the door, then to the hall, and I waved as she walked away. I stood there for a bit, rubbing my upper chest, gently up and down. It was a self-soothing technique, a way to touch my own heart when I needed it.

I was already thinking of therapists who would be a good match for Claire.

And I had another idea.

Back in my office, I retrieved Claire's file. I flipped through to the early pages and found the basic information about her parents, their job titles and workplaces, their addresses and phone numbers.

I dialed the number I'd been looking for, and I waited for the answer, biting my lip in anticipation.

Finally, a woman's voice said, "This is Tammy."

WHEN I FINALLY READ THE COMPLAINT, MY JAW DROPPED. I WAS SIT-
ting in Gloria Jamieson's huge office again. I wasn't officially back
from bereavement leave, but Gloria had called me in to warn me.
She'd seen the complaint first, of course, and wanted to prepare me
for the shock, I suppose.

The student had complained all right, but it wasn't about the
police invading our seminar, or the way I'd incorporated their
questions, and it wasn't even about the fact that I'd picked up
a boy on the side of the road. It was about my drinking, of all
things. A student was upset that I was drinking beer during the
seminar.

"Unbelievable," I'd said to Gloria. Something so minor, so in-
significant. "Are you serious?"

In response, she raised her eyebrows.

"But it's nothing," I said.

"Is it?" she asked, her tone implying it was indeed *something*.

"Gloria, come on," I said.

"Well. Were you drinking alcohol during the seminar?"

"I'm not going to comment on that," I said, which was the response Hal had instructed me to give after my DUI.

"Do you think it's acceptable to drink alcohol while teaching?"
she asked.

"No comment," I said. Obviously, this was all covered in the faculty conduct policy.

"Matthew, please," said Gloria. "Don't be ridiculous."

"We had a plan," I reminded her. "A three-pronged response to any concerns about the kid, harboring a runaway, the lapse in judgment, all of that. I was even going to talk about my son." My voice cracked on that last word, and my throat tightened up.

"Oh, Matthew," she said, placing her palms on the desk, as if reaching toward me.

"And how I wished there'd been someone at the pool who'd helped my little boy," I said. "A Good Samaritan there could have saved his life."

Gloria got up from her chair and walked around her desk. She stood next to me and patted me on the back, then sat in the guest chair next to mine. Leaning over her knees, she rocked ever so slightly, forward and back, as if massaging the invisible pain I'd expressed into the air. Gently, she said, "I think we may need to revise our approach."

To her credit, she sat with me and we worked out a plan. Afterward, I went back to my apartment and it felt so small, so cramped. During the funeral preparations, I'd been staying at Zenith with Claire and we'd been receiving visitors there. Now I was back in my campus housing and it felt strange. Somehow, I didn't belong.

Surveying my small living room, I recalled the seminar and all the students who'd been sitting there in a circle. Who was the one who'd accused me? It couldn't have been Lanie, Carl, or Maynard. They were the students who had participated most actively in the discussion. It must have been someone who didn't speak. Someone who was getting a poor grade. With nothing better to do than file complaints.

I opened the fridge. Yes, I had plenty of beer in there. As if to prove it, I took one out and opened it. Took a sip. Did I drink one or two during the seminar? Perhaps. I must have reached for it without thinking. I took another sip.

Gloria said she would do the best she could with the committee. But she also suggested I prepare myself for plan B. For example, a delay. Postpone the vote until spring. I didn't think it made sense. Maybe it did. But was that admitting fault, admitting defeat? What signal did it send?

I wasn't sure. She also suggested a bigger step: take the semester off. I really didn't want to do that, but if Gloria thought it might save the vote, I'd have to consider it. They'd call it administrative leave, but I could call it a sabbatical. Or bereavement leave. If I suggested it, as a preemptive measure, the committee would look favorably on my "willingness to be held accountable," whatever that meant.

My head was spinning and I wanted to feel normal. I decided to take a shower and shave. I got dressed as if I were going somewhere important, as if I were interviewing for a job. It made me feel better when I looked the part. So I wore my tenured professor getup. All pulled together, but approachable. Learned, but trendy. In reality, I had nowhere to go. My classes were being covered by teaching assistants.

I was alone in the apartment and pacing. I'd finished a couple beers and a made myself a quesadilla. I was thinking about Finn. I was thinking about Claire and the Zenith house. I was thinking about—there was a knock on the door and I opened it. There stood Doug.

"Oh," I said. "What is it, Doug?"

He smiled. "You didn't answer the buzzer."

"What buzzer?" I said, annoyed.

He shook his head as if I were a lost cause. "Someone's here to see you."

Doug stepped out of the way and there was Kira.

"Hi," she said, waving.

"Oh, hi," I said, wishing Doug had warned me. Fortunately, I was dressed up and looking sharp. "Come in," I said, opening the door for her. Her long hair was shiny and her smile was bright. "What a nice surprise."

"How are you?" she asked.

"I was just thinking about going for a drive," I said.

She frowned at me and tilted her head. She glanced at the can of beer in my hand and said, "How about a walk instead?"

I looked at the beer and set it down. "Yes, you're right," I said. I put on my coat and followed her out the door.

Doug gave me a thumbs-up as we passed his door. I put my hands in my pockets and followed Kira's lead, down the elevator, through the entry, and out to the front steps.

Once we were on the path, Kira said, "You weren't really thinking of driving, were you?"

I shook my head. "No. Well, yes, but only because I've been thinking about my house up there. And Claire."

"Well, that's good," she said. "But not the driving part."

"I get it," I said. She held my gaze as we walked, and I felt the urgency of her plea. I promised, "I won't do that again."

A few steps later, she asked, "So tell me what you're thinking. I've got some ideas too."

"You go first," I said.

"No. You," she said.

"Well," I began. "I've been thinking about moving back to Minneapolis. At least for a while."

"Okay," she said, smiling. "May I ask why? I mean, it sounds great, I just thought you really loved it down here."

"I do, but hang on. You like the idea of me moving up there?"

"Well, yes. Selfishly, I would like that," she said. "And I know Claire would love it."

"I hope so. I mean, she seems so independent."

"Oh, Matthew, she misses you."

I walked with that thought for a while. Kira had good judgment, which was something that I occasionally lacked.

"Good. I'll keep pondering that," I said. "Now it's your turn."

She swung her body toward me as she walked, as if building up momentum to share her ideas. Her whole body exuded energy and joy and I couldn't wait to hear what she was thinking.

Once Kira began, she couldn't stop, and her enthusiasm was infectious.

"We could start a partnership with one of the local foster care agencies, or with Rice County CPS, and students could volunteer to work with the kids."

"Wonderful," I said.

Kira listed multiple volunteer jobs for college students. It was a natural fit for sociology and I wanted to be a part of it. I said, "I think the college would support it."

She smiled. "If we could get St. Gus to make a financial investment, we could start a new transitional housing program."

"Fantastic."

She stopped walking and grabbed my arms. "You like it?"

"I love it."

Spontaneously, she hugged me. I hugged her back. Out of the embrace, I looked down at her, and she was looking up at me. She had a look of admiration, of infinite possibility, and I wanted to be worthy of her gaze. With sudden clarity, I said, "I'm going to quit drinking."

She pulled her face back, pleased and surprised. "Wow, that's wonderful," she said, hugging me again.

When we separated, we were both smiling. And as we walked back to my apartment, she tucked her arm in mine.

It was a feeling I quite enjoyed.

Forty-Eight
MATTHEW

TUESDAY, OCTOBER 6, 1992

AFTER MY MONDAY MEETING WITH GLORIA, AND MY TALK WITH KIRA, I'd been looking at Zenith in a new light. On my drive back to the Minneapolis house, I had asked myself questions: Could I live there? Would I be haunted? For example, Finn's nursery. When Finn died, he'd just graduated to a "big boy bed." All that furniture was gone now, of course, and it was just a room with an old NordicTrack and some boxes, the extra junk we needed to stash somewhere.

I remembered way back when Tammy and I first bought the house, before Finn, before Claire. Before it was a nursery, it had been our cozy room. We'd put a TV in there and bought the futon that could fold out as a guest bed in case my mom visited or Tammy's parents came to town (and they'd been welcome anytime— they'd helped us with the down payment, after all). It felt grown-up to have a guest room, even if it was just a futon and a TV. Mostly, we snuggled there after supper, eating ice cream sundaes and watching *M*A*S*H** and *The Bob Newhart Show.*

When Tammy got pregnant, we moved the futon/TV setup to the basement and the room became a nursery. But I'd forgotten that Claire had slept in the nursery when she was a baby. Somehow, I'd only associated Finn with it, but Claire had been the first nursery occupant.

Now, I stood surveying the room again. It was a bit small for a bedroom. It could be a TV room again. Or an office. *It could be my office*, I thought. I checked the closet. Nice shelves. I squinted my eyes, trying to erase the boxes that filled one-half of the room. There were two windows, so it got good light.

"Hmm," I said, shifting a couple of the boxes out of the way. I made a path to the other side of the room and stood there, checking out the view. "Not bad."

The walls would have to be painted. Baby blue was not suitable for a college professor. Perhaps navy or tan? Was there space for bookshelves?

I heard the front door open, and the screen door slammed.

"Hello?" hollered Claire.

"In here!" I hollered back.

I heard her clomp into the kitchen, open the fridge, then shut it. She shouted, "There's nothing to eat!" I had to laugh because the fridge was filled with pans of lasagna and fried chicken and tuna hotdish. There was plenty to eat. She hollered, "Where are you?"

"In the nursery—er—back here!" I called out.

Soon Claire appeared in the doorway holding a chicken leg. Seeing me standing among the boxes, she asked, "What are you doing in here?"

"I'm working on something," I said.

"What is it?" She took a bite of chicken.

Just then the phone rang. "Let's find out," I said, dashing for the phone. Claire followed me, curious enough to make her way into the dining room. We looked at each other, then I answered. After a brief conversation, I nodded and said, "Thank you, Dottie," and hung up.

"Who was that?" asked Claire.

"Dottie is the administrative assistant who works with Odin Bunderson, who is the chair of the Promotion and Tenure Committee."

"Oh," said Claire, pulling her chin into her neck like this was serious business. "What did she want?"

"Actually, I asked Dottie to set up a call with Professor Bunderson, that's what."

"How come?" She took another bite, ripping the meat off the bone, very much like a hungry animal.

"You'll find out," I said proudly. "Right now." I brought the cordless phone with me and sat down at the dining room table. I dialed the number and waited while it rang. Claire was leaning against the wall in the corner, eating her fried chicken. I pressed the speakerphone button so she could hear this. A good learning experience. Something big. I wanted to share it.

"Hello?" said a voice on the other end.

"Professor Bunderson, hello. It's Matthew Larkin."

"Yes, Professor Larkin," said the chair of the committee. "First my condolences."

"Thank you," I said. "And it's been an opportunity to appreciate the importance of ritual and connection, I think. The expression of grief across cultures. Family systems. It's helpful to put an academic lens on it."

Claire made a face, then smiled. Was she mocking me or did she like what I'd said? She gave me a thumbs-up, took another bite, and I smiled.

"I completely agree," said Bunderson. After a moment, he cleared his throat and said, "What can I do for you?"

As I walked through my proposal, Claire sat down and focused on me. She was no longer interested in the chicken; she was all ears and eyes. It was as if she was trying to telegraph something to me, that she trusted me, that I was on the right path. I told Bunderson I would proceed with our original plan, but I added more: I said I wanted to pursue alcohol counseling and grief therapy. And I had ideas for new research on the intersection of law and motivation theory, particularly in the context of Good Samaritan legislation.

Bunderson was silent, apparently taking it all it.

I said, "Odin, I hope you hear the passion in my voice. Please know that I'm committed to gaining tenure eventually, but I think it's best to postpone the vote until next year and that I request a sabbatical for the rest of this academic year."

Claire looked in shock.

"Considering everything," I said, gazing at Claire.

"I see," said Bunderson. "Well, I appreciate your thoughtful and robust proposal, Matthew, I do. Let me take it to the committee and get back to you."

"Absolutely," I said.

"I believe there will be a positive response," said Bunderson. "Candidly, I don't foresee any objection, but let's not get ahead of ourselves. I do need to bring it through the channels."

"Of course," I said, pumping my fist to Claire. Her eyes were wide and her mouth was hanging open. It was thrilling to make her feel as happy as she looked.

After I hung up, I felt a metaphysical release, a weight lifted from my shoulders. I stood up and in an instant, Claire was in my arms, and we were both laughing and crying like we didn't know what had just happened. And in a way, we didn't.

We were laughing and jumping around together, just like we used to do when something good happened, like when she got a part in the second-grade school play about a frog and a mouse who rode a city bus to a baseball game, or when she learned to do a cartwheel when we were on vacation at Wisconsin Dells, or each year of elementary school when she was named a Top Student, or when she came in second at the sixth-grade science fair. We danced. We jumped around.

And we were happy.

Forty-Nine

KIRA

ON TUESDAY, TAMMY LARKIN CAME TO THE COUNSELING OFFICE. I made sure she arrived at a time when Claire wouldn't be there.

My idea had been to pick Ms. Larkin's brain. Perhaps ask her to refer me to some potential local experts to help us develop policies, training, and enforcement in the areas of preventing sexual harassment and assault. As far as I could tell, this was something relatively new for high schools, even as advanced as we were these days.

When we talked on the phone on Monday, I'd told her that I knew she'd worked in compliance for a major corporation for many years. I was looking for someone who could develop policies for the school. And a training program for students and staff. And I asked her if she knew of anyone.

"I know lots of people, but this is my area," she'd said. "In fact, I could do it myself. I assumed that's why you called me."

"Oh, wow," I'd said. "Really?"

"Yes, of course. Why not?"

"I need someone tough. I need a pit bull."

At this, Ms. Larkin had chuckled. "Well, I've gone up against some of the most powerful egomaniacal jerk-offs in corporate America, if that's what you mean."

"Exactly," I said. "We need to get their attention."

As we ended the call, we'd agreed to meet in my office.

When she walked in on Tuesday, she was loaded for bear and to be honest, I was a bit afraid of her. We found a private conference room far from the Counseling Office. I didn't want any chance encounters. And I wanted to focus on what Ms. Larkin was saying.

This woman was amazing. She walked me through her proposal, with sample policies from her previous work, including training scenarios, tip sheets, and more.

"Wow. Are you a lawyer?" I asked. I hadn't expected such an immediate, thorough, and generous response.

"No, but I'm about as close as you can get to one."

I chuckled. She seemed to know her stuff. I was impressed and I told her so. She thanked me and asked me how I'd learned about her.

"Claire," I said. "We often have parents come in and talk about their careers, and I asked her about you and Matthew, um, that is, her dad, and she explained your impressive job. What you both did for work."

"Oh. That's nice," said Ms. Larkin, looking down and smoothing her lap. "And may I ask, why is the school interested in pursuing a training and awareness project now? Are there any special concerns you're hoping to address?"

This lady was sharp. I had to be on my toes. Carefully, I said, "We've had some incidents. It's clear we need to change."

Ms. Larkin nodded and made some notes. She asked about the administration's "buy-in."

I said I thought we could get it. I knew where the bodies were buried. I didn't say this, but I'd already talked it over with my supervisor, Cindy, and we'd strategized about an approach for the school district. And Mr. Peoples was on board. We were united.

"I suppose the next step is for me to write up a proposal for the principal," said Ms. Larkin.

"Yes, and about that," I said, remembering my promise to Claire. "I wonder if you might be willing to use a different last name. In your proposal or any of the communications or materials that have your name on them."

She raised her eyebrows. "Oh?"

"Because, I mean, Claire doesn't know we're meeting today," I said. "And I'm only basing this on my work with teenagers, but if students associate your name and hers, well . . ."

"—Claire would be embarrassed?"

"Maybe," I said, shrugging. "It's normal at her age."

Ms. Larkin nodded. "I get it."

"I don't know. Just an idea," I said, but I really hoped she'd go along with it because that would help to insulate Claire from any backlash. Not that I expected any.

"I can use my maiden name," said Ms. Larkin. "Actually, I'm starting a consulting business. The school will be one of the first clients in my new venture."

"Oh, that's wonderful," I said. "What's your maiden name, if you don't mind me asking?"

"Grant. Tammy Grant," she said. "Maybe I'll go by Tamara. I don't know. It's more powerful."

"Very strong," I said. "I love it."

"Yeah. They won't know what hit 'em," she said, adding a sassy smile, and we laughed.

We finished up and made plans for next steps. I walked Ms. Larkin/Grant down the hall and back toward the exit, thanking her again.

Before she left, she said, "You know, I wasn't too happy when the school disciplined my child without notifying her parents."

"Yeah, that wasn't cool," I said.

"Oh." She looked at me, surprised. "I didn't expect you to agree with me. I thought you'd defend the school."

"Nah," I said, winking. "I'm on the side of the kids, always."

She smiled at me. "Good. I like that."

We shook hands, like very civilized coconspirators. I liked her. A lot.

Fifty

SEAVER

SUNDAY, SEPTEMBER 27, 1992

AFTER GRADY HIT THE GUY IN THE BARN, I RAN AND HID BEHIND THE shed. I didn't know what to do. I was trying to find out whether the guy was dead or alive. I crept closer, behind a tree, and spied on the barn. I saw Grady moving around, in and out, to the front and the back, into the house and back outside to the barn, but I couldn't see the guy. Was he still on the ground? I couldn't see him.

Bucky must have smelled me. She walked toward me and nudged at me. I wanted her to be quiet.

I heard June call, "Dinner!" and I saw her standing outside the back door of the house. She was talking to Grady. I heard my name. June and Grady went inside the house, then they both came back out. I hunched down, taking Bucky with me to hide behind, and we moved closer so I could hear. Bucky stopped with me and leaned down to graze. I couldn't see the guy. He wasn't on the ground where he'd fallen, but how could he have moved? He'd been knocked out.

Grady said, "He's gone." I didn't know if Grady meant me or the guy. "He's not coming back."

June looked upset. She was turning in a circle, searching all around. She put her hands on her face, on her apron, and back on her face. Grady was just looking at the ground. June was kind of yelling at him then. She called my name. I crouched down. She called again, and Bucky looked up. I was afraid Bucky would get June's attention and she might see me.

I heard a crack of thunder, and I felt a drop on my cheek. Dark clouds were gathering and the sky was getting heavy. I wondered where the guy had gone. Or maybe he was dead. Had Grady killed him? Was I a witness? If Grady went to jail, June would be sad. I didn't want June to be sad like my mom. But Grady was only trying to help me. I didn't want him to go to jail. And what if the guy was still alive, was he looking for me? Is that why Grady told me to leave? Because he knew that guy would come back and do something bad? Get back at us?

I didn't know.

So I ran.

It started to rain, but I kept going. I thought of Adrian. I said his phone number over and over. I was headed to the highway so I could hitchhike to Minneapolis. To Adrian. To my mom. But then the hail started, and I needed a place to hide. That's when I saw the porch at the feedstore. I ran up there and crawled under a tarp. No one would find me there. I could wait it out, I thought.

My head got tired and I must have passed out. Next thing I knew, I was in a car, and I was afraid they'd take me back to the farm.

And I saw the light on in the barn. So I ran again.

Fifty-One

KIRA

THURSDAY, OCTOBER 1, 1992

THE NEXT TIME I TALKED WITH JUNE, SHE WAS DISTRAUGHT. I TOLD her I knew she and Grady had decided not to take in any more foster kids.

"I'm sorry," she said.

"No, I understand," I said, although I didn't yet fully understand. But now that we'd found Seaver and his leg had recovered, there was no need to point fingers. "You can't do it forever. And Seaver's doing well with his aunt."

"Well, that's good news," she said, but her tone was weary. There was something she wasn't saying. After a beat, she said, "Kira, you need to come down here. There's something you need to see."

"Okay," I said, but from the trepidation in her voice, I wasn't sure I wanted to. "What is it?"

"I can't say on the phone," said June.

"Well, that's not good."

When I pulled into the driveway, June was waiting on the porch as usual. Without speaking, I followed her inside and we let the storm door slam behind us. She walked straight to the kitchen and stopped. I leaned against the counter and reached for the pistachio jar. I unshelled one and tossed it in my mouth. Maybe doing something ordinary would make me feel more ready.

"So, what's going on?" I said, pretending to be relaxed.

June was standing behind the kitchen island, wringing her hands. She had a sober expression. "You remember the farm-hand?"

"Of course. The one who disappeared," I said, tossing in another pistachio. "On the same day as Seaver."

"Yes," she said, shifting her tone slightly at the mention of Seaver.

"What's going on, June?" The tension was killing me, despite the pistachios.

"All right," she said, motioning me to come with her. "Let's go."

She put on her mud boots, and we walked out the back door, down the familiar creaky steps, and into the yard. The ground was cold, but the sun was shining. At the sight of June, a couple of horses trotted to the fence, thinking she might give them an apple. She didn't. I patted Bucky and she trotted away.

June marched into the barn, muttering as she walked. I followed her as she led me to the side bedroom. The Sheetrock still wasn't taped or mudded. Inside, she turned to me and said, "I know the real reason why Grady didn't want Seaver coming back."

"Okay," I said, attentively. "I thought you both decided it was time."

"No—there's something else." She yanked on the pull chain to give us some light, then walked to the corner. She stood in front of a cabinet, and taking a deep breath, she opened the doors. Standing back, she pointed to the bottom shelf and I took a peek. There was a slim metallic-looking case there. A hard-shell silver briefcase, like I'd seen used for poker chips. I didn't say that because June was acting so strange. But it looked like a poker chip case.

"What's this?" I asked.

"It was his. The farmhand," she said. "His name was Jackson, by the way. Owen Jackson. And there's his wallet." She pointed to a small leather lump next to the metal case.

"He left his wallet?"

"Not exactly." She shook her head. "But Grady found it."

"He found it? Where?" I asked.

"Down by the creek," said June.

I made a face. "So he dropped it at the creek?"

She didn't answer my question. She said, "And there was something else."

"What, June? You're freaking me out a little."

"The key to this briefcase was in his wallet." She held up a small, single key. "The key to this horrible man's, Owen Jackson's, briefcase."

"Okay," I said, not sure what to make of it all. "Where's Grady, by the way? Does he know about this?"

"Oh, he knows," said June. "But he's not here."

"Where'd he go?"

"He went down to Iowa," said June. "To see his sister."

"Uh-huh," I said, adding, "Okay, you're acting very strange."

She put her hand to her forehead. "Well, I'm sorry, Kira, but this is a strange situation. Very strange." June looked as if she might faint.

I reached out to her and said, "Come, sit down."

I guided her to the edge of the bed, and she sat. Then she sprang up and looked behind her at the bed, as if it might be covered in spiders or sewage or something. When she saw the bed was perfectly clean, she sat again. "I'm sorry. Thank you."

"It's fine, June. My god, what in the world has gotten you this upset?"

She handed me the key and nodded toward the metal brief-case, still sitting at the bottom of the cabinet. "Open it," she said.

I shook my head, furrowing my brow. I knew we had to, but I didn't want to open the briefcase. I was worried what we'd find.

"Just do it," she said, as if reading my mind.

Finally, I approached the cabinet and lifted out the briefcase. I brought it to the bed and set it down between us. When I opened the lid and saw the contents, I thought I would vomit.

They were Polaroid photos. Of children. Dozens of them. Nothing naked that I could see. I flipped through the photos in disbelief. The children were facing away from the camera, which was focused on their behinds, with some of them bending over. There were also shots of children's mouths, close up, all of them eating something. Lollipops and Fudgsicles and ice cream cones. All of them children. It was disturbing, to say the least. Distressing that someone had done this.

When I saw the photos of Seaver, I gasped. I felt faint. I gripped the edge of the bed.

June's face was buried.

I kept looking for more. There were four or five photos of Seaver. Eating a Popsicle, standing by a truck. From behind.

I shut the case. June and I were both like zombies, staring into space. Nothing to say. Nowhere to go.

After a long while, I broke the silence. I said, "All right, well. I mean, I have to report it. I'll need the address from his wallet."

June nodded stiffly, her eyes wet and her mouth taught.

I continued, "The good news, if there is any, is that all these children have their clothes on. And, I guess, I don't see any evidence of touching or physical molesting. Just the creepy horrific photogra-phy, which, I mean, he must have had the kids pose or whatever. It looks like it to me, anyway. I'll ask my supervisor what else."

"Fine," said June, sounding completely spent.

"So this is why Grady didn't want Seaver back?" I said. "He was protecting him?"

"Yes," said June, nodding, letting tears drop. "I presume."

"And why you've retired as foster parents?" I said, rubbing June's back. She was sitting there in her mud boots and her cardigan, hunched over, as if defeated, soft under my hand.

"We had to," she said. "They'd never let us continue after this. Truth be told, we were going to hang it up anyway, dear. We've had our children. It's time to rest."

I was letting that sink in.

Suddenly, June perked up with a courageous voice and said, "If they put me in jail, I'll understand. But I will go to my grave swearing that I knew about none of this. For what that's worth."

I said, "Oh, I don't think you'll go to jail. They might ask questions, but . . ."

And then, as if she hadn't heard a word I'd said, June continued, fiercely proclaiming, "If they try to put my Grady in jail for what he did, I will fight them tooth and nail. He did nothing wrong, Kira. He did nothing wrong. In fact, he saved Seaver's life."

"What Grady did?" I said, "June, what exactly are you talking about?"

Fifty-Two

COLLEGE APPLICATION ESSAY (DRAFT)
by Claire Larkin

I wasn't there when my brother drowned. It took thirty seconds. Finn was only four years old. After he died, our house got quiet. My parents were angry but they didn't talk. Then Mom moved out and asked for a divorce. When my grandma Betty died, the obituary said she died from cancer, but I think it was also another type of poison: secrets and shame. My evidence is my own eyes.

As she was dying, we stood at her bedside to say goodbye, but it seemed Gamma was in another state of consciousness. For the last thirty minutes of her life, she was thrashing around in the hospital bed. It looked like she was fighting off an invisible attacker. The only sounds she made were the words No and the name of her brother. I asked the adults what was going on. Finally, my aunt told me that my grandmother's brother had sexually assaulted her repeatedly when she was young. At the time, no one knew or did anything about it. For many years, she carried it with her inside. Then, on her deathbed, she was apparently reliving it, and by reliving it, she was finally telling her truth. This had been her terrible secret, but now her dying body desperately needed to release it.

I am grateful to my grandma, because I don't want to die of secrets or shame. When I saw her struggling with the memory of her attacker, I saw myself, fighting off a real person, a boy at school. He sexually assaulted me and then made me feel bad about it and like the whole thing was my fault. I didn't want anyone to know. He made me feel small and ashamed. His friends laughed at me.

At first, I was afraid to tell anyone. What if they didn't believe me or thought less of me? But then I saw what happened to my grandma and I knew what to do. After Gamma Betty died, I started talking to a therapist. I have learned to talk about my sadness and anger and guilt. About Finn. About my parents' divorce. About everything. Talking about it has made me feel like I can breathe again. My therapist says the only bad feelings are the ones we don't let ourselves feel.

And that's why I want to be a grief counselor. So other kids who might be confused about secrets and shame can have someone safe to talk to. And I want to help other families deal with their grief and learn to express their feelings about divorce or a tragic death, such as the loss of a brother.

I'm also interested in weather science, and I might want to be a part-time meteorologist. Clouds and temperature patterns can teach us a lot about the movement of energy, and I plan to use these theories in my grief counseling, especially with kids.

My father has always told me about St. Gustaf College and how wonderful it is. Ironically, for that reason, I have resisted going there. Now I realize that St. Gustaf is the perfect place for me. An education at St. Gustaf will help me begin my journey to becoming a grief counselor. It will also help me face another loss: the years I was angry at my father.

Fifty-Three

KIRA

SATURDAY, OCTOBER 3, 1992

WHEN GRADY CAME BACK FROM IOWA, HE WAS DIFFERENT. HIS SKIN was gray. He oozed trauma. He looked sickly and vacant. He was changed, and it was upsetting to see him so low.

June believed he would get better. He'd been through a lot. With the police and everything. June believed in the healing power of time, and I did too. I'd seen it work in my life and in the lives of so many kids on my caseload.

But this was a biggie.

Even the police officers thought so. They had a lot of questions for Grady.

Grady had spoken freely with law enforcement. He told them how he'd heard the horse squealing outside the house, squealing loudly enough he could hear it over the football game he'd been watching on TV. And how he'd come out to the barn to see what was wrong, and that was when he'd discovered the farmhand, Jackson, with his arm around Seaver's neck. He described how Seaver was struggling to get away, and how Grady, without thinking, had grabbed the shovel and swung it, hitting the back of Jackson's knees. How Jackson had fallen, and he must have hit his head on the anvil, because Jackson went down hard and then lay bleeding into the hay. Grady said he'd told Seaver to get out, but he'd assumed the boy had run into the house. Then Grady went to find the horse, Bucky, who was apparently loose in the yard.

Later, June had come out asking where Seaver was, and that's when they realized he was gone. Grady said he went looking for Seaver, but couldn't find him anywhere. Then, when he went back to the barn, Jackson was gone too. The guy had simply vanished. He must have been well enough to get up and stumble away, because his white truck was still in the driveway. And all his stuff was left behind. And then three days later, on Wednesday, some field workers came to the house and said they'd seen a body on the acreage, by the creek. They'd led Grady to him. It was Jackson, but he was dead.

Grady and the field workers searched the dead man's pockets and found the wallet and keys, including the key to the metal suitcase. And that's how Grady discovered the Polaroid pictures.

The ugliness of this, and all the resulting trouble, had really spooked Grady. And it was understandable that he would want to quit.

But when Grady said he was thinking about selling the farm, I was taken aback. This farm had been his pride and joy. Wasn't there something else we could do to save it? I reminded him how the kids had loved to work with the horses and how good it was for them to have chores. I wondered if there was something we could work out with the college. A new chapter. I asked the Ogletrees to let me talk to Matthew about it.

For the kids on my caseload. For the college kids. For all of us. Either way, it could be a perfect marriage.

Fifty-Four

MATTHEW

SATURDAY, OCTOBER 24, 1992

I WENT TO THE PICNIC KIRA'S AGENCY SPONSORED FOR THEIR FOSTER kids, foster parents, and any parents interested in possible adoption. I wasn't there as a potential parent; I was there strictly as a friend. And Kira had explained that Seaver would be there with his aunt and he was doing well. So I went, and I was hoping to see Seaver, not that I expected him to care. I just wanted to see that he was thriving and well. Give me some peace of mind. And I suppose, I wanted him to know that I was a good person after all. If Kira approved of me, I believed, then that was a high compliment. It gave me a credibility I didn't know I'd needed.

The event was held at an apple orchard on the outskirts of town. The agency had reserved a pavilion with a large shelter because there was rain in the forecast, but on the day of the picnic, the sun came out and there was no sign of rain. After lunch, the agenda called for hayrides and a corn maze. Meanwhile, kids were running around the field surrounding the pavilion, where parents were standing in small circles, holding plates of pulled pork sandwiches and brownies.

Seaver's aunt Jen (and her boyfriend Jeff) were both in attendance, somewhere on the premises, but Seaver was standing by himself, holding his favorite toy. I approached him slowly to say hello. "You've got your Rubik's Cube, I see."

"Yeah." He glanced up at me and kept working it.

"You left it in my car," I said.

"I know. Ms. Patterson brought it back."

"Yes." I said, ducking as a Frisbee flew overhead, nearly hitting me. It landed twenty feet away.

Seaver ran to pick up the Frisbee. He tossed it back to wherever it came from, but his throw was weak and the disc wobbled as it sailed away then sank to the ground. We glanced at each other as we watched the Frisbee, as if we both knew I couldn't have thrown that Frisbee any better, and its shaky flight was an apt marker of our brief connection, a moment of shared empathy, and that was the end of our exchange.

Dogs chased after the Frisbee and were fighting over it, until June Ogletree called them away. Kira had introduced me, properly, to the Ogletrees, and I understood that June's presence at the picnic was merely as a mentor for new recruits, not as an active foster parent.

Seaver wandered off, vaguely waving goodbye as he left. I suppose that was the most I could have hoped for from a kid like that, so young, with so much on his shoulders. And who was I to him, anyway? Just a stranger who'd given him a ride one night. His caseworker's new friend. A clueless old guy. A dad.

I turned to look for Claire. She had come to help out, as a favor to Kira, but I think she also wanted to see her new friend Adrian, whom she knew would be there, and she'd brought her friend Becca with her. The two girls were standing by the lemonade table, peering at everyone and whispering. Their job was to keep the food table tidy and throw away any stray paper plates and plastic forks. I was proud of Claire and her willingness to volunteer. Since I'd gone on sabbatical, I'd obviously spent more time with my daughter and

I'd been impressed with the young woman she was becoming. I wasn't sure how much of that I could take credit for, so I took none.

Kira approached me, beaming her beautiful smile. Her face caused my face to illuminate. "Hi there," she said.

"Hi," I said.

She leaned in for a hug.

We released the hug and stood admiring the crowd. "A good turnout," I said.

"I'm happy," she said, and we smiled at each other.

"Me too."

After a minute, Claire and Becca approached us, carrying a tray of cups of lemonade. "Want one?"

"Nonalcoholic, right?" I said, winking.

Claire rolled her eyes and handed me a cup of lemonade. I took it. It tasted bland, but it was delicious.

Fifty-Five

CLAIRE

APRIL 1993

I'M READY FOR COLLEGE. I KNOW I HAVE TO WAIT A YEAR AND A HALF, BUT I'm ready. After everything that's happened, I've basically lost interest in high school. I mean, I still go to class and eat lunch with Becca every day, but I feel older than everyone and everything they do just seems so juvenile and stupid. I'm just ready to get on with it. Sometimes Dad takes me down to Northwood with him when he's doing research or going to a meeting. I like getting a feel for what a college campus is like. College kids are so much more mature than high school kids.

They moved Evan to a different biology class. They didn't tell me how that happened but I'm glad it did. I got a new seatmate, a girl named Zoe. She is obsessed with two topics: astrology and sheltie dogs. I'd never thought much about either of those things until I met Zoe. She talks a lot, so I listen. Her two shelties are named Bubba and John. I told my dad about it and he laughed. We are planning to get two kittens from the animal shelter, so we've been joking that we should name them Bubba Cat and Kitty John.

My mom designed a training program for my whole school. Luckily, Mom wasn't the person delivering the sessions. It was done by staff from other school districts and Mom stayed behind the scenes, thank god. I never told her about Evan, but she found the college essay I was working on. She read it, then told me if I ever wanted to talk, she'd always be there. I said I knew that already.

If I was going to talk to anyone, it would be Becca or my therapist or Ms. Patterson, or maybe Dad. He decided to take the year off from teaching, which was a surprise to everyone, especially me. Teaching was his favorite thing. But I like having him around. He's been living at the Zenith house, which meant that, during volleyball season, he could come to my games. Ms. Patterson came with him to a couple of games. They sat next to each other and it was strange to see them like that. But it was okay. I was glad they were there. They're working on a social work project for St. Gustaf and they're, like, really into it. I don't work in the Counseling Office anymore; they moved me to the library. That's fine with me; I love shelving books, and I've found some excellent resources on weather systems.

Becca and I talk about what college we're gonna go to. She wants to go far away, which would make me sad because I might stay close by. I don't know. I might go to St. Gus. Especially if they give me a good scholarship, which they probably will because my grades are going to be amazing. Plus, faculty families get some kind of discount. The only thing is, if I go there, I'm not taking any classes that my dad teaches. If I can avoid it.

Adrian might go to St. Gus and study food science for two years. Then he'll go to culinary school. He got a recommendation from that chef he met with. He's been doing sort of an internship with him, so that's awesome. Adrian cooks for me sometimes. I showed him my dad's recipe for wild rice soup and Adrian said it was good, but he added curry powder and it was awesome.

I'm still interested in meteorology. I was telling Adrian about it. He says I could be a professor. I don't know about that. I guess I could.

I've been teaching my dad about the troposphere, especially when we're in the car together. Last weekend, we were driving back home from a visit to Northwood. We'd stopped at Finn's grave and cleaned up the flowers. Then we went to a gas station and bought a couple of quarts of chocolate milk for the drive. When we got back on I-35 North heading home, I was pointing at the sky and naming various clouds: cirrus, cumulus, stratus. Dad was driving; his eyes were on the road, but he was listening.

I said, "Cirrus clouds are thin and way up high in the cold air, so they're made of ice crystals, whereas stratus clouds are low and thick."

"Uh-huh," said my dad, taking a sip of chocolate milk. "My favorite are cumulus."

"So, those are the puffy ones that form down low in the troposphere where the warm air rises and cools, then turns to water vapor. But I also like the upper atmosphere," I said, lifting my carton of chocolate milk and attempting to open it. I was struggling with the container and I'd stopped talking for a few seconds. Finally, I got it open and took a sip.

In the silence, Dad had been facing forward, focused on the horizon, so he hadn't noticed me struggling. And since I'd stopped talking, he thought I was done with my explanations about the jet stream and atmospheric temperatures.

He said, "Hey, is that all?"

I said, "What do you mean?"

He said, "Isn't there anything additional about formation patterns you can tell me?"

And I said, "Oh yes, I was just getting some chocolate milk, but I can keep going. I can tell you about dust particles and the water cycle?"

He said, "That sounds perfect, Claire. Please keep telling me, because I want to hear more."

And we drove the whole way home like that, just drinking our chocolate milk and talking. Talking about clouds.

ACKNOWLEDGMENTS

THANK YOU TO MY AMAZING EDITOR, SARA NELSON, AS WELL AS EDIE Astley, Laurie McGee, Stacey Fischkelta, Chris Connolly, Heather Drucker, and the entire team at HarperCollins. Thank you to my wonderful agent, Marly Rusoff, and to Julie Mosow for invaluable guidance and book genius.

In doing research for this novel, I gained incredible input and insights from Dick Senese, Brent Johnson, and Sonia Shewchuk, among others. I'm deeply grateful for beta readers Janell Stanton, Cassandra Wolfgram, and Mathea Bruns. Thank you to Makenzie Krause for putting the word out.

I also benefitted from the wisdom and support of fellow writers, particularly my Friday Morning Writing Group and the Loft mentor group. I'm forever indebted to superstar Pamela Klinger-Horn and the unbelievably welcoming community of local authors and booksellers.

Thank you to the many other book friends and readers who have encouraged me so generously. Special thanks to the MHC Book Club, at which Anne Jennen once shared a personal Good Samaritan story.

I'm also grateful to the team at Schaefer Halleen for believing in me and for tolerating my periods of disappearance when I needed to write.

Thanks to my family for always listening, reading, and cheering me on. I couldn't do it without you. And I'll never forget those hours we spent at the "old folks' home," sitting together in a circle and reading the manuscript aloud, chapter by chapter. Thank you, Larry, for being you: an eternal optimist, a smart reader, and an old softie. Thanks to Skyler, for sitting on the pages, just like a writer's cat is supposed to do.

ABOUT THE AUTHOR

TONI HALLEEN WORKED FOR MANY YEARS AS AN EMPLOYMENT LAW attorney. She was born and raised in the Midwest and earned a BA in women's studies from Mount Holyoke College, and a JD from the University of Minnesota. Toni won a Mentor Prize in fiction from the Loft Literary Center, and her writing has appeared in *Wigleaf*, *Structo*, *Gravel*, the *Star Tribune*, and elsewhere. She lives in Minneapolis with her family.

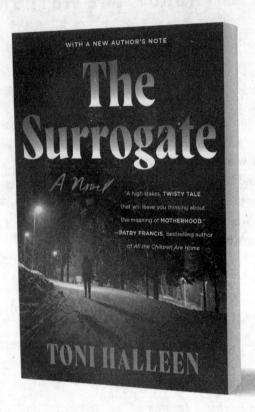